R. CHIGBUE-ONYEMEM was  in Lagos.

She graduated from the Unive Honours in Theatre Arts and also City Lit in Holborn, London.

R. Chigbue-Onyemem wrote and produced Drama and Women & Children's programmes for the Federal Radio Corporation of Nigeria and also freelanced at the Nigerian Television Authority as an actress.

She currently lives and works in London.

KILBURN
to
KIRIKIRI

R. CHIGBUE-ONYEMEM

SilverWood

Published in 2022 by SilverWood Books

SilverWood Books Ltd
14 Small Street, Bristol, BS1 1DE, United Kingdom
www.silverwoodbooks.co.uk

ISBN 978-1-80042-198-1 (paperback)
ISBN 978-1-80042-199-8 (ebook)

British Library Cataloguing in Publication Data
A CIP catalogue record for this book is
available from the British Library

Page design and typesetting by SilverWood Books

For my brother,
Christopher Chike Chigbue SAN OFR (1956–2001)
And in memory of my parents – the Late Hon. Justice VJO
Chigbue and Justina Chigbue

Prologue

We stayed at home in isolation with our front doors locked and enjoyed an unexpected holiday. All the churches, mosques, schools, offices, gyms, zoos, restaurants, most of the shops and all public places closed as we accepted the effects of lockdown lethargy and stayed indoors. People rested, read books, watched television, and cooked a lot of food. Abandoned offices were likened by many to the bridge of *Marie Celeste*. While millions of people went for long walks on deserted roads, others stayed at home and baked a lot of banana cakes and piles of banana bread until flour became a scarce commodity.

Druggies, scammers, fraudsters, foxes, squirrels, birds and wild cats took over the streets of North London as most people obeyed the lockdown rules and remained indoors. Brazen big and small thieves had a field day. They jacked up parked cars in broad daylight and stole the catalytic converters. Every day, we woke up to hear about another theft, and those of us that were not robbed nervously waited for our turn. Phones, laptops, iPads and doorbells were not spared. Unexpected intruders turned up at front doors.

As for me, I refused to remain on the sofa in that Covid-19-induced daze, watching television or trying to uninstall the weird antivirus programs and viruses that had stealthily invaded the privacy of my desktop and self-installed; instead, I prayed to Saint Rocco, the patron saint of pestilence and plague, and allowed a host of memories to populate my head.

The enigma that was 2017 wafted into my focus.

PART 1

1

2017

Trouble leapt like a million frogs.

I always loved Thursdays. They were my best days of the week and they always brought me good luck. I was born on a Thursday, christened on a Thursday, met my husband on a Thursday and married on a Thursday. When I was in the boarding school, we ate my favourite vanilla ice cream on Thursdays. I interviewed for my job on a Thursday and started work at the Headington local office the following Thursday. So, naturally, I assumed that the last Thursday of the month of February 2017 was going to bring me the usual good luck.

That critical Thursday turned out to be my *dies horribilis*.

It all started in suburban Headington, thousands and thousands of miles away from Kirikiri. A raging storm, Doris, was already battering the UK and all I wanted that Thursday morning was to be in the office before 9.30am because of a special announcement.

I was full of anticipation.

Excited.

Strong gusts of wind blew in my face when I leapt off Bus 283. They swayed my five-foot-seven frame and almost blew me off balance. They rattled and overturned the grey wheely bins at the entrance of the infamous alleyway that was between our office car park and Stanley Gardens. I lurched and jerked and steadied myself, and with my head bent down, rushed into the forbidden alleyway.

PING! Images of cracked skulls and mashed-up faces flashed through my mind. PING! PING! The gruesome pictures of Mary McGee's bandaged head and broken arm that still defaced the pretty white noticeboard in our staff canteen flashed before my eyes. Those images came and went in a flash. Yes, Mary was mugged in the alleyway a few months ago; and yes, her skull was fractured, her ribs were cracked and her right arm was broken, but that was not my portion, I told myself.

After a few staggering steps in the alleyway, I suddenly trembled convulsively. Premonition! I had an eerie gut feeling of imminent danger, but I knew that the only things that were at risk and needed protection from any mugger lurking in the narrow street were my second-hand handbag and iPhone 7 Plus. I felt the hidden pocket of my chocolate-brown, polka-dot midi dress where the phone was safely tucked away; and, as for my handbag, it was hidden under my navy-blue winter coat. So, with the furry hood of my duffle coat pulled over my hair, I staggered and rushed down the alleyway like a mad hatter.

About halfway through, I was forced to slow down. My path was almost blocked by a large, heaped, blood-stained duvet. On top of the dirty, colourful pile was a neatly folded bottle-green cardigan. I stopped and looked behind me to make sure their owner was not in the alleyway. Ada, you cannot afford to be mugged here this morning – PJ&PJ needs you, I told myself and ploughed on. I had to be in the office before 9.30am.

Deep down, I knew I should never have entered that alleyway, but that 9.30am announcement meant the world to me. Almost sixty members of staff from the twenty-one UK branches of PJ&PJ had gone for a promotion exercise, and I wanted to be in the building to hear the name of the successful candidate.

Hopefully, mine, I enthused.

Sleep eluded me the night before. I lay awake most of it, tossing and turning on my bed as I tried to work out how much difference the new grade would make to my pay cheque.

That bottle-green cardigan on top of the blood-stained, multicoloured duvet reminded me of Reon, a very bad teenager that I used to know – but there and then, I knew the cardigan could not have belonged to Reon because he lived in Putney, in South West London. Moreover, the last time I heard of Reon, he was incarcerated for handling stolen goods.

From time to time, I turned around to make sure nobody followed me because members of the public also used the alleyway. They would usually cut through our car park to access Helena Road.

I blamed my friend, Malika, for my lateness. She had flown in that morning and I had to stay back to let her into the flat before I left.

I finally heaved a loud sigh of relief when I staggered into the car park, but that relief did not last a nanosecond. My footsteps faltered and I almost tripped. A sight that I had never witnessed in all my years at PJ&PJ met my eyes.

"OMG!!" I exclaimed aloud and yanked my hood off with automatic alacrity.

At least thirty of my colleagues were out in the car park. They stood in huddles and were talking animatedly. I could tell they had been out there for a long time because most of them clutched empty teacups and coffee mugs in their hands, and Fish-face Eric and his best mate, Duncan, were trying to control their badly chattering teeth. What I could not understand was why everybody was out in the car park when the forecast storm was already drifting towards the east. Didn't they listen to the weather forecast? Earlier that morning, before I had set off for work, the weatherman on TV forecast stormy conditions, caused by Storm Doris; and while I dressed up for work, pictures of her damage in Shepherds Bush and Holland Park were shown throughout the morning.

Why were they in the car park? Could it be a fire or bomb drill, or was it the real thing? If it was the real thing, I had failed in my role as the fire and bomb warden.

I noticed two empty police cars parked on the double yellow lines in front of the office. Before I could blink, two more police cars screeched to a halt beside the office building. Two officers leapt out and rushed into the building. I knew right away it had to be something major.

Little did I know that the course of my kind-of-okay normal life was about to be changed forever and that my shortcut through the alleyway was my fast track to my proverbial hell on planet earth. The events that followed in very rapid succession that horrible Thursday shook my entire life and rendered my cast iron reputation at work in tatters. Those events set a new tone for the rest of my life.

Headington PJ&PJ, a London & Home Counties Branch of Peter Johnson & Paul Johnson Insurance Company Ltd was in an imposing five-storey building called Headington House in North London. We rented all five floors of the building from a private landlord – Mr Ariel Oppenheimer. Rumour had it that Mr Oppenheimer wanted PJ&PJ out so that he could knock the building down and replace it with a block of twenty-eight luxury two-, three-bedroom apartments with underground parking and landscaped gardens.

Our open-plan office, the Insurance Officers' room, was on the third floor of the building. We also had the conference room, the post room, the game room, the ladies' rest room, the stationery room, the staff canteen and the office of Mary McGee on the third floor. Mary was the Headington branch office manager. She was supposed to go on secondment to our head office in Watford, and the successful candidate in the paperboard promotion exercise would move into her room.

I hurried anxiously to the nearest group of colleagues, and approached Daisy and Peter C., the two lovebirds of the third floor. Oh, poor Daisy! She was trembling like a leaf and shivering badly. All she had on was a very light, purple linen blazer on top of a knee-length, banana-yellow dress, a pair of leggings and her everyday pair of tan, synthetic, quilted boots. How she could have worn such a flimsy, short cotton dress in the dead of the winter beat me; and I knew she would have clung like a leech onto Peter C. for warmth had there not been so many people in the car park.

"What is happening?" I asked anxiously.

"I haven't got a clue," Peter C. shrugged and replied, rather apologetically.

Typical! Peter C.'s surname was Cummins, but everyone called him Peter C. or Peter Clueless. Peter never had a clue about anything. He could not even hazard a guess why or how he had left his pretty wife of twelve solid years and their four children in posh Maida Vale for Daisy's dingy, one-bed flat on the Grahame Park Estate in Colindale. Peter Clueless. As usual, his long-sleeved blue cotton shirt was rumpled; and his crumpled, badly faded pair of blue jeans seemed like he had dug them out of a laundry basket.

"Dunno," Daisy muttered through chattering teeth and gave me one of those half-hearted, abrupt plastic grins.

I decided to hang with both of them. "I said I don't know. Dunno," Daisy repeated. She clucked her tongue, shook her head and walked off. Peter C. followed her.

Could it be because I walked through the alleyway?

I shrugged and made my way to the furthest group of smokers puffing away by the wall at the far end of the car park. I always knew smokers were nicer and easier to talk to; but before I could ask questions, the office manager appeared at the staff entrance.

"Can you go back to your desks, please?" she requested authoritatively.

16

2

We filed down the long corridor of the ground floor in total silence. All I could hear as we walked up the wide hallway was the staccato of high heels, low heels, kitten heels, winkle pickers, stiletto shoes and the crunching of Daisy's tan riding boots on the laminated wooden floor. I stole quick, furtive glances at faces for clues, messages or signs, but everyone seemed to avoid eye contact. We walked past the many staff noticeboards in silence. The huge, colourful portraits of Peter Johnson and Paul Johnson that adorned the white walls suddenly became portraits of interest. All eyes focused on them. I noticed Daisy almost bumped into Fish-face Eric while unsocially distancing herself away from me. I felt like I was walking along the longest, coldest, and loneliest corridor in the world, all by myself. I was super lonely.

Not in a million years would I have thought or guessed that the reason for the police cars and the evacuation of Headington House was me. I never assumed that the most sorrowful and worst period of my life was about to be launched.

The rage commenced. If I was asked to choose between

being attacked and beaten to a pulp on my way to work and the events that unfolded after that fateful Thursday morning, I would have very nicely opted for being mugged, beaten up or even murdered in the alleyway.

We walked on in deafening silence. Colleagues branched off to their various rooms without saying a word to each other and I soon got tired of trying to read blank faces for clues.

RING-RING-RING… Trilled a mobile phone in someone's bag or pocket. The hush was finally broken. I looked up to see whose phone it was. There followed a very brief exchange of glances, but no one reached into their bag or pocket to answer the call. That person ignored the phone. It rang and rang and rang until it stopped ringing.

We ascended the wide marble steps of the spiral staircase that seemed to go on forever. On the third floor, I walked through the doors and up the corridor to my open-plan room – Room 348. Mary McGee's office was the first on my left. When I walked past the closed magnolia door of her room, my thoughts shifted very briefly to the results of the paperboard promotion. In my mind's eye, I saw myself ensconced there one day as the Headington branch office manager and that thought brought a little smile to my face. After all, it meant all my financial worries would disappear. There would be no more struggling to make ends meet, and no more red bills.

If you are successful, I told myself and smiled again. I had big ideas percolating in my head for when I became the office manager. Things just had to change in Headington House. First of all, I planned to ban officers from eating at their desks; and second of all, I planned to stop them from stealing PJ&PJ's electricity by charging their mobile phones at work. In short,

I intended to show them that I did not win all those awards in 2016 for nothing.

Mary McGee and I had quite a lot in common – she won the best insurance officer award in 2015 and I won it in 2016. Both of us were in the same milk club on the third floor and both of us were North Londoners – she lived on Walm Lane in Willesden Green, which was less than ten minutes' drive from my beloved Kilburn. Four days earlier, after the 7pm mass at the catholic church on Quex Road, Mary was very excited when I told her the good news that I had heard on the streets about a proposal for a lift at her Willesden Green station and plans to also have the Metropolitan line stop there.

I must have been deeply engrossed in those thoughts in that short walk. I did not realise I was all alone on the third floor until I got to the door of Room 348.

Everyone else must have walked up to the fourth floor.

My first instinct on realising I was on my own was to turn back and run to the fourth floor, but it was too late. I was already at the slightly open door of my office and could see inside the room.

Shock. Fear. Petrification. An instant pain pummelled my tummy. It felt like someone hit my stomach with a massive physical blow.

"Aaargh!!" I exclaimed, transfixed by the door. My mouth remained wide open for the next few seconds and I found it pretty painful to close it after that sudden display of shock.

The spine-chilling sight that remained permanently seared in my mind for a long time sent involuntary shivers right through my whole body. I stood by the door, frozen, and felt myself almost passing out. The spectacle in Room 348 was like a scene from a movie. My skin registered instant goosebumps and my mouth remained hung open in awe.

Two uniformed policemen, plus Debbie Evans – the Human Resources Manager from our head office in Watford – and Mary McGee surrounded my desk. All the stuff from my drawers and desk were emptied and strewn all over the floor. I looked around and surprisingly, the other nine desks, nine chairs and twenty-seven other drawers in the room were all intact.

"Good morning, Mrs George," Debbie said aloud as I struggled to close my mouth.

Mrs George? How strange! Where was that coming from? Why Mrs George? I wondered. Nobody had ever addressed me as Mrs George in all my eleven years at PJ&PJ. We were not hierarchical at all and had always enjoyed the first name culture at the establishment. Deborah Evans was Debbie or Debs to everyone in the office, and I was Ada, PA or Pretty Ada to Debbie or Debs and everyone else. Most of the time, most people called me PA because they always said I was pretty and reminded them of Naomi the model! Not Mrs George!

It was all so surreal.

I didn't respond to Debbie's greeting – not because I did not want to, but because my mouth suddenly stopped working after I closed it. I could not open it and my voice was also gone. I felt a strange blockage inside me, like a large boulder had lodged itself between my pharynx and trachea. The boulder sat in my throat. Dumbfounded and motionless, still by the door, I tried and struggled to find my voice and muster some courage.

"What eee… What is going on?" I eventually stammered in a feeble and hoarse whisper.

No one answered. I was not sure they heard me; even I could barely hear myself.

I cleared my throat aloud and looked Debbie right in the eyes, waiting for an answer. My eyes darted back and forth from one end of the room to the other, like those of a cornered mouse.

"What's going on, Debbie?" I asked again.

"Em-em," Debbie stammered, slowly wobbling backwards from my desk. "We… We…were… We have…have…just finished conducting a locker search." She carried on retreating and finally stopped when she was by Daisy's intact desk. She looked at the policemen and very quickly added, "Not just your locker but a few other lockers on the first, second and fourth floors."

"I can't believe this. Everyone carried on to the fourth floor, except meee!!" I screeched, staring angrily at Debbie.

"Well, those were my instructions earlier on. About twenty minutes ago." She looked at the big, bright, purple Fitbit on her left wrist and added, "Maybe if you had come in earlier, you would have heard my instructions."

One of the two uniformed policemen who had been rummaging through the contents of my lower drawer by Peter C.'s desk immediately rushed to Debbie's aid, or so it seemed, followed by the second officer. "I am PC Dunne and this is my colleague, PC Martin," he said as he came up to me. My mouth dropped open again, and for some inexplicable reason, I suddenly started trembling again and wished the floor of Room 348 would crack open for me to fall in and disappear.

"Hmm," I grunted feebly, still scanning the room in a shocking daze. I felt my hands become all sweaty and I clutched my thumbs very tightly to prevent myself from reverting to my childhood coping mechanism. Ada, on no account should you suck those thumbs at work!

On hindsight, my reaction was possibly because I had never been in such close contact with a uniformed policeman. I restrained myself and hid both thumbs in two tightly clenched fists. My eyes welled with hot tears when I saw the tiny green–

white–green flag that was hanging behind my desk when I left work the evening before; it lay limp and lifeless on the floor. I saw my possessions carelessly littered for all eyes. My hand cream, a half packet of Hobnobs, my half-bag of sellotaped brown sugar, an unopened bag of cheese and onion crisps, plus my box of pink tissues and my favourite, unwashed, red coffee mug were all chucked into my wastepaper basket. The pile of unactioned ICs – insurance claims –that I had left in my in-tray the previous evening was gone.

Surely, this could not have been because I walked through the alleyway. After all, Headington was full of alleyways.

My brain and thoughts went into overdrive as I tried to figure out what I could have done wrong. More of my stuff was on the floor. I wondered whether to retrieve my pietà, my new 2017 A4 desk diary and my *Collins Pocket Dictionary*. It seemed like a hurricane ran through my desk and its surrounding area. A stone-faced Debbie shifted her position and went to rest against the radiator behind Daisy's desk.

She remained by the radiator, fidgeting with her antiquated silver Parker pen. From where I stood, still rooted to the same spot by the door, I felt her vibes of immeasurable disgust in my bones. It was common knowledge that Debs hated visiting local offices in the cold months. I also knew that she loathed large-scale conflicts.

What on earth were they looking for and how could Debbie violate my cherished and personal, tiny little office space and belongings so badly? We were members of the same lottery syndicate, for heaven's sake!

I felt my already painful stomach flip and my brain became chaotic like my desk space.

My line manager, Ramila Shah, stomped into the room from

22

the rear door, scowling. The frown disappeared when she saw me – it was replaced by sympathy and extreme sadness. Whatever it was, for the first time that morning, someone actually maintained eye contact with me, even if it was just for a nanosecond. Ramila was the nicest line manager I ever had in my entire life. She was kind to me from day one. In my first year at PJ&PJ, when I was a mere, timid insurance office assistant, Ramila had encouraged me to speak up at meetings – she would ask me very easy leading questions, like "Ada, we held the last meeting in this conference room, didn't we?" And she didn't stop at that; every time she had the opportunity, she would tell everyone who cared to listen that I was manager material.

That morning, when Ramila did not give me her usual broad smile and ask the usual "You okay, Ada?" I knew I was in big trouble.

Panic set in with a capital P. My eyes suddenly felt like they were about to pop out of their sockets and in an attempt to hold them in, I blinked involuntarily at an incredibly fast rate.

I noticed the coat rack was half full of coats and Daisy's working files were on her desk. Then I saw Debbie teeter up to me in her extremely high-heeled shoes, her face devoid of expression. With each slow step that Debbie took towards me, the strangely empty open-plan office suddenly grew bigger, wider and whiter.

At that time of the morning there should have been nine other insurance officers in the room on our tight-knit section. The room should have been filled with the aroma of strong coffee and freshly baked croissants from Lidl. The phones should have been ringing off their hooks, Ramila's Bombay mix should have been on top of the filing cabinet for all to enjoy, Daisy should have been brewing her fourth or fifth cup of tea or gossiping by the coffee machine, and Jason Gilberg's *Metro* newspaper should have been doing its morning round in the room. My thoughts suddenly became cloudy. I became dizzy. My head started spinning and the room suddenly started to rotate around me, like I had just come off a swing.

"May I be excused to go to th-the little room…? Th-the the bathroom?" I stammered timidly. I tried to steady my wobbly knees that felt like strawberry trifle. I had to get out of the room before I passed out.

Debbie looked at the policemen and Ramila before she reluctantly responded. "Yes, you may."

The bathroom suddenly seemed so far away. I steadied myself and headed for the ladies' toilets at the end of the corridor. I rushed into the nearest cubicle and crashed straight onto the toilet seat where I sat for quite a long while. I wanted to remain there forever and wished I could flush myself down the toilet and disappear in the sewerage system. When I finally came out of the stall, I stood in front of the wide, half-length mirror on the wall opposite the cubicles. I took five deep breaths in through my nose and exhaled through my mouth. I could not believe the vulnerable and wide-eyed Ada that I saw in the mirror was me. The black liners around my huge, soft, almond-shaped eyes were smudged and they looked large and scared. Big chunks of the arched eyebrows that I had filled in earlier on that morning with my dark-brown eye pencil were gone and the foundation and mineralised powder on my nose and heart-shaped face looked greatly disturbed.

Debbie was pacing back and forth along the corridor when I came out of the ladies. Hot tears welled in my eyes again. I knew Debbie very well and I knew she was hovering around the corridor to make sure I did not do a runner.

"Alright?" she asked.

I nodded in the affirmative. Debbie and I returned to Room 348.

Room 348 was empty. The policemen were gone. Ramila was gone and Mary McGee was gone. My computer and telephone were also gone. But most surprisingly, the treasured little picture of me at age eight was also missing from the place of pride which it had occupied on my desk for the last eleven years.

And there was more damage... My 2016 Best Staff of the Year certificate and my First Aid certificate had been ripped off the wall and flung onto the dusty part of my desk were my computer once sat. I could tell the certificates had been angrily and carelessly ripped off the wall because little pieces of Blue Tack were still stuck on the wall. If only they knew those certificates meant the world to me; especially the first aid one which I had obtained after a four-day practical course in Leeds.

How could they do this to me when I actually worked my socks off for PJ&PJ?

"Can we see you in Room 340... Mary McGee's room?" Debbie asked as she stomped off towards the office manager's room in her high-heeled shoes. I nodded and followed her up the corridor sheepishly like a lamb being led to the slaughterhouse.

I could not wait to find out what my offence was.

3

A very tall, painfully thin and pale gentleman, dressed in a dark-grey, undersized suit with the red PJ&PJ lanyard and dongle dangling around his neck, rose to his feet as Debbie ushered me into Room 340. He must have been in his late forties or early fifties, and about six feet tall, if not more. He wore a bright-red silk tie with a matching bright-red kerchief that peeped out of the left breast pocket of his short and tight blazer. The sleeves of his blazer stopped just above his wrists. He had pretty untidy beetling eyebrows, and his small, round eyeglasses reminded me of John Lennon.

"My name is Darren Murphy. I am the Deputy Head of False Insurance Claims, and also in charge of the PJ&PJ audit team in Watford. Good morning."

"Good morning," I muttered under my breath as I stood by the door wringing all the ten fingers of my sweaty hands. I could have sworn my heart rate was more than a hundred beats per minute because I felt it racing in my throat, in my neck and in my chest.

Without being told, as soon as I saw six unopened blank

cassettes, an audio tape recorder that had PEAL written on it and a square microphone nicely set out on Mary's desk, I knew my stellar career was under serious threat. There was also a thick red file on the desk.

"Mr Murphy, I shall leave Mrs Ada George in your capable hands," Debbie said crisply. She stomped out of the room and slammed the door shut.

At the far corner of the room was a shiny black box which I guessed was the container for the PEAL tape machine.

Why me? Surely, all of this could not be because I walked through the alleyway.

"Please, sit down," Mr Murphy said with what seemed like a chillingly evil smile.

I walked to the chair on the other side of the table and felt my blood curdle as I plonked myself on it. I couldn't wait to hear what my offence was. Mr Murphy's face looked vaguely familiar. I had a very strong feeling I had seen his heavily lined forehead and the unusually neat, side-parted, three-coloured hair somewhere before that day. His beetling eyebrows; the thinning grey, ginger and light-brown strands of hair that started in the middle of his head all looked very familiar.

Mr Murphy sat opposite me, and as he very gingerly unwrapped two of the blank cassettes, he told me that the interview was going to be recorded. After that it was suddenly quiet. All I could hear were the whoosh, whoosh, whirr of Mary's printer, the ticktock-ticktock of the white clock on the white wall and the loud beats of my heart pounding against the chair. I looked around Room 340. It did not look or feel like Room 340. Mr Murphy filled the room with his height and presence. Mary's Cheddar cheese ploughman's sandwich, her 500-millilitre bottle of spring water and her statues of Mary and Saint Therese of the

Child Jesus had been pushed to the furthest end of the desk. Mr Murphy placed the two unwrapped cassettes in the machine.

Cassettes! Why not CDs? I wondered. And six cassettes? Must be a very long interview. I must be in hot soup! I had not seen cassettes in a very long time…

BINGO! I remembered where I had seen him!

Darren Murphy had been on television… The dodgy car insurance claims' programme… He was the one that busted the biggest dodgy car insurance ring not too long ago. OMG! He looked a lot taller and thinner in real life.

Dear God, I don't want to end up being on telly!

Darren Murphy switched on the tape recorder, and as I watched his aquiline nose grow longer, and his dark, cigarette-burnt lips get thinner, his already elongated neck further stretched as he sat up on his chair. He cleared his throat and proceeded to fire questions at me with no explanation whatsoever.

"Can you please confirm your full name and staff number?"

"Ada Nneka George. 90-31-9991."

"What is your date and place of birth?"

"17 April 1979. Paddington. St Mary's."

"What is your nationality?"

"British."

"And what is your place of origin?"

"Nigeria."

As soon as I said the word "Nigeria", I saw something happen to Mr Murphy's piercing eyes. I was not sure if they twitched or if he widened or rolled them. At the same time, he flared his slightly bent nose, adjusted his already adjusted tie and very quickly regained composure.

"Did you say you were born in St Mary's in London or St Mary's in Nigeria?"

"St Mary's on Praed Street. In Paddington, West London. London."

"I see," he said and continued. "Well, I am here to ask you questions about your death in 2015…"

Hmmm? What? Death or debt? I was not sure if he said debt, as in that I owed money, or death, as in that I was dead. Neither death nor debt sat comfortably with me. Death or debt I wanted to ask, but I could not speak. I felt as if a fat, viscous sewer rat came from that filthy alleyway and sank its ugly, large, overgrown teeth deeply into my neck, grabbed an imaginary boulder in my throat and refused to let go.

My dark times commenced. Death or debt?

"… And to ask you about the three-quarters of a million-pound insurance pay-out that was made to your husband for your death. 750,000 pounds."

Three-quarters of a million pounds? "Hmmm?" I grunted. "Hmmm?" I grunted again.

I was livid and very displeased with myself because my voice was gone again at that very crucial time when I needed it most. I just could not speak. I did not want to look at Mr Murphy while I struggled to find my voice, so I remained on my seat, staring at the bright-red kerchief that peeped out of his left breast pocket. I sat staring without blinking until two big fat tears dropped from my eyes on to Mary McGee's desk. As if he was anticipating my tears, Mr Murphy quickly offered me tissues from a box that I never noticed was on the floor beside him. I ignored the tissues, but soon realised I needed them when the tears did not stop. I reached out to take the tissues, but something strange happened inside me. I had a peculiar light bulb moment. A light switch was flicked on inside my head and I saw bright orange stars, followed by an apparition of my late grandmother. My deceased grandmother performed magic. She waved a magic wand in my face and without any warning, the imaginary boulder that was stuck in my throat suddenly disintegrated into tiny cobbles.

"Hun? What? Pardon?" I waited for an answer.

The Nigerian-ness in me also surfaced out of the blue.

"Get yourself together, Ada," my dead Grandma whispered into my ears. Out went the pretty British Ada with the subtle British accent and in came the real Nigerian Ada with a deep, unalloyed, Nigerian Igbo accent.

"Pray, please, who did you say died?"

Mr Murphy simply continued, "This is a very serious interview and it is being recorded. If you want to ask for a friend or colleague to sit in with you, you are welcome to do so." I could not tell if Mr Murphy had noticed the switch because he did not change his demeanour.

He did not seem to understand what was happening to me.

"If you also want a copy of the typed record of this interview, you can send your request to me at the Watford Head Office in writing after this interview."

He passed a complimentary card to me and added, "Or an email at this email address."

I exhaled aloud, shook my head and shoulder, adjusted my sitting position and sat up straight. I reached out and took the card off him.

"Eh! Who did you say died? Which three-quarter million pounds? Who is my husband? Which husband?"

Mr Murphy ignored my multiple questions and switch of accents.

"Please. I beg of you, whose death?" I asked again in my very deep, original Nigerian accent as I sat up properly.

"Your death in 2015."

"Whose death? Me? My death in 2015?"

"Yes. You. Your death in 2015."

I raised my left hand, did a circular motion around my head with it and denounced death by clicking my middle finger and thumb aloud. Pop! The loud sound of my clicking thumb and finger went. At the same time I muttered, "God forbid" under my breath.

"It couldn't be. There must be a mix-up," I said aloud. "I am not dead," I said slowly and shook my head. "And I do not have a husband. In fact, I have not had a husband or seen my husband in a very long time."

"Indeed."

Indeed? I recognised the sarcasm in that word. That really angered me and my Nigerian instincts kicked in big-big time. I tried oh-so-hard to keep a lid on them. I folded my arms across my chest, turned my head and faced the PEAL tape recorder instead of Mr Murphy. I pursed my lips, unfolded my arms, and folded them again. I started to rock my entire body in a repetitive manner on the chair. Squeaky-squeaky and squeaky-squeaky… The chair squeaked every time I rocked my body. I liked the noise and so I kept on rocking.

Ada, shine your eyes. No more dulling. Don't be dull. Don't be tardy.

"Let me explain what has happened. This company has a policy of carrying out credit and criminal checks on all senior officers before they take up their positions."

"Yeees?" I asked and continued rocking. Squeaky-squeaky and squeaky-squeaky.

"As you were successful in the promotion interview…"

"Was I?"

Was that right? What a way to find out!

"Yes, you were… And so, we carried out the usual background checks on you. In the course of these checks, we found out that apart from your faked death, and other types of insurance offences, you also have a criminal record which you failed to declare to PJ&PJ… Plus, a lot of unpaid credit card bills."

"Me? Meee?? Are you sure it is me, Ada Nneka George, the daughter of Doctor Epiphany Chukwu?" I paused and waited for a reply, but got none. "It is not me, ooh."

When Mr Murphy still did not say anything, I leaned forward and asked, "Are you a policeman?"

"No. I am not a policeman. I am the Deputy Head of False Insurance Claims."

I sighed aloud. Sweat had started dripping from my damp palms. I refolded my arms and discreetly wiped my hands on my dress. I stopped rocking on the chair, unfolded my arms and sat back.

Mr Murphy opened the folder on the desk. He brought out a folded piece of paper from the first plastic wallet of the file. He unfolded it and held it up.

"Is this a photocopy of your birth certificate?"

"This is too mad! Utterly insane," I muttered as I read the details on the short certificate without taking it off him. It was a photocopy of my short birth certificate which I never gave to PJ&PJ.

"Yes. It is."

"Or is it someone else's birth certificate?"

Like whose? I wanted to ask, but changed my mind. "It is mine."

Next, he brought out a photocopy of my marriage certificate and asked me if it was mine.

Once again, I read the contents and replied, "Yes?" More of

32

a question than an answer.

Mr Murphy opened the folder on the desk. He brought out another folded piece of paper from the third plastic wallet of the file. He unfolded and held it up.

"Emm… Is this a copy of your death certificate?" He held the certificate up for me to read.

"What… My what?" I asked alarmed.

One would have thought I could smell rotten fish. I screwed my nose, squeezed my lips, elongated them, moved the elongated lips from left to right and from right to left. Then I raised my upper lip to slightly touch my screwed nose. I squinted my eyes as I read the details on the certificate and I sat perusing it for quite a while. The first line stated it was a certified copy of an entry in a register of deaths. It had my full name, Ada Nneka George written on it and it was issued in Lagos, Nigeria.

"No," I replied.

"Can you confirm if the name, the date of birth and the date of death on the certificate are yours, please?"

"Yes, that is my name and that is my date of birth. Seventeen, four, seventy-nine."

"The maiden surname of a woman who has married is given as Chukwu. Is that your maiden name?"

"Yes, it is. Chukwu."

"And the date of birth?"

"The date of birth is mine."

"And your date of death?"

"Date of what? Not mine," I hissed.

"Is this your death certificate?"

I shook my head. I took another look at the death certificate and shook my head again.

"Sorry?"

"No," I said adamantly and added, "How can it be my death certificate when I am right here?"

"Well, you tell me, Mrs George."

"I really don't know what is happening here."

"Well… I can expatiate and tell you what is happening here… It states here that you died in a car accident in Nigeria on 15 October 2015."

I shook my head again in disbelief and sat shaking it repeatedly for quite a while.

"Have you ever seen this death certificate? Your date of death is given as 15 October 2015."

For a split second, confusion set in. I, myself, became unsure whether I was dead or alive. I pinched my arm, felt the pain; I bit my inner lower lip and it hurt. I knew I was alive.

"No. Never. And I didn't die. I am not dead. I never died and I will not die," I cried in exasperation. "I could not possibly be dead. I swear on my father's life and to God who created me, I know nothing about all of this."

"Okay! So, who is Mr 'Orlu-wor-lee'?"

"Mr 'Orlu-wor-lee'?!" I shrugged my shoulders and said, "I don't know."

"How much did you pay him for this death certificate?"

"I did not pay any Mr 'Orlu-wor-lee' for anything."

And then the penny dropped. I stopped crying. "Oooh!!" I exclaimed aloud. "Oluwole?" I asked as I realised, he meant Oluwole, as in Oluwole the place. "Oluwole is a place in Lagos, not a person," I volunteered. "I don't know the place, never been there, but I have heard about it."

"How did you hear of it?"

"How did I hear of the place?" I asked.

"Yes. How did you hear of the place?"

34

"Hun!" I sighed. "When my former neighbour in Putney went to Nigeria many-many years ago, armed robbers visited his parents' house in the middle of his first night out there. They stole his pound sterling and British passport. He had to go to this place called Oluwole to buy his passport back."

"So, how did you get this death certificate from 'Orluworlee'? Did you have to bribe or pay anyone to obtain it from 'Orluworlee'?"

I ignored the last two questions.

"Well, we got our officers to go to Nigeria. They actually went to the office where birth and death records are kept and saw the Chief Records Officer whose signature is supposed to be on the certificate; he said his signature was forged. There is also no record of your car accident or death in any hospital or mortuary out there. No grave. According to the CRO, although the document and the stamp on it seemed to be from their official source, his signature was forged on this certificate."

"En-hen. See, that explains it all. I am not dead." I sat up and started soliloquising… "I mean… There is no record of my death in any hospital or mortuary. No grave… Nothing. Nothing. And I am here, living and alive…"

"Sorry? Oh well, this is the death certificate that was given to One Life Insurance Company Ltd."

"One Life Insurance Company?" I asked. "Who is that? Who are they? I know nothing about this, and I have never even heard of this One Life Company."

"Did you decide to exploit the insurance system because you know it like the back of your hands? After all, you have been working here for almost twelve years and I gather you are very good at your job."

"No comment."

"Who is Emeka George?"

"My estranged husband."

"Are you still married?"

"Sort of."

"What do you mean by sort of? Are you divorced?"

"No. Separated."

"How long have you been separated?"

"About twelve years."

"And you are not divorced?"

"No."

"And did you say you are separated?"

I nodded my head and pursed my lips.

"Separated for twelve years?"

I nodded again.

"Do you want to tell me about this separation?"

"Hmmm," I grunted, paused, sat up and exhaled loudly. I started a story that I had told countless times: how my husband and I attended TVU, Thames Valley University; how we married while we were students at TVU and how both of us returned to Nigeria after we graduated and set up a custard factory; how Mama, my ex-mother-in-law, gave me a lot of aggro because she heard embellished stories about how I made her son – that is, my husband – my errand boy when we lived in London. I also explained that the fact that I was unable to have children compounded my problems. Mr Murphy listened attentively as I narrated how Mama had brought to our home a housemaid-cum-junior wife to bear children for my husband in the summer of 2005; how we all lived together under the same roof for a while until I returned from our custard factory one evening and saw my husband and the young girl naked on our matrimonial bed.

"It was all too much for me. I came to England for a two-week summer holiday, a break from it all, and somehow remained here. I stayed on and never returned to Nigeria."

And then I became teary.

"Why England? Why did you not go to France, Spain, Italy, Germany, Luxembourg, Belgium or even America?"

Oh! How I hated the way he leaned back on Mary's swivel chair and waved his two spindly hands in the air with each country that he mentioned.

"Because English is our lingua franca in Nigeria."

"I see."

Ada, that was a silly and naïve reason. "And I came here because I was born in London," I added very quickly and wiped my tears away.

"Were you?"

"Yes. I was born here. I said so earlier. My parents sent me to my paternal grandparents in Nigeria when I was three months old. I did my primary and secondary school education back in Nigeria and then returned to attend TVU, Thames Valley University, in my late teens, and to unite with my boyfriend. He later became my husband."

"Husband or ex-husband?"

"Either one is fine," I snapped.

"When was the last time you saw your husband or ex-husband?"

"I have not set my eyes on that man since the day I left for the two-week holiday in August 2005, which was approximately eleven and a half years ago. I spoke to him very briefly – once when I rang to commiserate with him over the loss of his brother and that was it."

"We have a letter from him on your insurance file. He was the sole beneficiary. Plus, your five children."

"Five children?"

"Yes. Five children."

"Five children? I do not have any children," I retorted. "I just told you that my marriage ended because I could not have children. Not even one! Ask any of my colleagues here and they will tell you that I do not have children."

Mr Murphy ignored me and continued. "We also went to your hometown in Nigeria. To 'Ibutha'. To speak with your parents…"

"… You did what?" I cut in alarmed. "You went to talk to my parents in the village about this? For what?" I leapt off my seat.

"Yes. We did. We saw your father. Please, sit down, Mrs George."

I sat down as quickly as I stood up. "Seriously? You brought my old and aged parents in Ibusa into this? Why? What has this got to do with them?"

And My father? My dear Papa meant the world to me. This man did not understand how I revered my parents. That we were in awe of our parents. I pictured my old and grey parents' shocked faces at seeing unexpected English people in their parlour in Ibusa, and how scared and worried they would have been. I had to call them immediately to let Papa know that I was alive. There were so many things and problems I hid from my parents and never shared with them, and this would have been one of them. I loved and looked after Papa in my own little way and would actually do anything in this world to protect him and Mama. Anything at all. When I was growing up, Papa made sure I did not lack anything. He sent me to the best schools and there was a very strong bond between us until I met and married Emeka. He was my rock.

38

"I better ring my dad right away," I said as I whipped my iPhone out of my pocket.

Mr Murphy looked me in the eyes sternly and said very calmly, "Your parents, Dr and Mrs Chukwu are both fine, and they know that you are okay. They actually rang you while our officers were there, and they confirmed that you were well and alive once they got off the phone with you. They even confirmed that they spoke to you like an hour before the officers got to 'Ibutha'."

"I can't believe this is happening to me. This is all so surreal. You went to my village? To talk to my parents? To Ibusa?"

"I didn't go. My colleagues went."

"Your colleagues went? They crossed the line!! So why did your colleagues not arrest Emeka George while they were out there? He lives in Nigeria. He is not in London," I snapped.

"Did you fake your own death for insurance purposes?"

Ada, do not dignify that outlandish question with an answer. I sat there thinking about my dear Papa and wondering how I was going to prove to him, prove to PJ&PJ and prove to the whole world that I knew nothing about the death certificate. I knew that would be like getting blood out of Dracula. Little did I know that the insurance fraud was the tip of the iceberg.

Next, Mr Murphy brought out my picture; the photo of me at age eight that I noticed was missing in Room 348.

"Who is this in the photo?"

"Me."

"You?"

"Yes. Me."

Mr Murphy looked at the photo, then looked at me. He looked at the picture again for a long time and spoke: "This cannot be you in the photograph. The child in this photo has

39

tribal marks on her face and there are no tribal marks on your face."

"Oh, those marks faded ages ago," I replied nonchalantly.

"Faded?" he asked. "Indeed, they faded," he added very quickly and sarcastically. "Er… Are you the real Ada George or did you hijack someone else's identity?"

Unbelievable. I sat and shook my head repeatedly. I did not really know what to say.

Mr Murphy pulled out another document from the file.

It was an A4 document from his folder. He handed it to me. It was a photocopy of my expired travelling passport which I had not seen in over fifteen years.

"Is this yours?" he asked.

"Yes."

"Just out of interest: your middle name Nneka has two letter Ns on all these certificates, but Nneka is spelt as Neka with only one letter N on all your documents with PJ&PJ."

"Hm."

"Is there any reason why?"

"Yes."

I wanted to explain that when I had joined PJ&PJ, I provided my long birth certificate and passport as ID; that somewhere along the line, the typist who provided the office phone list for all the five floors, dropped one of the Ns in Nneka; that I did not bother correcting the typist then because I thought I was going to be in the company for a very short time and I didn't want her retyping and redistributing the whole list again just because of me.

"Yea?"

"PJ&PJ was supposed to be a stepping stone for me."

"Yes?"

"Hmm."

I thought that was it, but I was wrong. Mr Murphy very slowly pulled out two more sheets of paper from another plastic wallet in the folder and requested.

"Tell me about the car accident of 2014. The 4th of August 2014 to be precise."

"Car accident in 2014?"

"Can you please give me answers and stop asking questions?"

"I have never been involved in a car accident. I haven't even driven a car in over twelve years."

"So why did you receive the sum of £1,750 from a 'no win no fee' law firm for being in a car accident in 2014, if you were not involved in a car accident?"

It was all so surreal… It felt like I was at the bottom of hell. I had only owned one car in my whole life, a Toyota Corolla, and it was parked and covered in tarpaulin back home in Lagos.

"No comment."

"You received an insurance pay out of £1,750 for a bogus whiplash claim in the accident and another payment of £1,200 the following month for a burnt-out car. You paid these two cheques into your First Special current bank account."

I was speechless. "I don't even own and have never owned a First Special account," I finally said.

"Are you in financial difficulty?"

I did not reply to him.

"Where did the 365,000 pounds that was paid into your First Special savings account in December 2015 come from?"

"Whaaat? Three hundred and sixty-five whopping thousand pounds!!" I exclaimed.

"Yes. 365,000 pounds."

I wanted to tell him that I had never owned or seen such an

obscene amount of money in my entire life; and that if I saw such an amount, I might actually faint, but decided against it.

"Did you ever buy a house in Abbey Wood?"

I shook my head.

"Is that a no? Can you please speak up and also project your voice as the tape machine cannot see when you shake or nod your head?"

"Yes, it is a no," I replied firmly. "Never even heard of Abbey Wood," I muttered. "Where is Abbey Wood?" I asked.

I wanted to tell him that I had heard of Hadley Wood, Northwood, Cricklewood, Hazelwood, Falcon Wood, Petts Wood, and even Wormwood, but not his Abbey Wood; but changed my mind.

"Did you ever take out a Direct Bank credit card when you were in the university, on which you defaulted?"

"Not that I remember."

"In your first year at the university?"

"First year in university? Emmm?"

I remembered that one sunny Saturday afternoon, in my first year at TVU, Direct Bank had a stall on campus for credit cards. On that day, they gave out a free camera to any student who applied for a credit card. I signed up for the card to be able to get the free camera. I got it there and then, but never got the credit card.

"I remember applying for a Direct Bank credit card, but I never received it," I said aloud.

"You never received it?"

"No."

"Well, the credit card was sent to the home address that you provided on the application form, a Putney address."

"But I did not receive it."

"Okay. Let us assume you never received the card. Did you not get the monthly statements?"

"No. I didn't. I was in Uni doing my own thing as a fresher. I didn't do any follow-up with any bank. All I wanted was the free camera."

Mr Murphy paused for a short while and asked, "Are you still legally married?"

"Yes," I replied.

"Why is that?"

"Why?" I asked. "Why?" I repeated again, as if asking myself the question. "I wanted to take my time with the divorce," I said quietly.

Mr Murphy leaned forward on his chair, looked straight into my eyes and asked slowly, "Don't you think twelve years is a long time?"

I did not reply. There was a long silence. I wanted to tell him that my catholic church did not permit divorce, that I had a church marriage, a court registry marriage and an African traditional marriage during which Emeka paid a dowry of sixty-four pounds – but decided against it. There was no point. I knew he will never understand. I waited for the next question but none came. I remembered the address on the credit card application was my very first address in London; it was my Aunty Rhoda and Reon's address in Putney, South West London.

I cleared my throat and said, "The card, that credit card, must have been sent to my Auntie's address in Putney. It was my permanent correspondence for many years."

"Why do you have seven maxed-out credit cards?"

"I haven't… I don't use credit cards. I only spend money that I have."

"How many bank accounts do you have?"

"Two. My salary account and a small ISA."

"No other accounts?"

There was a long pause while he waited for an answer. I shook my head.

"Well, we have frozen all accounts in your name, except the salary account and the ISA where some of your salary goes into every month."

"You did?"

"Yes."

I shrugged. "Well, those are the only accounts that I have."

He paused and waited for me to say something about the frozen accounts but I said nothing.

"Do you have any holidays planned?"

"No."

"On no account should you travel out of England within the next twenty-eight days."

I did not say anything. Mr Murphy heaved a big sigh. I noticed for the first time that he was sweating profusely. He stretched like a cat and tilted his long body to the right. I thought I heard a very slight groan and a little click of a knee joint, but I was not too sure. He brought out a white handkerchief from the left pocket of his trousers and mopped the beads of sweat that had gathered on his forehead and under his nose. Next, he wiped the sweat from his neck and entire face and returned the handkerchief to the right pocket of his trousers. Very slowly, Mr Murphy returned all the documents to their individual plastic wallets. One by one, he placed them in the file.

There was another pause and then, Mr Murphy finally spoke.

"I must tell you that there are penalties for false and exaggerated claims. In the interim period, you are suspended with immediate effect…"

"Nooo!" I cut in and screamed. I could have sworn my colleagues on the upper and lower floors heard me. "I didn't do it. You can't do that. I didn't do them things. I didn't do them…"

"…while we carry out further checks into this matter. We are still waiting for some more documents. When we receive them, you will be asked to return for a second meeting. This should be no later than twenty-eight days from now."

"I didn't do them things."

"Is there anything you want to say before I end this interview?"

"It is not me, oh." I wanted to scream, but the words were stuck in my throat again. I suddenly became lightheaded, hot and nauseous. I placed my elbows on the desk and cradled my cheeks in the palms of both hands. Raising both eyebrows, pictures of a jobless Ada George roaming Kilburn High Road flashed before my eyes. Big and fat clear tears dropped straight from my hazel-brown eyes onto Mary McGee's desk. Mr Murphy hurriedly took the red file off the desk and held it in both hands; I was not too sure if it was because he did not want my tears falling on the folder… but then I was pretty far away from the file.

It was an indication that the interview was over.

"The tape recorder is now being turned off," Mr Murphy announced, and switched the machine off.

"Oh, by the way…" he started again after he had turned the machine off, as if he just remembered something. I became hopeful. I took both elbows off the desk, raised my head and looked right into Mr Murphy's eyes with hope and anticipation. "… The cheque for the 750,000 pounds is yet to be cashed. I will advise you to return the cheque uncashed as you have now risen from the dead."

"Hmm!!" I sighed aloud. Was that it?

"Or rather, if you could get your husband to return the cheque – it will make a world of difference to your case…"

The tears streamed down my face. Mr Murphy ignored me as he had done throughout the interview and continued.

"Your line manager is waiting outside this room to take your computer card, work identity card, dongle and entry card off you."

"This is so unfair." I sobbed. "This is so extreme and so unnecessary," I cried more. "Not fair," I wailed louder.

I remained in the chair hopeless and helpless.

"I said, your line manager is waiting outside this room to take your computer card, work identity card and entry card off you…"

I stopped listening because I suddenly needed to go to the bathroom. I tried to get up and out of the chair, but couldn't… My knees were wobbly, like jelly trifle. I felt my heart pounding; next, it started racing fast and furious as if my chest was about to explode. Without warning, pins and needles set in on both legs, and I was hyperventilating. The last four words, – "entry card off you" – were amplified and replayed right inside my ears nonstop. Darren Murphy's voice rang like a pre-recorded message. It sounded like Mr Murphy was stuck on those last four words – "entry card off you" – and he was saying the four words over and over again. All I could hear in my head was a loud and fast chant of "entry card off you" which became louder and louder and faster and faster. Darren Murphy, the painfully thin deputy head of false insurance claims remained seated and grew progressively fatter and fatter before my eyes. The room started spinning around me while he chanted those four words faster and louder, like someone in a trance. I mustered the strength and courage to stand, but I was still hyperventilating. My wobbly knees became shakier and my whole body felt boneless, spineless and weightless. I felt it and knew I was about to have a complete meltdown. At the same time, Mr Murphy's body continued to expand and inflate in his chair at a faster pace. He became monstrously obese and was about to explode. I knew I had to move away to avoid gut spillage. I did not want him to explode in my face because the thinner-than-a-rake Darren Murphy had morphed into a tall, hairless, very robust Humpty Dumpty with dangling thin arms. The last thing I remembered was me thinking that was it, that I was lifeless and that I was about to die. I attempted to make a move for the door before Mr Murphy finally exploded. Then, everywhere became pitch black. I slumped onto the floor as darkness enveloped me.

I must have held my breath until I passed out.

4

The sound of someone weeping and wailing aloud in some foreign language woke me up. It was that painful type of cry that depicted total inner pain. I opened my eyes slowly and saw a white pillow on which my head rested. The pillow was soaking wet and a strong, irritating odour of mixed, undiluted antiseptics choked the whole space around my face. It was the worst smell to which I ever subjected the external openings of my nasal cavity in a long time... And then the penny dropped! I was the one crying in the Nigerian Ibo language.

I closed my eyes again very quickly and attempted to slip right back into unconsciousness, but unconsciousness eluded me.

"If you could get your husband to return the cheque – it will make a world of difference."

My thoughts zoomed from one part of my head to another. Why couldn't they just stop the cheque?

Springy metals poked my back and I soon realised that I was on a hard white, single bed in the sick room of PJ&PJ. I was still in my coat and the shoes on my feet made me very uncomfortable. I had never worn shoes or winter coats in bed. I looked up. The very high ceiling above me was covered with a painting of uncountable tiny light-blue fishes. I lay staring at them for a long while.

How on earth could I have allowed myself to react so badly to the extent that I actually passed out? I had not had any fainting spells in over thirty years.

Who passes out at work?

Ramila later told me that I was out for two hours.

Dear God, please come and get me out of this mess. If you do get me out of this alive, I promise to give the church one hundred pounds from my salary.

I refocused my eyes on the tiny fishes on the ceiling and they had a calm, therapeutic effect on me.

How irresponsibly stupid and naïve of me to have thought that I belonged to PJ&PJ and that they belonged to me! In my mind's eye, everything was perfect and tops at work – after all, I was the health and safety rep, the first aider, the stationery officer and the fire and bomb warden. I had it deeply embedded in my brain that Headington PJ&PJ could not function without me for even one working day; and I sure did work my socks off for them. I had been told many times that I was an absolutely essential asset to the company and that was how I saw myself.

When I took up the insurance officer role eleven years earlier, the whole idea was for me to use it as a springboard to better jobs, but alas, I never left. After a couple of promotions, and once I was also able to act up as a manager from time to time, all plans to leave were abandoned. I decided to stay and work my way up the rungs of the ladder. I intended to remain in PJ&PJ until death did us part. I could not count the number of times I slept and dreamt of PJ&PJ. I just loved the company and

I believed they loved me too as exemplified by the many awards, rewards and recognition I received. I worked as hard as I would have done had the company belonged to my dear Papa. I was always one of the firsts at work and one of the last out.

My already exhausted mind went on overdrive with my thoughts flying all over the place. Pictures of my life literally flashed before my eyes as I lay on the thin mattress and my dislike for my husband, Emeka, went a thousand notches higher in such a short time.

The most annoying and nauseating midget on earth had once again destabilised my life!

I didn't even know he already had five children. Five children! Within twelve years!

I met Ibusa-born Emeka when I was sixteen years old. He was my first, my one and only, and my last boyfriend. Emeka! He finally ruined the only thing of value that I had on earth – my reputation. I knew that without a job I would be unable to pay my rent and bills; and would have to leave my lovely Kilburn and return to Aunty Rhoda and Reon's house in Putney. I pictured stacked up unpaid bills on the kitchen table.

It shall not happen, I thought. I knew where to go and what I had to do. And I was going to go there and do it right away.

I heard loud clip-clop of high-heeled shoes approach the sick room. I turned my face to the white walls of the room and pretended I was still asleep.

"Why so many policemen though, for one little harmless Ada?" a female voice asked. "I don't get it."

Ramila replied in a very low tone, almost a whisper. "They took it so serious because Ada works in insurance, and it is now being treated as both internal and external fraud."

"Eh?" As soon as I heard "eh", I knew the other person was

Neelam, the second first aid officer.

"Yes. And a full investigation is in progress. An audit trail analysis is being done as we speak on all her processed insurance claims, and they are currently looking at all her emails and the history of her telephone calls. Her computer was removed to check her internet searches."

"What do you mean?" I heard Neelam ask.

"They will look at the hard drive, her email traffic and her internet usage," Smart Ramila explained. "And even her itemised phone bills," she added.

"Wao!! That will take forever, although that does not explain all the policemen and cars."

Ramila continued. "Well, because Ada is very popular and has lots of friends in the building, Debbie, our overzealous HR manager of the year, brought in so many policemen because she thought it was a big syndicate, like organised crime. She thought a lot of people had to be locked up."

"What is your take on all of this?" I heard a genuinely disturbed Neelam ask.

"Well... I don't know!! It is not a straightforward case, but Ada is not really that sort of person."

In my head, I conjured a mental picture of Ramila shaking her head. She continued. "And besides, Ada loves this job. This is her entire life. How do you think she passed the senior manager paperboard promotion exercise and beat fifty-nine other candidates?"

"Yea, gotcha, but I still don't think she should have been suspended, though," Neelam added.

"I agree," Ramila concurred. Then she lowered her voice and I had to really strain my ears to hear her say, "There are so many aspects of criminal deception here. There is also a possibility Ada

51

is not really Ada George, that she hijacked somebody else's name and details."

"That is impossible. She was born in London."

"Yes. But how do you explain that photo of her in a village when she was eight years old? In that image Ada had two facial tribal marks… But…our present-day Ada has no facial marks."

"So?"

"Well, a scanned-over copy of the picture of the other Ada shows the two marks."

My heart sank deeper than the Titanic. I felt the hot tears flow from my right eye straight into the left one and on to the pillow. Even my very own Ramila doubted me. Suddenly, a tiny voice whispered, "Ada. Get up and leave." It was my late grandmother.

Both ladies were in a state of shock when I unexpectedly leapt off the metal bed. They must have thought I was still unconscious. I should have explained to them that my parents sent me back to Nigeria when I was three months old and that, as a child, I suffered frequent fainting spells and high fevers. That my illiterate grandmother got a native doctor to put the marks on my face when I was seven years old because she believed that the marks would stop my ailments – like the spell that I just had. I wanted to use my tears to scrub off the foundation and mineralised powder on my face for them to see the marks, but I knew that was not going to change anything. I headed straight for the door. The second first aider, Neelam, was talking but I was not listening.

Ramila followed me out of the first aid room; she looked pained and I could see genuine sadness written all over her face.

"Here, Ramila," I said as I took off my dongle and handed my name badge, the entry and smart cards to her.

Ramila did not take them off me; instead, she took my right hand and held it firmly in both hands, and spoke apologetically. "Ada, don't worry. I am one million and ten per cent certain that you will be vindicated. I know very little of this case, but trust me, it should be sorted out within the next one or two weeks." She paused and carried on, "I only know as much as you do. PJ&PJ had to ensure you have not perpetrated other insurance fraud." She hesitated and continued, "Hence you are being suspended."

I could not believe what Ramila was saying. She knew like everyone else in Headington PJ&PJ did that my husband, Emeka George, was in Nigeria. She knew we were estranged. She knew from the stories I used to tell her that Emeka wouldn't even know how to obtain a mere Oyster card in London not to speak of a death or insurance certificate.

"Is there a photo of the other Ada?" I finally asked.

"It is on the file. I am sure when you come for the second interview Mr Murphy will obtain a clearer photo."

"Is there anything I can do to help?" I asked.

"Awww!! No, Ada. I know an audit trail analysis has commenced on all your claims to find out what operations you performed in the last eleven years."

"Eleven years!!" I exclaimed. I took my coat off as sweat started dripping down my back. "That will take forever," I added.

"Yes, it will take quite a while, but certainly and definitely not forever."

"So, what do I do? I love my job and you know it. That is why I have never taken a single day off sick."

"Nothing. Are you home alone?"

"No. I have a guest. Malika. An old friend visiting from Nigeria. That is why I was late this morning."

"That's alright then. Just be patient. They were only able to

53

monitor your private phone calls for the last one month. I, hand-on-heart, know you are very professional and straightforward and I will keep saying it."

I started crying and said, "I didn't even know I was being monitored, and you never gave me heads up?"

"I am sorry, Ada. Give me your dongle, smart and entrance cards and I will escort you off the premises through the staff entrance."

I handed the cards, name badge and dongle to Ramila. My dream of working at PJ&PJ until the age of seventy or thereabout evaporated into thin air. I could not believe that I, the superstar staff and best employee of the year 2016, had been ejected like a jigger out of Peter Johnson & Paul Johnson. Deep inside me, I knew that was the end of my stellar career at PJ&PJ.

5

With my back hunched like the camel's ugly hump, duffle coat draped over my right arm and my second-hand Chanel handbag held carelessly in my left hand, I exited through the backdoors of Headington House and walked right back into the alleyway. No rush. No swagger. No hood and no fear of muggers. I just kept on walking with my back bent from the weight of the invisible heavy bag of sadness. I thought of my dear Papa. I thought of my Mum. I thought of my home in Ibusa. I thought of my pretty little sisters and I thought of my beloved Papa again. I knew I had let my dear Papa down and for the first time in almost twelve years, I felt helpless and thousands of miles away from my hometown. The rain blew in my face and washed away my tears as I embarked on the longest walk of my life back to Kilburn. If only Mr Darren Murphy could see me in the rain, with the foundation and mineralised powder washed off my face… And see the two little marks on my two cheeks. The last time I measured them, each mark was slightly bigger than a grain of uncooked rice.

I felt the rain drip from the strands of my Brazilian weave

that was plastered to my forehead, cheeks and neck. I felt and knew my wet dress was stuck to my bum and legs, but I didn't care. The bulk of hair on my head felt like a heavy wet mop, but I did not care.

No wonder people said Emeka was swimming in money, that he was an oil tycoon, that he was a realtor and always in the news. How could he be so mean to the wife of his youth?

I set off for Kilburn.

I kept on walking until I found myself on Cricklewood Broadway. I stood at the bus stop near McDonald's where I had a choice of many buses to Kilburn. The first one came, a Bus 32. I ignored it. I also ignored a second 32 and I ignored the Buses 16, 332, 189, 316 and another 32. I walked up Shoot Up Hill and passed Kilburn tube station. By the time I got on to Kilburn High Road, the rain stopped abruptly and the road was suddenly crowded.

I looked at the milling crowd on the high road, hoping to spot the identity thief that had turned my life upside down. I knew that finding my stolen ID was like looking for a needle in a haystack. A lost identity was not like a lost person, place or thing. After a while, when I found the noisy traffic, the blaring sirens, the lingering smell of cigarettes on the high road, and the milling crowd and shoppers too much for me, I turned off on to Victoria Road.

The gusts of wind soon subsided and I became enveloped by the peace and quiet and the light human traffic on Victoria Road. For a split second, my head seemed to disengage from the thoughts of the incident at work. I stopped and tried to decide on where to go.

The church or the police station? The church or the police station?

I decided to go to the Kilburn Police Station by Queens Park to report the theft of my identity, the false accusation at work, the injustice and the unfair suspension.

At the other end of Victoria Road, I crossed Salisbury Road and walked up to the front of the police station where I stood and spoke to myself: How many ears do you have Ada? What will you say to the policemen in there? You better not go in there if you love yourself. What if you go in there and it becomes another major investigation? If the people that knew you for over eleven years did not believe you, what is the guarantee that these policemen who do not know you from Adam will believe you?

I did a U-turn and headed home.

6

By the time I reached my rain sodden doorstep on Kilburn Station Parade my frozen ears ached badly from the cold. I struggled to use the numb fingers of my right hand to turn the key in the Yale lock anticlockwise. I pushed the door open and slammed it shut with so much force, all in an attempt to lock out Storm Doris and its ill wind.

What a freaky Thursday! I kicked off my wet shoes, picked up the four brown envelopes on the doormat and made my way to the front room. Malika's suitcases were still in the hallway. She always left her baggage there for the first few days.

Home was a poky little two-bedroom flat on Kilburn Station Parade. The front room was tiny and the curtains were threadbare. The second bedroom, which I sometimes called the box room or other times the guest room, was smaller. It could pass for my laundry room because I tended to dump piles of washed clothes on the single bed in there. My bedroom was slightly bigger, although it could just about take my double bed, a little bedside table, a small wardrobe and a small chest of drawers. My twenty-inch flat screen LG TV was on top of the chest of drawers and as for my long and narrow kitchen – it was the smallest kitchen I had ever seen in my thirty odd years on earth. One could hardly swing a cat in it.

I plunked myself on my battered and tattered, burgundy leather two-seater sofa and from nowhere, a very strange feeling came over me. My brain made a quick and instant mental switch. There and then in my mind's eye, my Kilburn flat that I had lived in for over eleven years and called home suddenly became my temporary accommodation, and a pink house in a little town called Ibusa in the faraway midwestern part of Nigeria where I grew up but had not seen in many years became my permanent home.

I walked into my tiny kitchen. It was filled with the lovely aroma of spicy jollof rice and fried fish. Malika was fantastic. Every time she was around, I cut down on the quantity of noodles and beans on toast that I consumed, and ate a lot of hot home-cooked food.

A yellow Post-it note was stuck on the rusty fridge door, which was almost falling off, and read, "Gone to Kilburn High Road. See you later. Ta-ta for now."

Malika and I grew up together, and although she was a few years younger than me, we were very close friends. There was a time everyone called her Amalimoyi. It was her real name, but many years ago she changed it to Mally, and later changed it to Malika when she went to college.

My trend of thoughts was very suddenly and rudely interrupted by the startling and piercing sound of the house phone.

"Grrr-grrr," it thrilled aloud.

I looked up at the clock on the wall. It showed the time was quarter to three in the afternoon. I allowed the high warbling

59

sound to carry on, but when it crossed my mind that it could be Malika, I picked up the receiver after the fifth ring.

"Malika?" I asked. It was not her.

"Good afternoon," a very loud, booming male voice said.

"Hello?" I greeted with askance.

"Can I speak to Ada 'Neeneeka' George?" The man demanded aggressively. His extremely loud voice seemed to fill the entire flat.

"This is Ada Nneka George," I replied slightly irritated by the deep sounding voice. I guessed whoever it was had deliberately amplified and adopted the intimidating voice.

What now? I felt like asking.

"My name is David Drinkwater and I am calling from LDRC. Can you please confirm the first line of your address?"

"Sorry, where are you calling from?" I asked in a typical Nigerian question-for-question style.

"LDRC... Can you please tell me the first line of your address?"

Ambulance chasers, PPI claims companies and grant scammers came to my mind. Grant scammers would ring private home numbers and ask people to apply for government grants for small businesses or home energy savings – but that was not all, they would also ask for advance fees. Very similar to the Nigerian advance fee – 'the 419 fraud'.

"15 Kilburn Station Parade," I replied.

"And your postcode and date of birth?"

"I am not willing to give you my date of birth as I deem that as giving too much personal information to an unknown caller."

"Fair enough. This call is regarding an outstanding debt of 8,321 pounds that you owe United Bank of London for a credit card at your previous address."

I felt like screaming but calmly said, "I think there is a mistake here. What is LDRC?"

"London Debt Recovery Company."

"Well, I think you have the wrong number because I have lived at this address for the last eleven years of my life."

"No. I haven't got the wrong number."

"Yes. You have."

"No, I haven't. I am not going to stay on the phone going around in circles with you. We are debt collectors and we have been instructed to collect the debt that you owe. Please note that if you do not make arrangements to pay this outstanding debt within the next fourteen days, legal action would be taken against you."

I hung up.

When the phone rang again, I picked the receiver up and replaced it immediately.

Mr Drinkwater's telephone call opened a floodgate of another set of calamities that occurred in very quick, rapid succession.

If a clairvoyant had told me that I would end up in Kirikiri as a result of the whirlwind hurricane that followed everything that happened that Thursday, I would have screamed "Shut the front door!" from the 72nd floor of the Shard.

Kirikiri is a small county, a stone's throw from Ajegunle – the former jungle city of Lagos. The Nigerian medium and maximum prisons are situated in Kirikiri. In all the years that I lived in Nigeria I never ventured near Kirikiri. The closest remote contact I had with Kirikiri was when I was in the secondary school and we had a couple of very intelligent girls that lived there. Unfortunately, the mere fact that they were from Kirikiri almost obliterated their academic prowess in my head.

7

I knew Malika was back from Kilburn High Road when I heard the front door rattle aloud.

"Hello Ada of London. How come you are home so early?" she called cheerfully from the hallway.

I got off the sofa and very slowly made my way to the door. As I watched a happy Malika bounce up the short hallway in her five-inch stilettos, tears dropped on to my cheeks and nose and straight into my mouth. I rushed straight into Malika's arms, crumbled and started sobbing like a baby. My shoulders heaved and my whole upper body shook vigorously with deep cries from my very inside. A shocked Malika embraced and held me for a bit, then she let go of me and stepped back. I saw alarm, shock and worry instantly plastered all over her face.

"What's the matter?"

"I am finished." I convulsed in sobs and used the back of my hand to wipe the dripping mucus from my nose.

"What is wrong? Ada?" She stepped further away and asked. "What is the matter? Is our dear Papa okay?"

I nodded.

"How is Mama?"

"They are fine."

"Your health?"

"I am fine."

"Your sisters? Aunty Rhoda and Reon?"

"Everyone is fine."

"What then?" she asked. "Come and sit down... Come on... Don't stand there... Let us go and sit down... Look at your swollen eyelids. What is the matter?"

Every time she asked me what was wrong, more hot salty tears dropped on my nose, mixed with the watery mucus and trickled into my mouth. Malika led me to the battered and tattered burgundy leather sofa.

"What is wrong?... Why are you doing this to yourself?"

I remained on my feet by the sofa and carried on sobbing.

"Ada. Sit down," she instructed sternly and stood over me like a mother would.

I perched on the edge of the sofa.

"Stop crying," she advised as she wiped my tears away with the right palm of her hand. "It is enough now. Stop crying."

Unfortunately, every time she asked me to stop more tears streamed down my cheeks.

"Did anybody die?"

"Nhm-nhm." I shook my head.

"Did you kill anybody?"

"Nhm-nhm." I shook my head again.

"So why are you crying? There is nothing from the heavens that the earth cannot contain. What is it?"

"I just had a phone call. A man called Mr Drinkwater from a debt collecting company rang to say I owed money." I sobbed.

63

"Yeees? And so? What else…?"

"He called on behalf of United Bank of London. Mr Drinkwater. He said I owed 8,321 pounds."

"Yes?" Malika asked. "What is the big deal?" She asked and waited. "I owe my bank in Nigeria over a 125 million naira and I can't see myself ever paying it all back before I die. Sooo…yeees?"

I stopped crying and kept quiet.

"Talk to me… Speak up."

"Towards the end of the telephone conversation Mr Drinkwater became very rude and aggressive. He said that if I did not pay within 14 days, legal action would be taken against me."

"Yes? You won't be the first person to go to court." How could Malika be so calm? "Not that they will cut your hand off or kill you! Or go for your mother because of your maiden name?"

I was amazed at Malika's nonchalant attitude.

"Or has anyone been murdered?"

"No," I said, paused and continued. "I never applied for or owned a United Bank of London credit card. In fact, I never even knew there was a United Bank in London. I knew there used to be a United Bank for Africa, UBA in Nigeria, but I am not sure if it still exists."

"Ada. You shock me." She paused for effect, looked at me with her two eyes wide open and continued with both hands on her hips and both elbows turned outward. "Have you ever heard of anyone that was locked up for owing money to a bank?" She paused and added, "And yes, UBA still exists. Google it if in doubt."

"Nhm-nhm." I shook my head.

"I owe my bank millions of naira and I have never ever been stopped on the road or in the branch for the debt… And bear in mind… I walk pass my bank at least twice a day as it is just two

64

doors away from my house in Lagos… Sometimes six times a day."

"But I don't owe any bank any money." I shrieked.

"You don't? How is that possible?"

"That is not all, oh. I was suspended from work this morning."

"What?" Malika shrieked as she took her coat off, plonked herself on the sofa beside me and flung her shoes off. "Ah-ah!! What is happening Ada? What did you do?"

"I didn't do anything. I don't know why this is happening." I started crying again. "It is not me. It is that Emeka." I sobbed as I explained what happened at work and ended it with the credit card that was sent to Aunty Rhoda's address.

Malika held me in her arms as I placed my head on her shoulder and stroked my frizzy and damp Brazilian weave.

"This same Emeka?" she screeched. I could see surprise and irritation written all over her face.

"Yes, oh. I just don't know what to do."

"Don't worry," Malika said after a long pause. "First thing tomorrow we will go and talk to a lawyer."

I nodded my head again.

"Let me get you a nice cuppa." Malika got up, headed for the kitchen and stopped halfway. From the kitchen door, she told me how oral history had it that Emeka's grandfather stole a goat from a neighbouring village and tied the goat to his back like it was a baby… Until he got home… About how he roasted and ate the goat with the hairs on because he did not want to leave any trace of the stolen goat.

I could not understand why Emeka would go as far as killing me on paper for money. By the time I had left Nigeria, he was already rolling in money from the custard factory that we set up together and he was already hobnobbing with the high-and-mighty big boys of Lagos. His slogan back then was that Lagos was not for wimps and slow coaches.

My relationship with Emeka George had started during my vacation job in the records and filing room of one of Lagos's state ministries. He was my mentor. He taught me how to put files away in alphabetical order in the filing cabinets that were labelled A–Z, and he also taught me how to eat groundnuts and roasted plantain for lunch. After work, he would escort me to the bus stop from where I took the bus back home to my auntie's house. Back then, Emeka lived on Montgomery Road, Yaba, with his oldest brother, Ignatius, an unmarried civil servant.

At the time I had met Emeka, he was already richer than most of his contemporaries. In fact, Emeka made and saw big money as far back as the early nineties. Back then, his brother, Ignatius, was among those in charge of evacuating the illegal Pompolo fishing community. Emeka became one of the main guys behind the demolition of the shanti town. He always bragged about how he and his men worked extremely hard to found the Orange Island. He said they destroyed plank houses, wooden shacks and boats and forcefully ejected the occupants of the town. Emeka used to brag about how he led the bulldozers that razed down Pompolo, how they fired indiscriminate gun shots in the air and how he and his men rendered most of the occupants homeless.

As a reward for successfully leading the demolition team, his brother gave him a gift of ten thousand naira. Back then, ten thousand naira was big money. Emeka used the money to buy Abananya made-in-Nigeria shoes and bags from the Lagos Island and sold them on the mainland to University of Lagos and Yaba College of Technology students. He more than tripled the money within a short time. Emeka bought and sold stuff for a long while, until one day his brother pitied him and used his connections to put him in one of the federal ministries where he worked as a filing clerk and that was where I met him.

Emeka and I had applied and attended the same university in London. Both of us excelled at uni. We married soon after graduation and achieved so much within a short time, including the remote construction of a three-bed house in Lagos.

We had returned to Nigeria when the house was completed and moved straight in there from where we started our custard business.

Malika returned to the living room. "Here is your tea, Madam," she announced as she handed the mug to me. The way she dragged the word "tea" brought a smile to my face.

"It is well," both of us chorused simultaneously as Malika returned to her position on the sofa. I took a large sip of the tea and it warmed me up nicely.

We were quiet for a long while. All sorts of thoughts ran around my head as I sat and watched Malika fiddle with the little gold stud on her nose.

I was brought back to my London palaver when Malika stopped playing with the shiny dot. She pushed her big boobs up with her two arms and broke the silence.

"Maybe if Emeka returns the uncashed cheque it will help."

I did not say anything. I wanted Malika to continue fiddling with the stud. Malika dripped in eighteen carat gold all the time. I sat and surveyed her total package and wished I had her kind of confidence. I wondered if PJ&PJ would have suspended such a confident person. She wore two neck chains; two large earrings on each ear; loads of bangles on each wrist; and a big, fat, oval ring on each middle finger. I met pretty and bubbly Malika – popularly known as the lady with the big boobs – through my younger sister, Vicky, and we struck a friendship that lasted a lifetime. In fact, she was very close to all of my five sisters – Vicky, Sarah, Angela, Margaret and Edith. Malika hailed from Ibusa as well, but she was a typical Lagos girl. She was very streetwise and had gained a lot of life experience over the years. She always bragged that she planted the proverbial toro (the old Nigerian threepence) in Lagos and that she was a typical Lagos girl.

"Even the marks on my face were an issue."

"Which marks?"

"These."

"P-please!"

"I know."

"Something similar to this happened to my step-sister and it took her ages to prove her innocence. You need to get yourself a very good lawyer quick-quick as today's events could drag on for a very long time."

"Emeka!" I hissed, shook my head and added, "That Emeka has brought me nothing but bad luck from when I first met him."

"I don't think you should accuse anyone straight away. Be careful," Malika advised.

"Why not? He is capable of anything and everything."

"You are right. Did he not disinherit his late brother, Ignatius's heir of her inheritance?" Malika hissed.

Rumour had it that Emeka's late brother, Ignatius, the civil servant, had built many houses all over Lagos in Emeka's name. He could not build them in his name because of his work. Unfortunately, soon after building all the houses, Ignatius died. I was already in London when the construction finished. Some people said Ignatius was childless, but Adanne, Emeka's oldest sister, said Ignatius had a child named Siobhan, that an Irish lady had for him. Adanne asked Emeka to go look for Siobhan after Ignatius's death and hand all the houses in his name over to her but Emeka refused.

"He is really evil. Is that why Emeka and Adanne don't speak?" I asked slowly.

"Yes."

"Oh my God!!" I exclaimed, even though I had heard a different story. I heard that they had not spoken for years, because Adanne was angry Emeka built a beautiful house for her, but it did not have a veranda.

Malika continued. "I also heard that Emeka sold all the properties that Ignatius built in his name and used the money to start his oil and gas business. Adanne was very angry; they had a big row, and do not speak till today."

"I see."

"Did you know that after you left Nigeria, he ran an empire of brothels? He used underage girls in the brothels and trafficked in women."

"No, I didn't know that."

We were both quiet for a while as I took in all the new gist about Emeka.

"You have to be extra careful in this age and time. There are many opportunistic thieves around," Malika advised.

"Have I ever lost anything since I came to London?" I asked. "Apart from the one-pound coins that little thief, Reon, used to steal from my coat pocket like twelve years ago?"

"No. Actually, you haven't."

"I ran into him the week before the last at Brent Cross Shopping Centre and gave him a tenner. I also gave him my house phone number and address in Kilburn. He promised to visit soon, but never did."

For a split second, I wondered if Reon had stolen the credit card that was posted to Aunty Rhoda's house but dismissed the thought. When Reon was about seven years old, he had a bad habit of searching and emptying the pockets of all hung coats, blazers and jackets on the coat rack and would nick all the coins from them at Aunty Rhoda's house.

His name was actually Leon, but it was changed by Aunty Rhoda because she could not pronounce the letter L. Every word she came across with the letter L was changed to letter R. Leon became Reon, the light switch became the "right" switch, blanket was "branket", Lloyds Bank became "Rroyds" Bank and blades became "brades". Funny enough, she also changed the words with letter R to letter L. Bread became "blead", and fried rice became "flied lice". Somehow, we all joined Aunty Rhoda in calling Leon Reon, and over the years, and over time forgot his actual name was Leon. Reon was my second cousin. His mum, Aggie, was Aunty Rhoda's daughter. Aggie lived in Nigeria. She had Reon while she was on a short holiday in London and left him with Aunty Rhoda when she returned to Nigeria.

"You need to think back to all the addresses you ever lived, where you shared the same front door and letter box with other tenants and the people you lived with," Malika advised.

"Apart from uni, the only two places I ever lived are here and Aunty Rhoda's."

"Has anyone else lived with you at this address?"

"Nope."

"And at Aunty Rhoda's?"

"Oh, there were loads of people, but they were all sorted paper-wise…" I replied.

"Reon's mum is back in Nigeria, so it couldn't be her."

"Tokunbo aka Adetokunbo was British, so it could not be

70

him. There was Binta – one girl that didn't have papers – but she came armed with the details of a dead British girl that was born here."

"Really?"

"Yes," I replied and added, "I also know that after she obtained the birth certificate for the dead girl, she went on to apply for a travelling passport in the girl's name."

"She did all of that?"

"Yes. I remember clearly, she went to pick up her British passport the day that Emeka and I returned to Nigeria because we all took the District line and parted at Earl's Court station."

"Who else?"

"Aunty Rhoda?"

We both chuckled when I mentioned eighty-year-old Aunty Rhoda's name.

"Anyone else?"

"Henrietta. She is very British."

"I remember Henrietta and her sisters, Diane and Theodora, were British. Anybody else?"

"None that I can remember."

Emeka! My parents had been totally against my association with Emeka because of his poverty-stricken background. I remember when I insisted that I was going to marry Emeka, my mum said poverty was hereditary and it was the best recipe for an unhappy married life because bickering, arguments and wife-battering were usually the order of the day; but I insisted and married Emeka.

"It is quite straight forward. Someone has to go and get the cheque off him before he cashes it. End of," Malika concluded.

8

An annoying sound of loads of tiny little feet were pattering right inside every part of my head; that coupled with the loud and irritating pitter-patter-pitter sound of the falling rain on the roof roused me from my dreamless and restless sleep. Malika's loud snoring from the little bedroom seemed to compete with the knocking of the wet drops coming from outside; and the mere dawning of a new day dampened my already damp spirits. The clock on the wall showed the time was ten minutes to six in the morning.

How and when we went to bed that night I could not remember. Malika always came armed with sleeping tablets which she took every night. I partook in them before I retired to my bedroom and anticipated I would sleep well, but alas, deep sleep evaded me. Most of the night, I dozed with my eyes wide open like those of a shark.

The sound of the falling rain on the roof soon stopped. I turned on my bed and pulled the cold curtains back. When I peered out of the misty window, I saw that tiny feathery snowflakes, which were being blown in different directions, had replaced the earlier precipitation.

My cluttered bedside table did not help matters. It was full to the brim. I could not believe I had amassed and kept so much stuff on such a small surface. Poor bedside table. There was the huge bedside lamp from IKEA, the Auriol weather station radio-controlled clock from Lidl, my alarm clock from Argos, my statue of Saint Therese of the Child Jesus, housekeys, a mobile phone, a pair of earrings, my black Fitbit, a stained empty teacup and four unopened envelopes. All on one little bedside table!

I looked at the four unopened envelopes and wondered what they were about and from whom the letters came from.

The first one was a reminder about my annual eye test from my optician, but the second was deadly. Words cannot describe what that second letter did to me. It was like those tiny little feet that were pattering inside my head became giant feet in wellington boots and trampled around in my skull, like ten big bulls in a tiny little China shop.

The letter was from another debt recovery company and the end bit read:

"The amount due is £12,666.21. If we do not receive the payment in full within five working days from when you get this letter, we will take legal action in order to recover the debt and you will undoubtedly incur interest on the outstanding balance. If we are successful with the court action our legal expenses will be added to your debt and you will have great difficulty in getting credit in the future."

Oh my God! Another debt of twelve-whooping-thousand, six hundred and sixty-six pounds and twenty-one pence!

There was a number on the letter that I could ring between 8am and 9pm, Monday to Friday. I knew without a shadow of doubt, that criminal proceedings in a court of law was unavoidable. I knew I would get a criminal record and wondered how my poor parents would take it all. Especially my dear Papa. My future looked bleak and blank.

Two old incidents flashed through my mind as I read the letter a second and third time. I remembered what had happened a few months ago – a cheque for fifty pounds came in the post for a survey I never participated in. I thought the company sent the cheque to me in error, so I sent it back to them. Maybe, if I had probed further, I would have found out then that there was a second Ada George. I also remembered how I wanted to redeem my reward points at the Mega-Drug store a couple of weeks ago and was told the reward vouchers had been emailed to me. I remembered they quoted an email address which was not mine. I should have done something then. A stitch in time always saves nine.

I knew it was time I looked for external help when I opened the third and fourth letters. In that third envelope, a brown one, was a penalty charge notice for vehicle registration number ADA001. It was for an alleged contravention of being in a bus lane. The letter stated that I had been caught on their CCTV camera and that if I did not pay within 28 days, they will serve an enforcement notice to the person that was the owner of the vehicle. I felt like a big tree fell on me and more little trees fell on top of the big one.

"MALIKA!" I screamed at the top of my voice. "MALIKA!" I called out again.

An alarmed Malika rushed out of the bathroom with soap suds on her face.

"What is the matter?"

I thrust the letter at her and stood watching her soapy face as she read it.

"Hmmm." She sighed as she continued reading the letter. "No problem," she finally said. "It says here that you can make representations against the penalty in writing so we will do just that in the course of the day."

"But the car registration is my name."

"So I see. But not to worry – they will have pictures of the driver."

I ripped open the last envelope. The fourth letter in brown paper wrapping was no better than the second and third. It read:

"Dear Ms George, following a recent review of our electronic record, it would appear that a balance of £1,043.65 is still outstanding. The balance outstanding is in relation to an account you held with The Fone Company. This line was disconnected on 01/02/15…"

I did not finish reading the letter. Without getting to the end of it, I reached for the phone and very quickly and furiously dialled their number on the letter.

"Phone-dot-co. Sue speaking. Can I help you?" Chirped the voice at the other end of the line.

"Um… Hello."

"Sue speaking," she repeated. "Can I help you?" the chirpy lady asked again.

"Yes," I replied. "My name is…"

"Can I have your account number, please?" the lady interrupted impatiently.

"Hellooo?"

The lady paused, and asked again, "Can I help you?"

"I do not have an account number, but I can quote the number on the letter."

After the initial formalities, the lady on the phone said I had an account that I failed to settle over 18 months ago. I could not believe my ears.

I put the land phone down.

What angered me most was the fact that I had not taken extra care to protect my identity all because I never thought anyone would bother to steal a Nigerian's identity.

My duvet-days commenced. I stayed indoors with my curtains drawn.

I shut the world out as I watched my weight dropped off like the autumn leaves.

I soon lost a stone and a half within a few days.

The nights that I always complained were too short became too long and seemed to go on forever.

I got used to staying at home.

I fell in love with Donald Trump as I watched him on telly day in, day out.

Jeremy Kyle, *Judge Judy*, the Kardashians, *Four in a Bed* and all the Housewives of Atlanta, Cheshire and New York became my favourite companions.

I also became an expert on Brexit.

Every morning I listened to Malika's horribly croaky voice as she moaned like a cat in agony, in her attempt to sing. I had never been a fan of shower singers, especially in the mornings but it didn't matter anymore. I listened to Malika singing the same song about patience over and over again. It soon stuck in my head and most mornings even before she started the song, I was already singing it in my head.

I cried when I felt like. No restrictions whatsoever and my headache worsened from lack of food and sleep with each day that went by.

One morning, I was about to reach for the last sachet of paracetamol by my bedside when Malika walked into my bedroom.

"What now?" she asked when she saw the tablets.

"What?"

"Why are tears streaming down your cheeks again?

"I have a splitting one-sided headache," I replied as I cradled my head in my hands. I didn't even realise I was crying again. I had cried so much to the extent that it had become my second nature.

"Put those tablets down. Now," Malika yelled. "You can't keep self-medicating, you know."

"But I just said that I have a splitting headache."

Malika shook her head and asked, "How bad is the headache on a scale of one to ten?"

"Nine and a half."

"Okay. Come. Let's go to the hospital, please."

"No, it is okay. I will go to my GP."

I thought of Emeka from my doorstep to the doctor's surgery. He had had no business committing insurance fraud because he was almost swimming in money when I left Nigeria. He had all the makings of a wealthy man. Over the years, I realised a few truths about marriage and got to know that whoever one married in their youth determined the course that one's life took for the remainder of their years on earth, whether they remained together or not. I realised that the fact that one had a successful marriage or an unsuccessful one was down to pure luck. My grandmother used to say it was like the "try your luck" draw at a church bazaar – that if a lady was fortunate enough to pick a man with a good and kind heart, there was a fifty per cent chance of a successful marriage; but if one was unfortunate enough to pick a mean, heartless, stingy and selfish man, the marriage was doomed.

Emeka was okay when we had lived in London but as soon

as we set foot in Nigeria he changed, especially after his mother came to spend time with us. She complained about virtually everything after we returned from London.

"You turned my son into your boy-boy," she screeched at me on a daily basis. "I heard that you made him do all the cooking... You made him iron your clothes... You turned him into your driver," She said.

When Mama realised that the list of offences yielded no response from Emeka, she proceeded to bang on about my inability to produce an heir for our custard factory and how Emeka should take on a younger bride that could bear him a son.

"Emeka, your father's lineage will not end abruptly," Mama said daily.

9

A notice that read "Thieves on mopeds are operating in this area" caught my eyes. They sure were everywhere. I made a mental note of all the health problems I was going to discuss with the doctor. I was at the medical practice as early as five minutes to eight and I was number four on the short queue.

The queue moved pretty fast and it was soon my turn.

I did not know or recognise the receptionists at the initial reception point. I wondered if they were new. All three of them looked young with the exception of the chubby, bespectacled one with a smiley face. The name on the stuck-on badge was May.

"Good morning, May. I would like to see Dr Mann, please."

"Morning. Is it an emergency?"

"Yes. Sort of."

"Well, if you don't mind waiting for like an hour."

"I don't mind," I replied.

"What is your date of birth, please?" May asked.

"17 April 1979."

"What is your surname, Ma'am?" asked the lady – her eyes fixed on her computer screen.

"George. First name Ada," I volunteered. I waited in anticipation of the next question which I knew would be the first line of my address, followed by what my postcode was, etc. but that did not happen. There was a long pause. After a few seconds, which seemed like an hour to me, she asked me for my postcode, and then the door number and street name.

May paused for a bit, looked up at me and carried on staring at the screen of her computer. I watched her type away on her keyboard with her long, curved, acrylic fingernails that were painted the colour of happiness and sunshine – colour yellow. I knew the chubby-faced, bespectacled lady was going to ask me to complete a form and re-register – as I had not been there in almost seven years – get me to see a doctor, cure my headache and bring me sunshine. I was oh-so-wrong. None of that happened.

May cleared her throat aloud and carried on staring at her monitor. Then she hacked a tiny little cough and carried on staring at the screen. After a pause which was longer than the first one, her facial expression changed into what I thought was between a frown and a question mark. She took off her glasses which had been perched on her nose, looked at me suspiciously and finally spoke.

"What is your medical number?"

"I don't know. But I know my NI number."

"That is not necessary. We don't need your National Insurance number."

"I know my passport number as well and my tax code."

"I don't need those either," she said abruptly and carried on staring at the computer. "For some unknown reason I can't seem to find any record of you on our system. When was the last time you saw Doctor Mann?"

"About six or seven, or maybe ten years ago."

"Have you had a change of names?"

"No."

"Have you moved addresses recently?"

"No."

"What is your previous address?"

"I have lived at the same address for more than eleven years."

"Have you just returned from abroad?"

"No."

"Do you have a medical card?"

"Yes, I do. It is at home."

"Do you have any form of ID on you?"

"Yes, I have my passport on me."

The lady took my passport off me and went away for a long time.

"Do you know your medical number?" she asked again when she returned.

"Actually, I just remembered I have my health number stored in my phone. Here," I said as I handed it to her.

"Let me search the national database." The computer whirred in the process. "Ah," she said and paused. "Okay." Another pause. "Em," the lady mumbled. "Let's see." She carried on muttering to herself as she moved the pink mouse on her table around slowly. She did a bit of typing on her keyboard, grunted and talked to herself again.

More typing.

Silence.

Muttering.

More typing.

She hummed to herself and typed again.

And then there was silence.

"We do not have your records at this surgery,' she said after what seemed like a very long time.

"It is not possible."

"I cannot gain access into your case note as our records here show it has been archived."

"Archived?"

I volunteered to complete a new registration form as I had not been there over three years but her response shocked me.

"No. You cannot complete another registration form as you are no longer on the national computer record.

I stared at her in bewilderment. Two large tears dropped from my eyes straight onto her counter.

"Are you, okay?"

I did not answer; I did not speak and I did not move. The receptionist got up, walked out of the reception point and came to the public area to meet me. By this time all eyes were on me and I could read utter disgust on the faces of the other patients. She led me to a quiet area of the room and handed me some tissue.

"Is everything okay?"

"I just don't understand why my record has been withdrawn."

"Take a seat. Let me make further enquiries." She returned to the reception point and stayed there for quite a while. I could not see what the receptionist was doing but guessed she was checking out stuff.

After a long while she came back to tell me that my records were previously transferred to a surgery in the south-east area of London and that she was waiting for the central office to get back to her. She was not sure if my case note had been archived or was just dormant.

I started reciting Psalm 23 over and over. I had just started the prayer for the fourth time when the receptionist returned.

"Our records show you as non-existent. That you are dead."

That was it. That did it. I shut down. I could not cry anymore.

I could not see Dr Mann because I was no longer on their register. From the corner of my eyes, I saw some of the patients in the waiting room look at me with disdain, or so I thought. With my head bowed in shame, I got up and very slowly made my way to the exit.

I left the surgery without looking up.

10

"Buckle up, please. Walk faster," Malika chided as we made our way to the solicitor.

"Sorry," I apologised, quickening my pace.

"Don't forget, I have to be home early to call my customers in Nigeria. Oh, and when we get there, please don't go banging on about your very many suspects."

"I won't."

"Just be specific and tell the lawyer about what happened at work, the phone call and the doctor's office."

"No problem. I will."

"Stick to the crux of the matter. Remember, our main concerns are the uncashed cheque, your stolen identity and the suspension."

"Okay."

I quickened my pace and was a few steps ahead of Malika.

"Slow down, please. We are not going to war."

I grimaced and slowed down.

*

Malika rang the buzzer. We were let into the building immediately.

"Remember we are also here for the death certificate. No out-of-point talk," Malika whispered as we walked up the dimly lit creaky stairs of a very old building towards the Maida Vale end of Kilburn High Road.

There were books everywhere in the room. I did not expect such a big, brightly lit room in the small and narrow dingy building. I could not see the four walls of the room. In place of them were bookshelves full of law books from the floor to the ceiling. And there were volumes on the desk, the floor, on top of the filing cabinets, on the sill of the little window. Everywhere.

Mr Bernard Benson rose to his feet and greeted us. He was also not what I expected. The first thing that caught my eyes was the snowfall of dandruff on the collar of his faded, baby-pink T-shirt and all I wanted to do was reach out and brush them all off. I was not sure he was a solicitor as he kind of looked a bit unkempt and unshaven. He was dressed too casually – ripped faded skinny jeans plus the T-shirt. Bernard Benson was of average height with a little ponytail at the back of his egg-shaped head.

His handshake was very firm. After the initial preliminaries, I listened as Malika told the solicitor everything. One would have thought Malika worked with me at PJ&PJ.

Mr Benson chewed on his lower lip as he waited for Malika to finish her narration.

"It is a shame this happened," he finally said and added, "We will see what we can do to help you."

"Thank you," Malika and I chorused.

"Did you not have any inkling something was wrong?"

"No."

"Do you always shred your bank statement, et cetera, before you dispose of them?"

"I tear them into tiny pieces, not shred."

"Do you share your front door with anyone?"

"No."

"Do you suspect anybody?"

I remembered Malika's warning and slowly shook my head. "No," I said.

"I know quite a few officers at Watford PJ&PJ. Who is the officer in charge of your case?"

"Mr Darren Murphy."

"Daaaren Muuurphy?" Mr Benson said thinking aloud. "I don't know him."

He gave me a form to complete; I also did a written summary and signed a letter of authority that enabled Mr Benson to contact PJ&PJ. Malika and I waited patiently while he rang around. He finally located Mr Murphy, spoke to him for a while, and asked for a record of the interview.

"The belief is that because you work for an insurance company it was easy for you to exploit the system and manipulate money from another insurance company," Ben said when he came off the phone. "They are waiting for some more documents from some banks and a mortgage company...There are five children, a husband and a hefty pay-out of three-quarters of a million pounds. The birth certificates for the children have been obtained and you are down as their mum. They also found out you had a criminal record for driving a motorcar without insurance."

I shook my head three times. "It wasn't me," I protested.

"They have got the papers for two properties in Abbey Wood and you sold one of them just before you died. A law firm in Manchester paid money for the property sale into a bank account in your name."

I sat and shook my head again and again in shock.

After a long pause Ben said, "Don't worry. I will accompany you to the next meeting. Mr Murphy has got my details. He will contact me as soon as he has a date."

I could not just lie in bed waiting for the next meeting. I knew I had to do something. I also knew that some proper motherland intervention would make a difference.

Gingered by those last words by Mr Murphy – "If you could get your husband to return the cheque – it will make a world of difference." – I looked into Malika's eyes as if she held the keys to my salvation.

"Yes. You have to go to Nigeria for some serious prayers," Malika advised as if she read my mind. "And I mean it," she added. Almost screaming. "Did they confiscate your passport?"

"No," I replied. "But Mr Murphy said I should not leave London."

"Em… Is Mr Murphy a policeman?"

"No."

"I think you should take a break from London. Take this to your father in Ibusa."

"But…"

"I… That is my opinion. The decision is yours," Malika said with an air of finality.

An unexpected teardrop fell straight onto my nose. Then I started… Boohoo… Boohoo… and cried nonstop.

"Stop please before you start crying blood. It is enough," Malika advised. "I mean… You can go if you want to… We don't know how long all of this will take… But I can assure you that it will take a long time because of the complexity of the whole matter."

I sat thinking for a while and finally nodded in agreement.

"Then you will also be able to confront Emeka and retrieve the cheque."

"I concur."

"Yes. And you can also bring back your baby pictures, your graduation photo, et cetera."

"Yes, oh… And my First Holy Communion and Confirmation photos. They will show I had the marks from when I was a child."

"And your parents will see you and know that you are alive."

"You are right, Malika."

"And you get to see your beloved Papa as well."

"Aww… You are so correct. And see Mama, too," I said after a long pause. "I need to get out of London as soon as possible before I lose my sanity."

"I concur."

"What if my name is on a list at the airport?"

"Then you come back home."

"It is not that straightforward. I could be detained at the airport."

"That is a possibility, but I think you should go home."

That night, for the first time in twelve years, I felt I was thousands of miles away from home. I could not understand why my parents did not tell me that they had visitors from England.

I fell asleep and dreamt I confronted the ID thief. I was in the Central Middlesex Hospital in Park Royal with a cracked skull, similar to Mary McGee's, waiting to see a doctor. When the nurse called for Ada George, I got up and so did a very fat lady. The confused nurse asked who Ada was and both of us chorused, "Me."

The fat fake-Ada was dripping in gold jewellery – nose stud, lip ring and four hoops in each ear. Her nails were like claws painted in a shocking pink colour.

To my utmost shock she muttered, "There are so many crazy people in this country," and walked off.

I woke up angry. I wanted to go back to my dream and ask her, "How very dare you call me a crazy person... Crazier woman – body and soul and name and ID and face snatcher?"

PART 2

PART 2

11

NIGERIA 2017

East or West – home is best.

What a trek, I mused, mopping my face and neck with my drenched face towel. Sweltering in the back seat of the battered green taxi that I boarded at the slope in the oppressively hot ancient city of Benin, I found myself looking right into the gaps of the driver's short, unruly dreadlocks.

Everything had happened so quickly, but my spirit was slightly lifted because I was homeward bound. I was going to my beautiful, hilly, sunshine town to retrieve the yet-to-be-cashed cheque from the thieving Emeka, to track down the ID thief and to see my parents. I knew my dear Papa would summon Emeka's family immediately and they would ask him to produce the cheque. I also planned to collect my childhood photographs and scrapbooks that showed me with the two marks on my face. I shifted my gaze from the driver's untidy hair to the dashboard of the cab. The car clock showed the time: it was 4.46pm and I saw the driver's name. Show-Boy-Ten-Ten. It was visibly displayed on a big, white placard on the panel above the dashboard.

The determination to retrieve the cheque by hook or crook before it was cashed was irresistible, even though I did not have any special modus operandi in mind. All I knew was that I was prepared to crawl, walk, fly or swim to the cheque. I did not care if it cost me my last drop of blood.

Luckily, I had made it through Heathrow Airport. I thought I would be delayed at the service counters on my way out of London but nobody cared about me.

I saw the fixed smile on the gum and kola-nut chewing Show-Boy-Ten-Ten through the rear-view mirror and marvelled at his happy, reckless demeanour as he hummed the hymn *Amazing Grace* over and over while speeding along the highways and byways of Delta State in the midwestern part of Nigeria. His body language revealed a personality that had no cares or worries in the world. For a split second I wished I was him; although, if I could drive, it wouldn't be the way he drove with just one hand on the steering wheel and the other being blown by the wind with his elbow on the driver's window. That one elbow remained rested on the window as its owner sped past bushes and forests, entering and exiting little towns and villages. He was the first and only person I saw that could hum a hymn, smile, chew gum and chew kola-nut all at the same time.

I sat sandwiched between two passengers – seated on my right was a plump, unevenly-toned, gum-chewing female passenger with chipped and split fingernails; she was like a chicken with a bleached neck. In my little head I named her Fanta-face-Coca-Cola-body, because of her multicolour. Her face reminded me of a peeled banana while her ears and the rest of her body, especially her hands, resembled the outer layer of a kiwi fruit. What a contrast to the smartly dressed elderly man on my left. He looked like a typical insurance officer. His black three-piece suit, dazzling white shirt, the big yellow tie and the large spectacles all reminded me of Darren Murphy.

After two different air flights, one international and another local, I was finally on the two-hour drive to Ibusa.

My hometown always held a special place in my heart. I loved it out there, regardless of the unbearably hot weather.

I cringed as Show-Boy-Ten-Ten dangerously overtook every single vehicle on the road. It was obvious he was out to show us his driving skills.

"Mister Driver, I beg you please slow down," I appealed humbly when he very recklessly overtook yet another lorry.

"Madam, chill-lax!" He laughed aloud.

The Fanta-face-Coca-Cola-body lady sighed in agreement with me – she shifted her body towards the window and hissed, "Life does not have a duplicate, oh."

"Madam, make you take a chill pill," Show-Boy quipped. There was a bit of silence and then he asked in pidgin English, "Are you JJC? Journey-just-come?"

When nobody replied, he reduced the speed for a very short while, maybe like a couple of minutes – after which he looked at me very sternly through the rear-view mirror, smiled and said brashly, "Madam the Madam, please next time take a sleeping tablet before you join taxi at our motor park."

He blew a huge, round, green bubble with his green chewing gum; burst the bubble, stepped on his accelerator and drove furiously faster than before.

"This is Onitsha by air service. We fly like aeroplanes on this road." He increased the volume of his *Amazing Grace* cassette, sneezed loudly, shouted, "Bless me, Show-Boy-Ten-Ten!" and overtook another lorry that had "Slow and steady wins the race" in scrawny capital letters at the back.

Barely a second later, he honked his car horn noisily and shouted "Up me!" as he overtook a little red Nissan Micra.

"This is Onitsha by air motor-plane." He stepped on the accelerator, gathered more speed, winked at me through his mirror, smiled and hailed me "Madam the Madam."

"Driver, I beg drive slowly," the insurance-officer-looking gentleman appealed calmly.

Another thing that irritated me was how Show-Boy kept fidgeting with his face cap. On the highway the visor cap was back to front, but once he drove through the small built-up towns, he would slow down and change it and the visor would be in front – I really could not understand why he did that and did not want to ask him.

Eventually, I made a conscious effort to ignore Show-Boy-Ten-Ten.

That trip to Ibusa had cost me an arm and a leg, because I did not buy my ticket ahead of time. I had to empty the little savings in my ISA to be able to break Mr Murphy's don't-go-abroad rule. In my head I planned to stay for seven days. Malika was God-sent. She warned me not to fill my parents' address on the landing card in Nigeria, because thieves and dodgy people could lay their hands on the cards and visit later at night to ask for pound sterling and dollars.

On arrival at Murtala Muhammed International Airport, I had looked around to see if there were any suspicious-looking people, but I did not see any. All I saw were happy and friendly strangers. Every single person I encountered greeted me with a smile and they were all ever-so-willing to help. In fact, I had not seen so many cheerful faces in the last twelve years.

I thought of my father. My dear Papa. Doctor Epiphany Chukwu. He was a very proud and perfect gentleman, with his hair always neatly combed and parted on the side. He loved spending most of his evenings by his fishpond; but I knew there would be no fishpond that evening as he would be by the gate as usual, waiting for me with open arms.

I pictured him speaking with his pointed Fulani nose stuck up in the air, threatening fire and brimstone on Emeka. I imagined my dad screaming, "Go and bring that scallywag here. Bring that pauper, that wretched son of a palm-wine tapper."

Show-Boy sped past sun-drenched bushes, shacks, vast lands, hawkers, motels, petrol stations, various towns, highways and junctions. I closed my eyes and recited the Hail Mary with my rosary beads. I must have fallen asleep while reciting the rosary because a sharp jolt and a sudden change of the car's gear woke me up. I opened my eyes and saw our car and all the vehicles on our side of the road desperately driving in reverse at top speed.

The chewing gum flew out of Fanta-face-Coca-Cola-body's mouth and stuck on the top of the passenger seat's back in front of her. She was chanting, "Jesus, oh. Jesus, oh." I later thought she was lucky that the gum did not land inside Show-Boy's unruly dreadlocks.

"St Christopher, patron saint of travellers, where art thou?!" the insurance-officer-looking gentleman on my left side screamed at the top of his voice.

All the cars on the highway drove dangerously in the reverse, at top speed, back to Benin!

"Armed robbers or kidnappers are operating in front," Show-Boy explained hurriedly as his eyes met mine and he saw my mouth hung open. I was speechless, watching mesmerised as he frantically drove on in the reverse gear, and at top speed. His concentration was on the cars behind him as he did not want to collide into them. He finally slowed down and turned into a big open parking lot in front of a lot of stalls and plenty of small eateries. Most of the cars before us had also stopped there.

"Did you see them?" I finally asked Fanta-face-Coca-Cola-body beside me.

"No. God forbid. Thank God, I didn't see them," she replied.

"Madam, in Nigeria, you don't have to see, oh. When you hear carry-carry, you carry and you better carry with them quick-quick before you carry last or they carry you," Show-Boy explained.

"Whoa!" I exclaimed.

"Yes, oh. Nobody tells the blind man in Nigeria when there is a war. Once he hears running footsteps, he runs with the people. This is Nigeria, aka Naij." Show-Boy opened the door and ran out to speak to the drivers of the other parked cars.

Fanta-face-Coca-Cola-body, Insurance Man and I remained seated in the car for over thirty minutes. When Show-Boy finally returned, he started the engine. All the other vehicles took off very slowly – one after the other, in an orderly convoy with all the headlights of the cars' turned on. Those headlights were left on for the rest of our journey.

Show-Boy drove along like a tamed and well-trained driver as he told us what happened.

The kidnappers or thieves had driven two cars at top speed in front of the driver of a BMW 7 Series; they stopped some yards ahead of it and blocked the road with their two cars, thus forcing the BMW driver to stop. Two other cars formed a roadblock behind the BMW and boxed it in.

Show-Boy concluded the story by saying, "All the moto behind the blockade thought outside the box quick-quick and reversed quickly. That is it. End of story."

All four of us laughed at the abrupt end of the tale.

Show-Boy remained in the convoy for the rest of our journey. The lady stopped chewing gum, the man on my other side carried on looking out of the window, and my eyes remained wide open. I started the first decade of the rosary beads again.

Halfway through the third Hail Mary of the first decade, I paused to think of my modus operandi. I had my M.O. planned in my head. I will spend seven days in Nigeria, no more no less. It would be quick. Sharp and with military precision:

"Arrive at parents. See my parents. Go see my sisters – if possible. Go through the family albums. Retrieve pictures that showed me with the marks on my face. Get my parents to send for Emeka and the cheque. Take cheque off Emeka and return to London. Quick turnaround. Bish-bash-bosh!"

I forgot that man proposes, and God disposes.

12

I must have fallen asleep because when I opened my eyes, I gratefully realised we were by the Oboshi stream which was at the entrance of Ibusa. The red sand on the untarred sides of the road told me I was finally in my compact town.

My spirits lifted when I saw the beauty of the setting sun in its golden splendour shine on our beautiful stream.

Ibusa stood pretty tall like a beautiful maiden in high-heeled shoes.

I started to sing an old school song about my journey home, about seeing my parents and about seeing my home sweet home again.

I pictured my mum summoning all the prayer warriors at St Augustine Catholic Church for a night vigil in our house and, for the first time in weeks, I felt safe.

When we were small, we were told unceasingly that no one could ever attack Ibusa, because the people were always prepared for any form of assault, be it from the waters, air, or land. I knew that the combo of Mr Murphy and PJ&PJ and the British police could not touch me in Ibusa because it was well-fortified. It comprised about nine villages and a number of streams on its borders. In the olden days, people swore by and worshipped the main stream – the Oboshi – and they actually flew to her patronage in times of trouble. Prior to the introduction of tap-borne water, Ibusa residents frequented Oboshi day and night and spent long hours there – fishing, bathing, doing the laundry, processing their cassava, socialising, trading by barter – before finally filling their calabashes with water which they carried on their heads back to their villages.

Papa always told me, that the people of Ibusa were beautiful and proud people who always had each other's backs. They were their brothers' keepers and always helped one another.

Legend has it that every Ibusa person was a descendant of an Isu prince named Umejei. He founded Ibusa. According to oral history, Umejei accidentally killed a friend in a wrestling match. Following the death of his friend, Umejei was smacked with a death penalty. In order to avoid hanging, he fled from the land of Isu with a small group of escorts – filled with sorrow and sadness. His father very sadly, hurriedly bade him farewell. He gave Umejei a gourd of traditional potion and instructed him to settle wherever the gourd fell.

Armed with the gourd from his father, Umejei set off and headed west. He travelled for days with his entourage. In the course of his sojourn, after journeying for a reasonable number of days, the gourd fell down and broke at a spot between the Oboshi and Atakpo streams. Umejei settled there and that area is the town now known as Igbo-uzo, Igbuzo or Igbo bi na uzo – which means, the Igbo people that lived on the way. When the English man came to Africa during the colonial days, they found it difficult and awkward to pronounce Igbuzo, as there is no word with the letters G and B combined in the English vocabulary and so Igbuzo became Ibusa.

My happiness increased as Show-Boy drove up the hilly road, and my eyes livened up when I beheld the land on which I was raised. Nostalgic memories flooded my being when we passed the general hospital, the post office, the bank and St Augustine Catholic Church. I remembered how my sisters and I walked up the road after confession every Saturday morning. My spirits soared higher and higher as we kept driving along Ibusa High Road and passed the groundnut seller, the roast corn seller, the pear seller, the off-licence wine and beer stores and assorted kiosks.

Gone were most of the sun-baked mud houses and their rusty corrugated zinc roofs. They had been replaced by beautiful, modern storey buildings. By the time we turned onto Isieke High Street, my happiness amplified, and I – unbelievably and surprisingly – actually forgot all about the London palaver as we passed the homes of famous Ibusa personalities: the school principal, the judge, Professor Abua and Onyenkuzi, the teacher.

"Home sweet home," I declared, as the taxi driver finally drove up the uneven, untarred, bumpy lane that led up to our compound in Ndike village. He slowed down and brought the cab to a stop in front of our house. I heaved a loud euphoric sigh of relief, adjusted the sleeves of my blouse, and slipped my bare feet into my dainty, metallic-gold sandals in readiness to get out of the car. I stretched my arms, stretched my legs, stretched my entire stiffened body, made a loud throaty and stretchy sound and proceeded to disembark from the cab. I looked at my watch. My journey door to door took twenty-three and a half hours.

"Thank you, Ma," a grateful Show-Boy-Ten-Ten chirruped as I handed him the taxi fare and a very generous tip. When he saw the hefty tip, he grinned from ear to ear, quickly took off his cap and bowed his head in appreciation.

I smiled.

"Ma, please next time ask for me at our motor park. Just ask for Show-Boy-Ten-Ten. I am the only Show-Boy there. No rival. No equal. I drive faster than cheetahs. After 999, the police number, it is me – 10-10-10."

A truck loaded with big water containers drove past and I marvelled at the drastic change. I smiled again with my lips drawn back. In the past, it would have been women and children with buckets, basins and calabashes of water trekking to and from the streams.

"Madam, here is my mobile." Show-Boy handed me a pre-written number on a scraggy piece of paper.

"Thank you." I accepted the piece of paper out of courtesy and tucked it in the side pocket of my second-hand Chanel handbag.

13

Suitcase in one hand and my good old, faithful handbag in the other, I finally stepped foot once again on the red soil of Ibusa. The good old slanted wooden sign board with "Dr and Mrs Chukwu's Residence" written on it was still in front of the house, but there was no Papa or Mama at the big, rusty iron gates!

The entrance was locked and the compound look deserted. I knew I was home and that it was dinner time in Ibusa because of the familiar aroma of fried plantain from one of the many houses that hit my nostrils. Our house, which used to be the only posh storey building in the neighbourhood, was dwarfed by newer and bigger villas.

Papa was never not at the gate.

I looked at the locked gates and then the walls. The high cement panels, which were topped with barbed wires and broken glass and bottles, looked shorter than they used to be when I was a child. Just as I was about to bang on the large, red iron gates like we used to back in the days, a female voice screamed excitedly from behind them.

"She is here! She is here!"

The gates were flung wide open and Eliza, our good and faithful servant, a middle-aged woman, rushed out to meet me. Her feet were bare and she held a wooden spoon covered in what looked like *egusi* soup in her right hand.

"Welcome, oh," she hooted at the top of her voice and almost knocked me down as she rushed at me and embraced me in a big bear hug. She relieved me of my suitcase and bag.

When I entered the compound and saw the wide expanse of beckoning land between the gates and the big, light-pink house, I knew I was home and dry. Our old place was still the same. Papa's ancient, butter-colour Mercedes 350SL was in its usual spot under the big *dogonyaro* tree – albeit covered in fallen leaves and birds' poop.

With a fixed, warm smile on my face, I trailed behind our one and only Eliza as we went past the mini roundabout and headed for the main house. The big, evergreen guava, mango, *udala,* pawpaw and *dogonyaro* trees were still as fresh as they were when I had last seen them about twelve years ago. It was under those trees that I clapped my hands and played Ten-Ten, closed my eyes and played Boju-Boju ("Close your eyes, close your eyes") and Who Is In The Garden with my sisters when I was a child. I saw the hibiscus trees from which we plucked the hibiscus flowers that were our pretend-meat when we made our play-play, sand-sand food.

"*Nnua*. Welcome Ada," Eliza repeated excitedly in Ibo and English, grinning from ear to ear. I had not seen such genuine happiness plastered on anyone's face in years.

"Thank you. How are you?" I asked excitedly.

"Fine, thank you. How was your journey?"

"Not too bad," I responded. "How are Mama and Papa? Where are they?" I asked slightly worried.

"Oh no, they are fine. They have been waiting all day. Mama woke up at four o'clock this morning. She killed the fattest brown hen in the compound and we just finished making your favourite soup."

"*Egusi*-melon seeds, right?"

"Yes. And she went to the big market and bought Lipton tea, St Louis sugar cubes and Peak milk for you."

"Oh no, she should not have bothered."

I glanced around again. The light-pink house was still standing, but the compound looked deserted. All the panes of the louvre windows were open, but the faded pink paint was cracked and peeling off the walls.

And then Mama appeared.

"Thank you my dear Father Lord for your generosity to me."

Mama sang aloud from the porch. I watched as she hobbled and danced towards me with a walking stick. She sang:

"Thank you Alpha and Omega. You are so good to me. Thank you, my miracle worker."

I rushed straight into Mama's arms and melted like a candle wax. Mama flung the walking stick away. Tears of joy rolled down our faces. And at that instant, I felt a big weight drop off my body and fall on the ground with a big thud. It was as if Mama removed from my body the heavy cloak of sadness that I had worn for weeks. I stood still and looked Mama up and down with eyes full of immeasurable gratitude, love, admiration and a bit of sadness – all rolled into one. My London Mummy had shrunk. Her big matronly bum was gone, and gone were the size 40D boobs. She looked smaller, shorter, fragile and weak. Mama was like a paper doll. When she flung her walking stick away and hugged me like a mother bear, something happened and that thing made me realise I had been suffering from love deprivation. Mama's wrinkly arms and stooped frame did it, even though I was scared she would fall down. Mama clung on to me and wouldn't let go for a long time. I remained in her embrace and inhaled and relished the scent of good old dry crayfish and stockfish from her white and purple corn-patterned wrapper and white blouse. She eventually let go, but I rested my head on her bony shoulder and remained motionless in that position for a few more seconds.

My sweet Mama. My Tea Mummy. My London Mummy was old and grey.

She stepped back very slowly, stood very shakily with arms akimbo and looked at me from head to toe, pride oozing out of both eyes. Next, she raised both arms like a bird spread its wings, turned her palms up facing the sky and raised her eyes up to the heavens.

"Thank you, God," she said aloud and inclined her head in reverence.

I felt like a brand-new baby. Tears of joy welled in my eyes again. I stood still and allowed them to roll down my cheeks. Mama wiped my tears of joy away.

"It is enough, my child," she said as she patted my back and carried on wiping my tears.

I finally heaved a sigh of relief as loud as I could.

"It is enough, my daughter." Even when the tears were gone, Mama carried on wiping my face with her bare hands that smelled of crayfish.

"Stop crying," she muttered. "It is enough, my daughter. I know your eyes have seen pepper. It is enough."

We very slowly walked towards the house as she carried on talking.

"At first, we thought you were dead or in prison. Papa told

those visitors that came to see us that we do not steal in our family. He told them that stealing is not in our DNA. He told them that we don't look for money; that money looks for us. And he told them that he and I went to University of London and Durham University respectively."

"Where is Papa? Where... Where... Where is he?"

"He is in his room upstairs; he went up to lie down not too long ago."

"What? Sleeping? Why?" I asked.

"Just resting. Stop panicking, my child," Mama replied casually.

"Mama, you forgot your stick," Eliza called out behind us as she brought the cane up to Mama. "East or west, home is best," she added with a wide, semi-toothless grin.

"Hmmm!" Mama sighed as she stopped to collect her walking stick.

"Don't forget to lock the gates," I called out to Aunty Eliza.

"No problem here, oh. We are safe here."

"Really?" I asked sarcastically and went back to shut the gates.

"Yes now. You forget Mama taught almost every single child in Ibusa, and Papa delivered most of them or their parents."

"True. Where is Papa?" I asked again as I walked back from the gates and caught up with Mama and Eliza.

"Upstairs," Mama replied.

"Is everything okay with him?" I asked in a panic as we entered the house.

"Yes, he is fine." Mama smiled.

The entire house was filled with the tasty aroma of her *egusi* soup.

"Your dad just went up for a short nap. He waited downstairs for a long time," Mama said calmly.

*

"Ada Girl. Welcome my child," I heard Papa croak from the bedroom in a weak and slurred voice. I rushed up the stairs.

A small, frail Papa sat in a brown wheelchair beside his bed, clad in an oversized, light-blue, guinea brocade shirt.

"Papa!!" I was shell-shocked.

Old age, sickness and pain were written all over his small, wrinkly face. He was thin, frail and tiny. A Zimmer frame and a second, black, folded wheelchair waited beside his big king-size bed. The room was overloaded with the smell of camphor and mothballs which permeated the air.

Nobody told me my father was ill. Nobody told me he had started using a wheelchair. Nobody told me he had a stroke and another stroke and another stroke and a fourth stroke.

I put my handbag on the table beside the unlit kerosene lantern and slid down to the carpeted floor beside him.

"My daughter, welcome," Papa greeted as he paused to gasp for breath. "Your father is tired."

"Good evening, Sir," I said slowly as I reached for his tender, bony, right hand and held it tightly.

Nobody told me he was ill.

"Your father is tired. My strength is finished," Papa said slowly.

I went down on my knees, cradled my father and part of the wheelchair and cried like a baby. I watched tears that I had never seen my father shed in my entire life drop down his sunken cheeks, and on to the bib that was rested on his laps. There and then, I resolved to visit my parents at least twice a year.

I blamed myself. If only I had come earlier.

I held on to him tightly.

"Ada! Stop crying. Your dad's tears are tears of joy. He is

109

happy and relieved to see you, and also glad that you are alive and not in prison."

"Yes Ma. Any tissue paper here?" I wiped my tears away with the back of my right hand.

"Yes. In your father's bathroom."

There were all kinds of stuff on Papa's little table in the bathroom. I shook my head and sat on the toilet seat as I used to when I was a child. I counted: six little jars of Aboniki – the menthol balm; five bottles of Morgan's hair pomade; three bottles of his favourite Aramis aftershave and two half bottles Vaseline baby oil. On the low bathroom shelf, there were at least six tubes of Colgate toothpaste in a pink oval shaped plastic container.

And then Mr Murphy popped up in my head. The bottles of hair dye reminded me of him. I just could not understand why the marks on my face had once again become a big issue. If only Mr Murphy knew what those facial marks had done to Mama. I was eight years-old when she had returned from London and saw the marks on my face. Mama was livid. She cried for days. I can never forget how she rubbed olive oil and Vaseline petroleum jelly on the marks every blessed day all in attempt to get rid of them. The marks never totally disappeared, but they eventually faded with age and were not as prominent as they were when I was younger. As I grew older, I found ways to mask and cover them with layers of foundation and compact powder every time I went out. I wished I had told Mr Murphy my life history, especially about how my parents had met in London and I was mistakenly conceived and born within ten months of their meeting; that both of them went to study in England and within the first month of them meeting my mum became pregnant with me; that I was parcelled to Ibusa when I was barely three months old and grew up with my paternal grandparents in an imposing house in our little Ndike village. I did not lack anything when I was growing up. I had many children and lots of toys to play with in our massive courtyard. I wished I had told him that I was very well read, that I attended Sacred Heart Primary School and went on to Methodist Girls' High School for my secondary school education.

If only he knew that the missing picture of me at age eight was taken in our village the day my father, Dr Chukwu, and my Tea Mummy returned from London.

And if only Mr Murphy knew that my father went on to become a distinguished medical doctor, while Mama became a teacher and later the headmistress of different schools at different times.

Strangely, I had never begrudged my parents for sending me to Ibusa as I understood it was because they needed to concentrate on their studies – although, ironically, eleven months after I was born, along came Vicky. My other sisters – Sarah, Angela, Margaret aka Margo and Edith – came thick and fast and, thankfully, all six of us had privileged upbringings.

I was eight years old when all of them returned from England, and the minute I set my eyes on my London Mummy in her floral, multicoloured sunray dress, I fell in love with her. I admired so many things about her, including her love for tea. For a long time, I called her my Tea Mummy and my London Mummy.

I snapped out of my London thoughts and walked back to Papa's bedroom. Clutched in my left hand were torn pieces of hard, light-pink toilet paper.

I glanced up and down Papa's room. Suitcases were stacked one on top of the other in one corner; at the other end, there were three big silver trunk boxes that my parents brought back from

London three decades ago: two old-school, brown, cardboard portmanteaux; a Ghana Must Go bag and three televisions.

I made a mental note to declutter before I left. He didn't need such a crammed room in his state of mind.

"Mama, dinner is ready," Eliza announced as she set down Papa's food. "I set the table for you and Ada."

"Bring Ada's food up here," Papa said.

Eliza left to get my food. We were all quiet for a while, and then Papa spoke.

"As you can see, it is just your mother and I in this massive house. All of you left."

Eliza returned with my food.

"Ada will eat from my plate," Papa said slowly.

I proceeded to share Papa's plates of fufu and soup.

"I will be full of energy tomorrow morning," Papa promised and with a weak pat on my back he said, "Welcome Ada of London. Welcome my child."

14

Mama and I helped Papa downstairs.

"I am a lion," Papa said quietly, adjusting his light-blue brocade shirt. The pressing lines were still on the shirt. I could tell Mama and Papa had made an effort with his dressing.

The living room looked smaller – the furniture was tired and archaic.

"All my mates are dead and gone. All I read in the newspapers these days are the obituary columns," Papa said as we eased him on to his favourite chair.

I could not believe my father, the great Doctor Chukwu, was confined to a wheelchair. The pomp and pageantry when my father in particular had returned from England will remain etched in my memory. There was jubilation everywhere. I joined a small group of children in our Ndike village and we lined the untarred road. All of us – the children in our compound – shook our tiny waists as we danced and waved our little white handkerchiefs in the air.

The white paint on the walls of the living room had become

a dark shade of magnolia, and it was cracked and peeling off the walls. I could not understand why my parents kept so much stuff. There were books, which my sisters and I read when we were in school, on the bookshelf. My *Sweet Valley High* books were there, as were books by Barbara Cartland and Jeffrey Archer. There were the *An Anthology of Longer Poems*, Dr Spock's baby book and Chinua Achebe's *Things Fall Apart* that my parents read.

"*Jagua Nana*," I read out aloud. "*Chike and the River...*" I was still reading the titles of the books in the case when we were all suddenly plunged into darkness, and the oscillating fan slowed down.

"NEPA," we all chorused National Electric Power Authority as the oscillating ceiling fan slowed down and finally stopped.

"Eliza, turn the generator on for two hours," Papa called out feebly.

"Welcome to Nigeria," Eliza screamed back sarcastically.

For a few minutes the only source of light was the moon; and then the generator came on with a loud roar and there was light. The noise became stronger as the other generators in the neighbourhood kicked in. The deafening sound of the machines all over the village drowned our voices and we had to scream at the top of our lungs to speak and hear each other.

My parents told me about the visit from the PJ&PJ officers. They told me about the warring families in our village and they told me that Emeka was very kind to them. They told me about the armed robbers and about the Fulani herdsmen in Ibusa, but added that they never disturbed the Chukwu household.

I told them my London story and that I just had to confront that lying and thieving Emeka. Strangely, I noticed they did not pass any comment about Emeka.

I looked around again and saw the retro rotary-dial phone

with a padlock on the dial. I knew the house phone had not worked in the last twenty-five years and I could not understand why it was still there or why they even had a lock on it. There was a blue Jerrican at the far end of the parlour. I saw the old Remington typewriter, on which I used to learn ASDFGF–LKJHJ, on top of the little table at another end of the room, a place it sat from over twenty-five years ago, and beside the table was another bookcase that was full of *Childcraft* books. Mama's bouquet of plastic flowers that had been there since they returned from England was on top of the bookcase and beside the bouquet were her various figurines. There were more rows of books on a third unit. Crickey! I could not believe they kept the Enid Blyton bedtime stories too.

I must help them declutter this living room, I thought to myself. The twin-deck hi-fi system on a little table and the big pile of vinyl records would be the first to go, followed by the figurines, the potpourri, the display unit and the old almanac of the royal wedding of Princess Diana and Prince Charles.

"Your room is still how you left it. Eliza has dusted and aired it for you. She has also given your toilet and bath a good wash," Mama said.

"Thank you, Ma."

I remained on the sofa in the living room for a very long time. I got out the dusty, old photo albums that were stacked on top of the wooden table by the windows and trawled through them. I very slowly and carefully extracted photos that I knew would help my PJ&PJ case. I removed a copy of my First Holy Communion photo that showed my face with the two marks and removed the dog-eared pamphlet by the side that showed Ada Nneka Chukwu as number six on the list. I retrieved my convocation and graduation pictures that showed my face with the marks. I found my first picture with Emeka that showed my facial marks. After that I made a phone call to Malika and finally dozed off on the settee.

I was awoken by mosquitos buzzing in my ears just as Mama and Papa were about to retire to their bedrooms.

My bedroom was exactly how I had left it. I chuckled to myself when I found my old scrapbook with the funny, glued-on photos in one of my bedside drawers.

I forgot about work and did not remember P. Johnson & P. Johnson until I was in the bathroom and the generator suddenly went off.

Emeka just dented my life! I never planned to be single at my age. Mama and Papa had been together for almost forty years.

I remembered the story of how they had met: Mama won a scholarship and set off for London to study Education. Just before Mama left for Lagos to board an aeroplane to England, my paternal grandmother (who was to become Mama Doctor ten years later) tied a parcel of food, black soap, native straw sponge and dry pepper together, which she gave to Mama to deliver to her son, Epiphany in London.

Mama had arrived in London in the early hours of a cold, wintry morning in January, when the whole city was covered in snow. Armed with daddy's phone number, she rang him from the airport and went straight to his room in his student digs on Bravington Road by Queens Park, West London, to go deliver the parcel. When Mama got to the flat that Papa shared with three other students, she found him in bed very ill with the winter flu, and out of concern and worry for her town's boy, she stayed to nurse him. She cooked hot and spicy pepper soup for him morning and night. When Papa finally recovered, Mama

116

did not go to her students' hostel. She stayed on in Papa's flat and before both of them knew it, she was pregnant with me. Nine months after Mama arrived in London, on one cold and grey London morning, a day when God seemed to be doing overtime on Praed Street in Paddington, the product of the liaison, Ada, my humble self, was born at St Mary's Hospital. Mama said I was a very pretty, chubby baby; she said her delivery was the easiest the hospital had ever witnessed and that I came out looking very much at peace with my surroundings.

When the news of my birth had reached my paternal grandfather, he was livid with anger and instructed that I should be sent to Ibusa immediately.

In accordance with Grandpa's instructions, at the tender age of three months, I had been parcelled straight to my grandfather's house, where I spent the first eight years of my life in a happy, hardworking family, until I left for my birth parents' when they returned from England.

Mama had said sending me to Nigeria was the most difficult thing she ever did in her entire life.

I had become seriously ill with extremely high fever at the age of seven, a few months before my parents returned. My grandparents tried everything to bring the fever down, from a cold bath to feeding me *dogonyaro* leaves and cows' urine, but nothing brought the fever down. They sent for the village's native doctor who instructed them to strip me naked. In the course of his healing ritual, the native doctor used his blade to cut two incisions on my cheeks and two incisions on my chest. The marks on my face were a little, short, vertical line on each cheek and both incisions were supposed to cure the high fever. My temperature finally lowered, but, unfortunately, the marks remained permanent on my face and chest.

On hindsight, I should have wiped the foundation off my cheeks that day and shown Mr Murphy the faded marks. Who knows, the interview might have been terminated and I might have been exonerated.

How I wished I had just done that!

In the silence of the night broken by the sound of a hooting owl, a lone goat's bleating and crickets' chirping, the moon illuminated my bedroom; and when I heard another mosquito buzz in my ear, I knew it was time to jump on my bed and slide under the faded duvet.

At exactly two o'clock in the morning, the table fan in my room suddenly squeaked and started working and I heard the fridge in the kitchen return to life with its loud hum.

NEPA finally decided to restore power supply.

15

Being back on my childhood bed in my childhood room enabled me to sleep like a bug in a rug. My town and its old, rustic charm encapsulated the therapeutic village feel that I sorely needed. Not even the very loud cock-a-doodle-doo from a cock that crowed nonstop from a few houses away from ours got me out of bed. I eventually woke up to the melodious tunes of the colourful birds that sang sweetly in the mango trees. I flung open my windows and from the vantage point of my first-floor bedroom saw a new town. The roads, grounds and the tin roofs of the pretty little bungalows opposite our house looked very clean. Uniformed road sweepers were at work. For a brief moment, listening to the birds chirping sweetly made me think of relocating to the village; but I dismissed the thought immediately on the grounds that if I ever did, I would be classified a big failure because I already had a failed marriage in the kitty.

As soon as I heard Eliza's melodious voice from the back yard, I jumped out of bed and made my way to the bathroom. I listened to her singing happily.

Her voice was still as sweet as it used to be. I wondered how she could be so happy after all she had been through in life. Eliza had lived a very tough and hard life. First, she experienced and was impacted by the Biafran Civil War. She lived in bushes and refugee camps for over a year during the war. After the war, she faced a second war – a domestic war – in her husband's house. There she had lost two upper front teeth and an eye.

There was a gentle knock on the bedroom door.

"Morning, morning," Mama chirped, popping in her head. "Did you sleep well?" she asked.

"Yes, Ma. Good morning, Ma."

Her wrinkly, made-up face split into a grin as she leaned on her walking stick and looked around my bedroom.

"Sometimes I wish this house was filled with children again and we were all back in time!" she said nostalgically. "But I know it is not possible," she added sadly.

Mama's face was covered in brown powder. She was dressed in a frilly, white lace blouse; and two red, up-and-down jumping horse patterned long wrappers, which were tied around her waist. Her eyebrows were shaped nicely with a very black-coloured pencil and she had on very bright, shocking red lipstick. I knew Mama would soon perch on the chair in my room and that she could remain on the chair and talk for the next one hour or more.

"Where are you going all decked and dressed, Mumsie?"

"I am all dressed and waiting for your sister, Vicky."

"Dr Vicky?" I asked excitedly. "Is she not in Abuja where she lives with her husband?"

"Yes. She is."

"So?"

"Is today not Friday?"

"Yes, it is Friday, Mama."

"Your sister video-calls me every Friday at ten o'clock. So, I wake up early and get dressed for the call."

"You dress up for a video call?"

"Yes, I do."

"Well. You look nice."

"Oof," Mama exclaimed and sank into my bedside chair. In no time, I found myself narrating all my calamities and woeful tales to Mama again. She listened attentively and did not for one second interrupt me, or say I already told her everything last night. When I finished, she sighed and shook her head.

"My body had been talking to me for a very long time, but I refused to listen. Everything that happened to you in London touched my body," she said after a long pause.

"It is okay, Mama."

She cleared her throat and spoke slowly. "Hm," Pause. "Ada, my daughter." Another pause. "There is a new development."

"What happened, Ma?"

"I have a feeling your father wants you to go back to Emeka from the way he spoke last night."

"Whaaat?" I screamed. "Hell no! No. No. No. I don't know about that at all."

"I know. He forgot about his very own sister, your Aunty Lucy that returned to Sunday, that wayward, adulterous, fraudulently rich and abusive husband of hers. She is neither dead nor alive. That is no marriage. That is hell fire."

I nodded in agreement.

"If you had children and returned because you have children from him and because you wanted a father figure in their lives I would understand."

Mama stopped talking – maybe she realised she was talking too much. She kept quiet and both of us smiled when we heard

Eliza downstairs in full-throated glory, belting out a song.

I was besotted. I stretched on my bed and opened the window wider.

"Up youuu, Aunty Eliza," I hailed.

"Yep!! Up me," she replied excitedly.

"I don't understand how she could be so happy at this time of the morning. Always happy."

"She would be," Mama replied with a smile on her face.

"How old do you think Elizabeth is?" I asked after a short pause.

"She was born soon after Queen Elizabeth the Second came to Nigeria in 1956. Her full English name is actually Queen Elizabeth."

Both of us laughed. Aunty Eliza was a permanent fixture in our house.

"Don't worry, my child. Get up. Go and pour water on your body. From now, it is all about you. Bathe, comb your hair, tidy yourself, spray your lovely perfume and carry on with your life. The two Johnsons are not the only employers in this whole wide world."

"Okay, Ma."

I went with the flow of things. My London palaver became secondary and was clouded by the household talk which was Emeka's wealth. I knew things were hard in Nigeria, but I never thought a day would come when I would hear my father say repeatedly that Emeka was a very good boy.

Money sure talks.

16

Papa sat in his wheelchair at the dining table, surrounded by his brethren, my five uncles. They were in a meeting. Papa's face seemed more wrinkled, compared to the previous night.

"Good morning, Sirs," I greeted with both hands behind my lower back.

"Morning our child. Welcome our child," they chorused.

"Ah, Ada of London! When did you arrive?" a surprised Uncle Dennis asked.

"Last night, Sir."

"How is the Queen?"

"She is fine, Sir," I replied with a smile and my hands still behind my lower back.

"And Meghan and Harry?" Uncle Gilbert asked with a broad, unclely smile on his face.

"They too are fine, Sir," I smiled.

Eliza rushed in, genuflecting and removing what she could of the breakfast dishes. I cleared the remaining and headed for the kitchen with her. We sat at the breakfast table in the kitchen for almost one hour while the meeting took place. Over my morning meal of fried yam and egg omelette, I wondered how my parents could have covered the kitchen table with a floral plastic material in this century.

"I heard them talking about you staying on and returning to Emeka," Eliza whispered.

"For real?"

"Yes… But… How about your load in 'Kiriborn'?"

"Kilburn, Aunty Eliza," I corrected. "Not 'Kiriborn'."

"That is not my 'consine'."

"And it is not 'consine'… It is concern."

"Okay. I have heard. I am just worried because if you stay, who will go and bring home the load you left in 'Kiriborn'?"

"Don't worry about that. I am not staying."

She grinned and showed the gaps that two front teeth once occupied. Strangely, Eliza was not angered about her lost teeth and eye, but I was livid for her because she survived the Biafran Civil War, came out intact after eating bush rats and snails while in war camps. Neither Kwashiorkor, Harold Wilson syndrome nor malnutrition pushed her into one of the shallow graves, but a loveless marriage trumped all those misfortunes. Her marriage to her abusive husband after the civil war maimed her.

"Will you go back to Emeka?" Eliza asked.

"Hell no. Will you go back to Uncle *KWALI-NGWONGWO-GI?*" We called her ex-husband Uncle *KWALI-NGWONGWO-GI*, because every time they quarrelled, he would tell Aunty Eliza to pack her load of rubbish, which he called *ngwongwo*, out of his house.

"God forbid," she hissed. "But what if Papa says it is a must? You know he has got a very weak heart and he is just recovering from his fourth stroke?" she added.

"Well, then I will if I have to. If that is what I will have to do to keep Papa alive, then I have to. I can't disobey my elders and Emeka's dowry is still on my head. But first of all, I have to get the insurance people's cheque off him…"

"Is Papa's life not more important than the cheque?"

I did not reply.

"Which is more important to you? Papa's life or your job?"

"Papa's life, of course." I wanted to add that I did not anticipate this and that my integrity was also at risk here. But I also knew deep inside me that I would sacrifice the job at the drop of a hat for Papa's health. I loved my dear Papa more than all that PJ&PJ business and would do anything to protect him and keep him alive.

"Oh, I see… You have your agenda?" Eliza asked, interrupting my trend of thoughts.

"Yes, definitely."

Both of us smiled.

Papa was on the phone. His brethren were gone. I watched his tired eyes open wider and glaze over. He was gasping for breath as he clung on to his phone with a shaky hand. I could never understand my parents – I had agreed to everything they wanted: I mean he had arranged a meeting with Emeka's family and I was okay with it; he wanted me to return to my husband for traditional reasons and because his sixty-four pounds dowry was still on my head, and I was fine with it; he wanted me to forget about London and the yet-to-be-cashed cheque and I was okay with it. I was prepared to do anything to prolong my dad's life – besides, I could never disobey my aged father.

I watched the mobile phone slide from Papa's hand onto the floor after he terminated the call.

He started speaking. He stammered and dribbled as his speech became more slurred.

My youngest sister, Edith, and her Intended had been kidnapped in America.

The kidnappers had just called and they wanted Papa to pay the ransom to their brother on the Orange Island in Lagos. They wanted fifty million naira.

The whole kidnap story didn't sound right. I couldn't understand why kidnappers in America would want their ransom in naira.

Papa was not allowed to tell anybody about the phone call and he was not to go to the police or phone Edith and her Intended. If he called their phones they would be killed. He was also not allowed to tell anybody outside his household about the kidnap.

"I don't have that kind of money." Papa cried feebly as his phone pinged. I picked the phone up and saw a photo sent from a strange Nigerian phone number. It was a beautiful studio portrait of Edith and her very handsome black American Intended.

Another message came in: "Pay now to save their lives," it read.

I could not believe what was happening!

"We don't have that kind of money," Mama cried. "Our only hope would have been Emeka, but we are already on his monthly payroll." Papa nodded in agreement.

Emeka? Emeka's payroll? I could not believe my ears.

The phone started ringing again. I pressed the little green phone.

"Hello?" I bellowed. The line was dead.

My father had changed in so many ways. I could not believe my parents were on Emeka's payroll. This was the same Papa who had been up in daggers when I was going to marry Emeka. His exact words were that Emeka was from a wretched family and that all wretches were wife beaters, and that poverty was the best

126

recipe for an unhappy life. He said that many years ago, during the Nigerian Civil War, Emeka's grandfather and family were so wretched and poor to the extent that when people ran into the bushes to hide, Emeka's grandmother ran into the bush with their pot of soup on her head.

My sister's kidnap overshadowed my matter. We were instructed not to call Edith and Papa mandated that I remain in Nigeria while we sorted out Edith's kidnap.

"Now you definitely have to go back to your husband. He is a very kind man. He brings us Ovaltine, Bournvita and Milo every month. He is the one that we will go to for the ransom," Mama said quietly.

"Seriously?" I muttered under my breath.

"Please, obey your father. We don't want him to have another stroke. Please, my child," Mama pleaded.

My phone rang just when I was about to say something. It was Ben, the solicitor. I excused myself and stepped aside to listen to his update.

"… Their findings also revealed that you are in a lot of debt and they concluded you need the insurance money to pay off your debts and go and start another life in Nigeria… I normally do not handle such cases… But I know you are innocent not just because you are a Nigerian and I have Nigerian blood in my veins, but because I can tell you are a million per cent innocent… We will file an ID theft affidavit and also create an ID theft report… I will contact the fraud prevention service and ask for a protective registration… I will file a police report, and obtain a copy of the report and a crime reference number… It is a slow process and the onus is actually on you to prove your innocence… But we need to put a special alert, like a red flag on your credit reports so that extra steps are taken to verify your ID in future before credits are extended in your name..."

I was not really listening because he was not saying what I wanted to hear.

"What is the worst-case scenario?" I finally asked.

"If you are found guilty, there will be a termination of your employment, a record of your details on the insurance offenders' register, followed by criminal proceedings in a court of law. Anything could happen, including imprisonment."

I picked up my phone and started deleting all my old messages. When I finished, something told me to call Edith's number with my Lebara phone. "After all, the kidnappers don't know you are in Nigeria," the bold voice that sounded like my late grandma's voice said. That was one voice I always obeyed. Without thinking twice, I pressed the button to unlock my phone again, pressed contacts, searched for E, scrolled down, picked Edith out of the top name matches and without another thought, pressed call.

Edith answered immediately.

"Good morning, my biggest Sister," she greeted cheerily. "Do you want to drop and I ring you back, London penny-pincher?" She laughed. She always said that every time I called her.

"Edith, how are you?" I asked slowly.

"I am good. Just about to go do my grocery and then go to the dry-cleaner's to pick up my clothes... If I am not too tired. Put the phone down and I will call you back right away."

I kept quiet. I couldn't understand what is happening. This girl did not sound like a hostage.

"Where is your Intended?" I asked slowly.

"Lazy dude... He is in the bedroom, snoring his head off."

I was confused, shocked, relieved and happy all at the same time. I kept quiet.

"Edith, where are you?" I finally asked in a whisper.

"Ada, are you okay?" She asked after a short while. "Where else would I be?"

I kept quiet.

"Okay, I am in your beloved Kilburn," she teased.

"Seriously, where are you?"

"Ada, you are beginning to scare me. I am in my God-given apartment in God's own country. Just had my soft-boiled egg and oats. When are you leaving for Nigeria?"

"I am already in Nigeria and I've seen the beautiful portrait of you and Mikey."

"That was quick. I only sent the picture last week."

"You did? Who did you give it to?"

After I told Edith the problem on the ground, we were able to work out what happened. Edith had sent a picture of herself and Mikey to Papa by regular post and some Nigerian crook must have intercepted the letter and photograph.

"But how did they know Papa's phone number?"

"I did ask Papa which of their numbers to give to Mikey to call them."

"Oh, I see. Now you can call me back on my Nigerian SIM." I gave her the number and hung up.

My MTN phone started ringing on my way to Mama's room.

"Mama, you and Papa have been four-one-nined. Your daughter is on the phone hale and hearty. Edith. Hold on, please."

Mama sat up in bed, her mouth wide open.

"Hold on, oh. Let me explain the situation to Mama... Ah, okay, you tell her yourself."

I gave the phone to Mama and left. I did not want to witness their reaction.

*

When I returned to Mama's room she was not there. I could hear her and Papa laughing aloud in Papa's room. The joy and glee in their eyes made me feel like someone just gave me a gift of millions of pounds.

"God bless you, our Ada," Both of them chorused, and before I could say amen Papa's phone started ringing. I snatched the phone from him.

"Is that Adolphus from the Orange Island?" I asked and continued talking. "This is Dr Chukwu's daughter. Please do not ever call this number again. I just spoke to my sister and she is very fine."

"God punish you," Adolphus said and hung up.

I blocked Adolphus's number immediately and returned Papa's phone to him.

I never really liked siestas. I never took short afternoon naps because they always induced bad dreams, but my tired brain, the warmth in Ibusa town and the midday meal of aunty Eliza's pounded yam and *egusi*-melon seeds soup sent me straight to sleep. I was in the in the middle of a beautiful dream of me being in the White House as President Trump's guest, when I was woken by the loud, ear splitting and deafening drone of an aircraft that whistled past the house. The clock on the wall showed the time was quarter to three in the afternoon.

"Did you hear that?" an excited Aunty Eliza asked as she rushed into my bedroom.

"I did. What's that?"

"That's your husband's private helicopter. That is how we know he is in town."

"So, it is true?"

"Yes, it is. His landing pad is on the outskirts of his village."

"Hmm, this is loud and it sounds so near, like it is descending and about to land in our parlour." I laughed. "He must be the most annoying and irritating millionaire in the whole of Nigeria."

I could tell from the airspeed and altitude of the helicopter that it was headed for a nearby pad. Soon after, I heard the loud chants of "Son of the soil. The river that never dries out," by the local urchins.

"Hmm, did he come because of this meeting?" I asked.

"Yep," Eliza replied.

She returned to the kitchen.

17

The show had to go on.

The meeting of elders from both families – Emeka's and mine – was a pretty short one. It was held right inside Ndike village under the tallest tree in front of my grandfather's house. There was a little wooden centre table, on top of which were a little saucer of kola-nuts, a little bowl of garden eggs, a saucer of Nigerian peanut butter, kegs of palm wine, one bottle of Schnapps, one bottle of Remy brandy and a bottle of illicit gin, Ogogoro.

All the elders sat in a semi-circle under the tree. Their eyes shone with wisdom.

"Greetings our fathers," we all chorused, and without wasting time, the meeting commenced.

I sat anxiously and waited to see the thieving ID hijacker.

Ko-ko-ka, ko-ko-ka. I heard the familiar sound from the past before I saw him. Those heavy, confident thuds hit the ground and I knew the yet-to-be-cashed cheque was a few feet away. My heart started beating fast. Boom-boom-boom. As the heavy, confident stomps of chunky heels drew closer, I took deep breaths, and waited. My whole body hummed. He hit the ground – Ko-ko-ka, ko-ko-ka. I knew those footsteps – the deliberate stamping and knocking of heels on the ground.

The smell of his ageless and timeless Aramis cologne wafted in as mixed emotions kicked in and my tummy became instantly colonised by a thousand and one butterflies.

When I set my eyes on Emeka, something inexplicable and strange happened inside my body. I never thought I would ever set my eyes on him again.

I was in love at second sight.

Emeka took my breath away.

He and I had unfinished business and my wise father knew it.

I could not believe myself. There and then, I knew that I did not allow my love for Emeka to die before I buried it. Many months later, I wondered if my dad knew something I didn't when he insisted that I went back to Emeka.

I could tell immediately that Emeka's callous theft of my identity and the £750,000 had catapulted him to a very high level. Staggering wealth was plastered all over a well-nourished, fresh and clean-shaven Emeka. He looked the epitome of big money and I could tell that his impeccably tailored, pure-white, guinea brocade shirt and trousers that exuded charm and wealth were sewn by high designers paid from the fraudulently obtained money. He looked the picture of respectability in spite of his shorter, fatter, rounder and stouter stature.

Emeka went straight to my uncles, bowed and greeted them. Next, he went to my parents, held both arm rests of Papa's wheelchair, tried unsuccessfully to go down on one knee and he kissed my father's hand. After greeting my mother, he struggled to get up – he pulled an empty chair up to where they were and sank into it beside them. From their side he winked at me and did the shape of a heart with his two index fingers and two thumbs. I nodded.

The family meeting did not last more than an hour. After a lot of deliberation, Emeka's mum was blamed *in absentia* for causing all the palaver in our defunct matrimonial home. The elders, especially my father, decided and instructed me to return to Emeka.

I could not believe my ears.

Just like that? And nothing was said about the cheque? And no apologies? Nothing.

My parents had dealt with a lot of children-palaver in the past years and even if I wanted to protest or argue, I couldn't. Protesting was not part of our Ibusa culture.

Anyway, I had my own plans. I was definitely going to stoop to conquer.

I knew the only way I could get the cheque was to enter Emeka's house and heart.

At Papa's request, the elders gave me twenty-eight days to go and tidy up my affairs in London and return to Nigeria, because Papa told them that the English man gave me work and that I should be allowed to go and resign properly. It was adjudicated that, from Ibusa, I would follow Emeka back to our matrimonial home.

The meeting came to an end as the shadows on the porch announced the sun's departure.

Back in my bedroom, I cried and cried and cried until I could cry no more.

18

Stooping to conquer.

From my bedroom window upstairs, I watched in awe as a convoy of big, black, identical SUVs with dark-tinted windows nosed up our drive and meandered into the compound. All five supercars had their front headlights on full beam. They circled the mini roundabout and very slowly came to a halt so the middle big car parked directly in front of our porch. I could tell that was not the first time those vehicles had been driven into our compound because the chauffeurs drove with so much ease and familiarity and there were precise gaps before and after the cars in the middle.

It was the morning of the following day after the meeting, and Emeka had come to take me to his prestigious mansion in Ikoyi, Lagos as mandated by the elders.

What a waste of workforce, I thought as I watched many bald men in shiny black suits, white shirts, matching red ties and big earpieces rush out of the black, shiny cars. One of them rushed to open the back door of the third black SUV. The other men formed a circle around the big black car and stood in silence, in precise military posture.

Poor men. They remained standing at attention for quite a long while, with their necks and heads erect and straight as their mate held the door open. Eventually, a bald, clean-shaven, short and portly Emeka leapt out of the SUV – Emeka had later told me that he had been on the phone all the while the men waited. His tummy bounced up and down when he landed with style and balanced on the ground. His very short legs made him look like a big fat toad.

Pot-belly syndrome. Emeka stood still for a bit, adjusted his shirt, raised his shoulders and puffed his chest out. Finally, he raised and held his arms away from his body as if he had boils in his armpits, or had applied shaving cream to the armpits. Next, he pushed his tummy up and strutted up to the front door majestically.

My brain went on overdrive. All sorts of ideas were percolating in my head. Emeka must have multiplied the three-quarters of a million pounds in such a short time. I could not wait to ask him so many questions about his wealth. Surely, he could not have become a millionaire, or possibly a billionaire with a private helicopter, a large fleet of luxurious cars and an empire of properties all over Nigeria, USA and Dubai from our mere custard factory.

"Ada Girl," Papa called out from his bedroom.

"Yes, Daddy."

"Come. Come. Your husband is here."

I walked across to Papa's room.

When I saw the roly-poly waddle towards me with his tummy like a drum, I thought he had definitely swallowed the cheque.

Despite the fact that he appeared neckless because his chin

skipped the space where his neck should have been and dropped straight on to his chest and shoulders, I still saw the old, cheerful face. The kind mouth and lucky-kissing lips that attracted me to him from day one was still there. Again, he was impeccably dressed in nicely tailored, over-starched, white guinea brocade trousers and a richly embroidered large top. I noticed his shoes were also pure white.

"Ada, how are you?" Emeka asked with a wide grin on his face.

"Good. Thank you. And you?" I asked.

"I am perfectly fine."

I was not prepared for what happened next. He kissed me fully on the lips, very quickly, smiled mischievously, and raised both hands as if those imaginary large boils under his armpits had grown bigger. Next, the naughty boy tapped my backside lightly, dimmed his dreamy eyes, raised both arms again and waddled down the stairs like a big fat pregnant she-goat.

Cheeky sod.

Papa wheeled himself along the hallway ever so slowly. I made a mental note to ask Mama to make one of the rooms downstairs comfortable for Papa so he wouldn't have to move up and down the stairs. I walked up to him, bent down and hugged him tightly.

I was at my most vulnerable and I made a very big decision to please my parents, especially my dear Papa. I chose the easy way out and decided to go tidy up and return to Nigeria.

I logged my almost empty suitcase down the stairs, and held on to my second-hand Chanel bag and a Ghana Must Go bag that contained my graduation pictures, old diaries, scrapbooks, university pictures and a very old, framed picture of me aged eight.

Mama met me at the bottom of the stairs.

"These two parcels are for you and your Aunty Rhoda.

Crayfish, *egusi*-melon seeds, dry pepper and a bit of dry fish."

"Yes, Ma. Thank you, Ma." I put my stuff down, genuflected and took the parcels off Mama.

Emeka grinned widely like the lucky cat that got the best cream. He looked happier than a lark and prouder than a peacock as he led me to the cars. That broad conspicuous smile on his face lingered a bit too long and for the first time in years, I noticed that he was handsome in a funny way.

19

The high security convoy glided out of my parents' compound and we set off for Lagos.

I took a deep breath. I could not believe that the ordinary Ada George of Kilburn who was used to the Bus 32 and the Buses 16, 189 and 139 was in such a cavalcade of luxury, bulletproof, powerful cars.

Initially, there was an uncomfortable silence in the car. I sat and compartmentalised all the recent incidents in my head and tried to work out the best time to discuss the three-quarters of a million-pound cheque; but by the time we hit the highway, the conversation started and flowed nonstop. In less than ten minutes I got to know that Emeka was into oil and gas, real estate and manufacturing, and that he was a multi-billionaire. Emeka later told me that the five armoured Range Rovers cost him 178 million naira each; and that there were ten security men in total – five civilian bodyguards and five private, mobile policemen in our convoy. All five mobile policemen were armed with Heckler & Koch machine guns. Emeka said he had five weekend suitcases in one of the Range Rovers as he sometimes changed up to four times a day because of the heat.

"I decided to go by road because my pilot fell sick and is unable to fly us back to Lagos," he whispered into my ear.

I tried very hard not to say a word about the cheque in the presence of the driver and bodyguard as Emeka and I carried on like we were never apart for almost twelve years. It was like we just continued from where we stopped and before I knew it, I was asking questions.

"Is it true you have five children?"

"Yes, it is."

"I am sorry about Brother Ignatius. Please accept my sympathy."

"Thank you."

"How is your sister, Sister Adanne?"

"Don't know. I don't talk to her."

"Why is that?"

"She stopped speaking to me first of all, because I did not include a veranda in the house that I had built for her... Enough about me. What is this dodgy thing I hear happened to you in London?"

I was shocked he knew. I was not going to discuss it with him until we got to Lagos.

I narrated everything to him, but omitted the fact that he was my number one suspect.

"Wait a minute." Emeka's eyes lit up. "Towards the end of last year, I got a WhatsApp message from a very pretty lady about a cheque for thousands of pounds in my name. She said I was about to make big money. They wanted to deposit a large amount into my account and I will get a percentage."

"OMG!! Do you have her phone number? Do you have the message?"

140

"Yes, I actually do. I thought she was a four-one-niner. Her initials were ABG. She looked very beautiful in her display photo. Very pretty girl with plenty rings on her nose, lips and ears. She had marks similar to yours on her face."

"Oh my God! Oh my God! Oh my God!! Show me," I screamed and screamed and screamed and carried on screaming.

"Calm down. It is not here. It is on my old Samsung phone and the phone is in my Ikoyi mansion. Don't worry, I never delete my messages. Never."

I felt hope and happiness bloom inside me.

"Don't worry. I will show you the message when we get home."

"Phew!!" I sighed.

After that, I became very comfortable in Emeka's company. There was no awkwardness or pretence. Emeka was in his element as he posed and showed off all the way to Lagos. We carried on talking as all five chauffeurs drove at breakneck speed, until I dozed off with my head on Emeka's broad, fleshy shoulder. The shoulder felt so comfortable, boneless and soft like the Dunlop pillows we had first bought for our Lagos house when we returned from London. Emeka and I had sent most of the things we used to set up home by cargo; but the curtains, carpets, rugs, settees, mattresses and Dunlop pillows were bought in Nigeria.

I must have dozed off with my mouth open because when I woke up, I felt a pair of eyes on me and spittle was dripping from the corner of my mouth.

"How about our marriage certificate?" Emeka asked from nowhere.

"I should ask you."

"I am asking you," Emeka said with all seriousness.

"Dunno."

"You don't know?"

"No, I don't," I replied slightly irritated.

"The last place I saw it was in your vanity case."

"Then it will be in your house."

"Nope. The last time I saw the case, it was in Aunty Rhoda's basement."

"Then it will be there," I replied, just wanting to go back to sleep.

20

Soon, we were by the Costain Roundabout on the Lagos mainland, on our way to Ikoyi on the Lagos Island. There were people everywhere.

Bulletproof Range Rover numbers one and two ascended the Eko Bridge; but, just before our car neared the bridge, Emeka screamed at the driver.

"No. No. Do not ascend the bridge. Go straight to Kirikiri."

Kirikiri?

The driver swerved the car and made a sharp detour for the Iganmu area. All the other SUVs ascended the Eko Bridge except ours. We headed towards Iganmu.

"What is happening?" I asked Emeka.

"My mother is at the Ikoyi mansion with that woman, Obiageli, my baby wife. Let us go to my palatial country estate in Kirikiri."

"Oh," I said quietly.

"Yes. Don't worry – you will like it there. It is modelled on the American White House," he said as he stroked my Brazilian hair. "And it is actually more comfortable than my Ikoyi house," he added and rested his right hand on my lap.

"The Kirikiri Maximum Prison is just round the corner from here," Emeka said as we weaved along the potholed roads of Kirikiri. We drove past the Kirikiri market, past loads of side streets and lots of local urchins until we turned onto a fairly narrow, tarred lane without houses on either side.

"Prince E. George Drive," I read out aloud and looked at Emeka with askance.

He smiled proudly. After about a quarter of a mile we drove up to a big-gated estate. The two grand iron gates had the words "White House" boldly written in gold. Other signs on the gates read: "Private estate", "Trespassers will be prosecuted", "No thoroughfare", "Beware of the dogs" and "No loitering and no malingering".

"This is my humble sanctuary," Emeka announced as we passed yet another quarter mile or more of a tree-lined driveway.

The barbed wire fences were at least twenty feet long and the gates were monitored by two uniformed gatemen and two mobile policemen. The driver meandered through the sweeping gravel drive slowly. The first-generation palatial mansion was set within a seventy-acre estate in Kirikiri. The display of grandeur and wealth was a far cry from Emeka's less privileged background of an Ibusa palm-wine tapper's son.

"I just bought the two properties behind the back garden last week."

"Why?"

"I want to turn this area into a little money village."

Two well-nourished, mean-looking, black Alsatian dogs roamed the grounds of the estate. I looked at Emeka again with suspicion, but he avoided eye contact.

"Private jets are not a luxury in Nigeria – they are a necessity," Emeka explained proudly when he saw me staring with admiration at the tennis court and helipad.

I smiled. Midlife crisis!

We soon passed a red sports car that was ostentatiously parked off the mini roundabout of the sweeping drive and our driver deliberately slowed down. I could tell they did this showing-off exercise on a regular basis.

"That over there is the Ferrari 458 Spider and that gleaming beauty behind it is my black, convertible Porsche," Emeka explained slowly with fake humility as he pointed to a posh Ferrari that sat on the long driveway.

"Hmm." I exhaled aloud when our car finally came to a halt in front of a sprawling, magnificent, white mega-mansion. Once I set eyes on the edifice, and after all the attention-seeking flashy cars that I had seen, I was convinced, without a shadow of doubt, that Emeka did not steal my ID or fake my death. At the far end of the compound, a Rolls-Royce Phantom Coupé was parked in front of a massive car port.

"Close your mouth," Emeka instructed and added, "This is my den. My second office. My stress-free holiday home-cum-guest house."

I didn't even know my mouth was open in awe. I just couldn't believe it all.

Our car finally slowed down. The two big overweight Alsatian dogs wobbled over to the car. They wagged their tails nonstop and jumped up excitedly. I could tell they were delighted to see Emeka. I watched with admiration as he stroked their ears and patted their backs.

Sorry, Ada. Emeka did not do any fraud in your name.

Wrong target.

Emeka proudly pointed to various doors as we walked up the ceramic and stone-tiled floor of a huge hallway. He grabbed my hand and led me into the main part of the most immaculate and pristine house I had ever entered in my entire life. The dazzling bright lights from the ceiling and from the floor and table lamps, together with the chandeliers and spotlights hanging from the high ceilings lit up the entire front room. Everything in the front room was pure white and spotless, and the plump and plush sofas were all white as well.

Men and women, most of them in uniforms, appeared from various parts of the house. They all formed a neat wide semi-circle and stood at attention.

"Good evening, Sir. Welcome Ma," they all chorused at the same time.

I could see Emeka felt taller than his five feet and two inches. He introduced the cook, the gardener, the laundry man, the housekeeper, the steward and, finally, the personal assistant. His PA. He announced her with an affectionate smile on his face. "Her name is Udo, which means peace," he said slowly. Udo wore a big, low V-neck, banana-yellow boubou. I noticed that her fingernails were painted in the same colour. Udo stood out. She was very pretty with fair, flawless skin.

"Is dinner ready?" Emeka asked.

"Yes, Sir." The cook replied.

"Udo, please show Madam the master bedroom. I will go and see what is for dinner."

21

Dinner was a banquet. There was an incredible amount of matching silver on the twelve-seater dining table. Assorted food was nicely presented in expensive porcelain dishes. The rays of light from the huge Swarovski crystal chandelier were mind blowing, and the aroma of a mixture of soups filled the room and tantalised my senses. I couldn't remember the last time I sat at a proper dining table to eat.

I was still oohing and aahing when my phone rang. It was Daisy from work. She called to say they had advertised both my old and new posts. After the phone call I was down for a bit, but that did not last long as I got sucked into Emeka's wealth.

"Among the supercars are my Maserati, Lamborghini, Ferrari and my Porsche."

Oh, shut up, I hissed in my head.

"See why I love Nigeria? My dear, anyone can become a multi-billionaire within a short time in this country. The family yacht is at the back of the guests' chalet."

OMG! Shoot me, I wanted to scream.

"Emeka, how about the phone with the WhatsApp message?" I finally asked.

"It is in the Ikoyi mansion. I will bring it over tomorrow."

Emeka was not the ID thief. The next person I had to check out in Nigeria after seeing the WhatsApp message was Reon's mum. I refused to admit to myself that the Nigeria trip was fruitless. I still had to find the thief.

I watched Emeka gobble up all the food between panting and grunting. Then it started to rain, accompanied by heavy thunder and lightning.

After dinner, we retired to a private sitting room that led to the master bedroom, and there Emeka took me on a beautiful trip down memory lane, about when we lived in London and our days at Thames Valley University.

"Stop plying me with alcohol," I screeched when Emeka refilled my gold-rimmed champagne flute yet again.

"I want to get you drunk so that you can tell me where your monies are," he laughed.

We avoided talking about our break.

"I will take you on a grand tour after breakfast tomorrow morning. Big is beautiful."

"Why Kirikiri though?"

"Because this is the only place where I could get so much land. Where else will I have so much space to do all of this in Lagos? I also have a piano room with a grand white piano, a snooker room and a study in this house."

"You have done very well."

Emeka nodded and refilled my champagne flute yet again.

"Stop plying me with champagne," I slurred and laid my head on Emeka's shoulder like I used to when we were in TVU.

"How much does JJ pay you after tax?" Emeka asked out of the blue.

"Emm." I was not too sure whether to say or not. "I take home £2,500 after tax."

"Is that all? Two and a half thousand pounds only? Forget about JJ and London and their chicken change. Just stay here… I will write and send them a cheque for their miserable seven-hundred and fifty thousand pounds."

"It is not JJ." I laughed. "It is PJ&PJ. Peter Johnson and Paul Johnson."

"Dumbos!! How they could think you faked your death for such a miserable amount of money beats my imagination."

"That job means the world to me, you know, and it pays my bills."

"Just stay in Nigeria. If they have ten heads per neck, let them come and arrest you here and we will show them that khaki and leather are not the same. I can very comfortably pay double your salary every month, tax free. In fact, bear with me…"

Emeka rushed across the handwoven Turkish rug and dashed out of the living room. He went across to the bedroom and returned with a wad of fifty-pound notes.

"Here. Ten thousand pounds for starters."

"No. Thank you." I gasped.

"Don't be silly," Emeka said as he stuffed the money into my handbag.

"If I had an account in Nigeria, I would have paid the money into it."

"But you do."

"No. I don't."

"Yes, you do. Our joint accounts are still live. I have been running all accounts in both names as they were."

"Well, I have to go back and clear my name," I protested, and added, "I can't leave the life I have led for almost twelve years just like that. I have to find the thief."

"And what will happen if you don't?"

"There will be very serious consequences. I am alive. I need to prove to the world that I am alive. I have to find the culprit. I can't abandon my London life just like that. My love for London is very deep and my love for Kilburn is even deeper."

Emeka listened, but not attentively. All I could see was lust in his eyes.

I sipped endless champagne and hated myself and what I was doing. Every time Emeka pinched my bottom and boobs, I wriggled and giggled on the plush leather sofa like a teenager. He nibbled at my ears and in his baritone voice whispered "Sorry… please forgive me. I am begging for forgiveness." into my ears. The pure love in that living room was electric and I was surprised at myself and the rate at which the rush of adrenalin fuelled a strange kind of lust for my ex-husband.

When Emeka planted a lingering kiss on my lips, the last twelve Christmases rolled into one special day. Next, he cradled me in his short, strong arms and whispered between short kisses. "We have a lot of catching up to do." Kiss. "Forgive me for treating you so bad." Kiss. "Forget about London and the two Johnsons." Kiss. "You have got me." Kiss. "My love for you will never die." Kiss. "I will pay you double of your wages every month." Kiss, kiss, kiss.

His fingers traced and moved exploringly to every part of me. He started from my eyes, nose, ears, mouth, forehead, cheeks, throat, breasts… All the while he kept professing his love for me.

"I love you, Ada," he whispered for the umpteenth time.

*

I will never know how I made it to the lavender-scented master bedroom. I vaguely remember that he took our shoes off and helped me into my nighty. I also fuzzily remember that he tucked me into the immense, luxurious, king-size bed like he used to do before he had become obsessed with my inability to have a baby. I remember he turned off the lights and held me in his arms. I remember how we gyrated to our star-record of old "Sugar Bum Bum" as the bedside lamp grew dimmer and dimmer; and I remember me purring like a kitten.

And then, all of a sudden, I started sobbing. I cried so much as it all came back to me – how my computer suddenly froze the evening before the morning of the event at work. It was really weird. I could not click on or open any of my icons and I could not log off or shut the computer down.

"I can't believe somebody would have the heart and liver to take out so many credit cards in my name," I said in between sobs.

"Ada. I have told you to forget about London. I am a wealthy man. I will take care of you," a tired Emeka advised. I guess all he wanted was action and sleep.

The tunes and sequence of the music were very familiar and for a split second I wondered if that was Emeka's CD from our uni days. From "All Night Long" to "Three Times A Lady" to "I Will Love You Tomorrow" And I waited for "Sugar Bum Bum" I knew Emeka was also waiting for us to pump and rump to "Sugar Bum Bum" like we did in our TVU days, and once the chorus began our hearts, souls, bodies and temperature became the sweetest things on earth. I journeyed from Kirikiri to paradise, from paradise to heaven and floated in and out of the clouds as Emeka and I aligned our bodies with the sparkling stars up above the world.

I did not know when I drifted off to the best sleep of my life in my ex-husband's arms.

22

Happiness has a short life span and a very lean body.

My sleep was suddenly interrupted by vibrations. I thought they were part of our love making and unconsciously started moving my body to the rhythm of the droning. It was when they stopped and started again, I realised that the vibrations were from a mobile phone that was on silent. Emeka's mobile phone.

"Emmy," I whispered tenderly, eyes closed. He did not answer. I was lying on my tummy. I reached out my right hand to wake him up and felt an empty, cold space of the bed. "Emmy, your phone," I muttered half asleep. There was no reply. "Telephone, oh, Emmy," I called out, thinking he was in the bathroom.

There was no reply.

"Emmy. Emeka."

I sat up. Alarmed. I wiped my eyes and put my hand on the empty right side of the bed, wondering where he could be.

The music had stopped playing. All I could hear was the rhythm of the pouring rain on the roof. The clock on the wall showed the time was a quarter past two in the morning. The mobile phone started vibrating again. I stumbled out of bed and headed straight for the en suite bathroom but Emeka was not there. The phone kept on vibrating. I stepped out of the bedroom and its private sitting room, and headed straight to the minibar in the main living room.

There was no Emeka.

I became frantic and walked barefooted on the red plush-carpeted hallway of the first floor. I passed the paintings and chandelier on the long corridor, passed the dining room, three living rooms and the snooker room, but Emeka was nowhere to be found. I was afraid.

I kept on walking. I went pass the study, the library and many guest rooms, but still no Emeka.

Little did I know that my new-found joy was about to evaporate into thin air.

I wandered around the mansion aimlessly, looking for Emeka, or at least someone who could help me, until I heard the loud squeaks of a bed in the last room on the left. I heard the faint familiar "Sugar Bum Bum" music from the room. I did not in my wildest dreams think one of the occupants and participants would be Emeka.

The strained breathing and panting from within were all familiar. I pushed the unlocked door open and beheld my clinically obese Emeka pounding away on top of Udo, the beautiful PA. My chest hardened. I shut the door, turned around and left.

It felt like Emeka stuck a knife into me, twisted it and ripped out my insides. I could not breathe. It felt like I was suffocating. I wanted the floor of the hallway to cleft for me so that I could sink to the bottom of the earth and hide there forever.

"It is not what you think, my dear," I heard a breathless Emeka call out behind me.

I ignored him. I stumbled back to the bedroom where I slumped on the bed and took deep breaths in and deep breaths out. I refused to cry. I had shed enough tears in the last few weeks. Not one more tear was I prepared to shed. I did not want to be labelled a cry-lady.

"It is not what you think," a panting Emeka said repeatedly as he ran into the room with just his boxers on and the top and bottoms of his pyjamas in his left hand.

"You are disgusting," I hissed. "Your phone was ringing," I said, pointing to his phone.

"At this time? It is 2.25am!"

And the phone started vibrating again.

"Hello?" he barked at the phone.

I will never forget that phone call. The look on Emeka's face will remain etched in my memory bank until I die.

He was sweating profusely even though he was naked and the air conditioner was on full blast. His face was badly contorted and all I could see were alarm and panic and deep pain in Emeka's eyes. Shock was plastered all over his face as he listened.

"Fire?" he bellowed. "Fire? Nooo!" He exclaimed. "What?" He asked. "Oh my God… Oh no." He repeated "Oh no" again. Next, he flung his phone and pyjamas on the floor, slid onto the bedside rug, and sat there with his back against the bed. He looked really silly and comical in just his boxers; like a naked Humpty Dumpty that had a great fall.

I did not know whether to bend down or slide onto the floor as well.

"What is happening?" I looked down at a comical Emeka and asked.

"Ada, I am finished," Hotshot Emeka started crying.

"What is happening?"

He looked up to me helplessly and said, "I am finished, Ada. That was the French man next door to me in Ikoyi, shouting fire! Fire! My house in Ikoyi is on fire. He has called the fire brigade but the fire is raging. My family is okay. They are all on the road and the neighbours are trying to drive all my cars out as we speak. I am finished. Oh my God!"

I was shocked by the fear written all over Emeka's face.

He reached for his clothing on the footstool. "God, I know you are angry with me. But please forgive me. Ada, please forgive me." He pulled his white brocade trousers on in a state of panic. "Please, forgive me," he pleaded with tears running down his face and ran out.

Sleep became the farthest from my bleary eyes. I felt hollow, empty, and deserted as I stood in the middle of the strange, massive bedroom. I stood by the door and blamed myself.

The size of the room and the echoing sound of silence were scary. I was all alone in a strange room in an unfamiliar house in the middle of Kirikiri. The tears started to flow. I walked up to the long mirror on the wall, changed the contour of my face and said aloud, "Your life is now worse than it was last week and terribly messed up, you foolish Ada Chukwu-George. How could you be so stupid and naïve?"

Somehow, with the divine intervention of God I made it through the night.

PART 3

23

Everything happened so fast. Virtually everything.

A broken Emeka returned from the Ikoyi house just before 7am. At that stage, all I cared about was the phone that had the other Ada's WhatsApp message in it. After that, I would bolt… Scram, vamoose, disappear.

I took one look at Emeka when he walked unsteadily into the bedroom and I knew that he was finished. His delightful, dreamy, come-to-bed eyes were just droopy and sunken in pain. His hands and short, pudgy, sausage-like fingers and his big forehead were all smudged with soot. His pure white guinea brocade trouser and top were covered in dirt and smears of ashes. When he plonked himself beside me on the chaise longue, I almost choked on the strong, stifling smell of smoke from his clothing.

"When I got there, the whole building was engulfed in flames. I watched and listened helplessly to loads of mini explosions as the windows shattered and popped like a bonfire."

"Oh, my actual God!!"

"Yes. I recorded it on my iPhone and by the time I left an

hour ago, the whole building was still covered in plumes of smoke and there were still visible pockets of fire."

"Oh my God."

"Yes. The devastating fire ripped through the entire mansion. It broke out about 1am."

"Whoa!! Thank God no lives were lost."

Emeka nodded in agreement.

All I wanted to do was to ask about the mobile phone with the message from the other Ada, but dared not.

At what stage do I ask? If only I had asked him to send for it yesterday.

I looked at his phone very briefly and the sight of the flames that I saw in the sneak peek of the video was very disheartening. The ones that belched out of the windows of the upper storey remained seared on my mind for a long time. Tears ran down on Emeka's fat face. I cradled what I could of his fat, lumpy body in my arms. He rested his big head on my bosom and wept like a baby.

I saw a deflated, drawn and haggard Emeka replace the roly-poly Emeka of yesterday. Gone was the obese braggart that blatantly displayed ostentatiousness barely twenty-four hours ago. Gone was the puffed-up chest and the previously elevated shoulders had very quickly dropped to the normal level of shoulders.

Even his rich-man swagger disappeared.

"I am finished. I have never seen a thing like this in my entire life. All my valuables are gone, my precious paintings, my porcelain, my silver. I lost everything. Oh, including that Samsung phone."

When I saw tears well in Emeka's eyes, I started crying. We cried and cried and cried. Emeka clung on to me like he used to in our university days and I rubbed and patted his back as we sobbed together.

If only he knew that I was actually crying for me, crying for the burnt phone, crying for my life and crying for the messy situation I found myself in.

After a while we stopped sobbing and remained in the room in perfect silence. Emeka nodded off, and all I could hear were his heavy breathing and the sound of my beating heart. I couldn't abandon him in his present state and return to London.

And then there was a loud rat-tat-tat on the door.

"They are here," a sleepy Emeka whispered into my ears. He jumped up in fear and shouted "I am coming." He straightened his shirt and added, "I will be with you shortly."

"They?" I asked, confused.

"Yes, Obiageli... Mary-Obiageli, plus my mother and the Ikoyi house-helps. They are all in the private living room... I will send the house-helps to the servants' quarters." He sounded really tired.

"Your Mum? As in Mama Ibusa?" I asked astonished.

"Yes, my mum. My mother."

"And your baby wife?"

"Hmm." He grunted, avoiding eye contact. "I just mentioned her name. Yes. Obiageli. Mary-Obiageli. She is here." He sighed out loud and added, "Man proposes, God disposes."

Unbelievable! There and then I knew that the fabric of our reunion and the dynamics in the Kirikiri household were about to change forever.

"I have to send the driver to the market to buy them clothes as they are all in their nighties and pyjamas. They will also need shoes and slippers. They ran out without shoes on their feet."

"I am so sorry."

"Oh, don't be, it is not your fault. The fire alarm that caused me over a million naira to install just failed to go off," he hissed.

I could not stop thanking God we did a detour and came to Kirikiri. I felt sorry for Emeka. I also felt sorry for Mama and Obiageli. I knew they would be devastated by the loss of their home and belongings. I did not know how I was going to face Mama, especially under the given circumstances.

"I lost four dogs – two Doberman Pinschers and two Alsatians. They died from smoke inhalation in their kennels because I was not there to rescue them."

Emeka grabbed a wad of naira notes from under the bedside table and headed for the door. I got up to go with him, but he signalled to me to stay behind.

"Wait. Let me tell her you are here. We don't want Mama to have a heart attack when she sees you."

Later that morning, I was in the living room upstairs eating a peeled orange and on the phone with Malika. Naturally, the romp with the PA had become irrelevant in the scheme of things. Malika was telling me how bailiffs came around and how she did not answer the door, when Mama, Emeka and Rita, the house-help barged into the room.

"Malika, let me call you back," I whispered into the phone and quickly hung up. "Good morning, Ma," I greeted.

Mama ignored me, walked past me and headed straight for the other settee where she plunked herself and dropped a black nylon carrier bag by her side.

"Good morning, Ma," Rita muttered and went to stand behind Mama.

"Morning," I replied.

"Rita, please take Mama's bag to the first room on your right," Emeka instructed.

Rita reached for the carrier bag but Mama jumped up and snatched it from her. She looked at me with disdain and said, "Over my dead body will I sleep under the same roof with a runaway wife. Take my load to one of the bungalows at the back."

"Mama, this is not the time for this, you know," Emeka chided her as he walked out of the living room.

"Do you want me to sleep under the same roof with this prostitute that went to London to sleep with all sorts?"

Mama got up and left the room. Rita followed her.

Mama, an imposing fat woman, a lot taller and fairer than Emeka, did not hesitate to show that her dislike for me was still there. She and Mary-Obiageli made their presence felt straight away. Both of them swanned around the mansion and barked out order after order – left, right, centre and all over the estate.

In the nights, a terrified Emeka went around the mansion turning lights off. During the day he spent most of his time at home, on the same chair, repeatedly-watching the eight-minute-long gory video of smoke bellowing from the Ikoyi house. All I could do was watch as tears streamed down his face.

A large, bosomy Obiageli carried her fat chubby cheeks – each almost the size of a puff-puff doughnut – her bosom which comprised boobs that were the size of two massive, voluptuous watermelons and her bulky lower booty all over the estate. I had never seen a big bum like Obiageli's before. It was huge, and it rolled and hopped and bopped up and down like ocean waves every time she walked around. I could not understand what it was that Emmy saw in the girl. Everything about her was big. Apart from the humongous bum, boobs and cheeks; her teeth, nose, mouth and even her ears were huge. I always thought ears never grew, but hers did.

Then Ben, the solicitor, rang.

"I have been doing a bit of digging as insurance fraud affects us all," Ben said. "I found out that there is a portfolio of at least three rental properties across London in your name."

"Really?" I asked. I was stunned.

"I plan to do a trace on the £360,000 which was recently paid into a reward account in your name. This whole thing will take between six to twelve months…" And the line cut. Between six to twelve months?

In the bedroom, I could hear Emeka in the bathroom. He was reciting an act of contrition in there. "… Oh my God I am very sorry for all my sins…" I looked in and saw his face was covered in soap. For a split second I thought he had lost the plot. He sat on the edge of the bath with his soapy face, praying. I knelt beside him, closed my eyes and also started my silent prayers about the cheque and my stolen ID right there.

"God is punishing me for all the evil things I did over the years."

"Wash the soap off your face." I advised.

24

Days flew by. Everybody adjusted to life in Kirikiri.

In the afternoons I went a-rambling in the tranquil rose garden, and the evenings were spent in the bedroom where I packed, unpacked, arranged, scattered and rearranged my suitcase and handbag. I was constantly checking my handbag to make sure my passport, ticket and the brown envelope that contained the wad of fifty-pound notes from Emeka were tucked away in the side pocket. As for Emeka, he lost his mojo. His delightful, dreamy, come-and-do eyes became droopier and droopier by the day. He still spent most of his time on the bed or the chaise longue watching the recording of the inferno on his phone over and over. The latest video and pictures on his phone showed the only things left in the compound were shells of burnt-out exotic cars and a burnt-out mega-mansion. His luxurious and flamboyant life flew out of the window. When he was not on the bed or the chaise longue, he was in the downstairs living room where he ate loads of chicken legs and popped and knocked back bottles of champagne as he liked.

His weight ballooned very quickly. For some unknown reason, he clung on to me like he did in our university days.

The volcano erupted.

The mere thought of being grilled again by Mr Murphy sent shivers down my spine… And then like a bolt out of the blues, a tsunami of shocking events occurred in rapid succession in our very toxic Kirikiri mansion.

Disaster struck that hot afternoon. It was the first of my last two afternoons in Kirikiri.

I was very quietly minding my own business and making my way down the wide, rugged staircase at the back of the mansion very slowly, when I heard loud and quick click-clacking of high-heeled shoes behind me as someone pounded down the stairs. I quickly stepped aside for whoever it was to pass. It was her. Obiageli.

"Husband stealer," she muttered and hissed as she stormed pass me angrily in another hideous, frumpy red dress and a pair of clumpy shoes.

I ignored her.

Next, she stopped, turned around, looked me up and down with disgust and muttered "Gold-digger." I wanted to tell her that she was the gold-digger. She was the one that married an already married man and was parading herself as Mrs George, but I decided against it. She carried on down the stairs and for reasons best known to her, she suddenly decided to make her way back up after she reached the bottom of the stairs.

As she made her way back up, she called me all sorts of names with every step she took.

"Idiot. Runaway wife. Divorcee. Gold-digger. Shameless girl. Husband snatcher. Gold-digger. You have scored zero. We will send you back to your London empty-handed."

"You are the husband stealer. You found someone else's property, grabbed it and you want to die with it," I said very quietly.

"Ada, do not step on the lion's tail, be it dead or alive."

I turned around and climbed back up the stairs – two steps at a time; if I could take three steps at a time I would have.

I returned to the bedroom.

A few minutes later, Emeka and I were watching The Kardashians when out of nowhere Mama burst into our private living room armed with a bottle of water.

"Emeka, my son." She put the bottle of holy water on the arm of one of the leather chairs and raised her blouse to reveal her braless, pancake-like breasts. She cupped both flat breasts in her hands –one in each palm – faced Emeka and continued. "Ada and I will not sleep together in this house tonight. My ears are full. One of us will have to leave today. It is either I go or she goes."

"What now?" Emeka asked.

"Your baby wife is in tears." Mama grabbed the bottle of water, opened it and started sprinkling the water all over the living room, all over Emeka and all over me. I could not believe someone could be so troublesome. "She has started to accost your baby wife. She called her a husband snatcher."

"Husband stealer," I corrected.

Emeka lost his rag. "Why would you do that?"

"Madam been-to-London, please carry your two left legs back to your London. Leave our Nigeria for us," Mama screamed. "You want to reap where you did not sow," she added. Her eyes were bloodshot.

And then Obiageli burst into the room sobbing like a baby.

Her whole body, especially the honkers on her chest, were shaking.

"Please, warn her, oh. Emeka. Warn her. I came to stay here because of children. Warn her for me, oh." She cried. The tears fell out of her eyes, but could not flow properly. They gathered on and remained stagnated on top of both fat cheeks.

My eyes welled with tears. I excused myself and headed for the bathroom. I remained there for a very long time. When I eventually returned to the bedroom, they were all gone. I spent the rest of the evening rearranging my belongings yet again. I shifted the wads of fifty-pound notes into the right-side pocket of my Chanel handbag. Next, I charged my iPhone and my power bank; and finally, phoned Malika to find out if there was any post from PJ&PJ.

I was about to return to the bathroom, when Akpan, the cook, knocked on our door.

"Dinner is ready," he popped his head in and announced.

25

The Last Supper.

The lovely aroma of jollof rice and fried chicken filled my nostrils. For the first time in days, my mouth watered as I walked down the hallway to the grand dining room. I always wished we could eat in our bedrooms in front of out televisions, or at different times, instead of having to sit stiffly like over-starched linen shirts at the table.

Obiageli and Mama were already at their usual positions at the dining table. Mama's face was long as usual and Obiageli sat there stroking the stem of the largest silver candelabra. Emeka soon trundled in breathing heavily. Every time I saw his huge, chicken-and-champagne-populated tummy, I felt like sticking a pin into it. I watched his eyes light up as he surveyed the array of foods and assorted dishes at our end of the table. He took his seat at the table and grinned from ear to ear, opening dish after dish. The table was laid for four. Emeka always sat at the head of the table. Mama and Obiageli always sat to his left while I sat to his right. We sat on the first four chairs of the twelve-seater, oak dining table. Emeka was dressed in an immaculate white jellabiya. I could not understand why a careless and excessive gobbler like Emeka that always dropped food all over the place wore a pure white outfit to the dining table. To me, it was just plain silly. Emeka, Obiageli and I placed our mobile phones on the dining table.

Suddenly, my phone started ringing. I looked at the screen and announced.

"International call. Do you mind if I get this? It is my solicitor from the UK."

"Oh, that is mega important. Please answer it," Emeka advised. I picked up the phone and excused myself.

"My solicitor called to tell me the meeting is in a few days' time," I announced as I returned and sat down.

"Ah, good timing," Emeka replied.

"Yes… I told him it was fine as I will be in England in a matter of days."

"Coolio," Emeka replied as he massaged his potbelly.

I watched Emeka fill his gold-rimmed champagne flute with his favourite bubbly. Next, he heaped his big flat China plate with a mixture of three different soups. When he opened the big dish of pounded yam and scooped a big mound of it on to his plate, I cringed at the thought of him demolishing all of it. He looked up at me and smiled.

"Round one," he announced to us as he took large gulps of the bubbly.

And I watched as he refilled his champagne flute. Next, he rolled up the sleeves of his jellabiya, washed his right hand in the little silver metallic bowl on the table, shook the water off his hand and balanced to massacre the food… Emeka never used the cutlery on the table. His mastered art of eating with his right hand

and fingers was first class. I watched as he cut lump after lump of the pounded yam. It was the case of a beautiful dining table witnessing ugly table manners. His sequence of consumption beat my imagination and I could not understand how such a short man could have such a voracious appetite.

His standard order at all dinner times was food, bubbly, food, bubbly and food, bubbly. It was always food with the right hand and a bubbly with the left hand. I wanted to advise Emeka to leave the champagne until he finished the spicy *egusi* and *agbono* soups which he kept mixing recklessly; but decided against it. After all, his mother was there and besides, I didn't want him asking if I was his mother. It was all so sickening and most irritating. Well, the apple does not fall far from the tree. Emeka got his insatiable love for food from his mother, I told myself. Obiageli and I were okay, but one would have thought Mama and Emeka had not eaten for days.

My phone started vibrating again on the dining table. I looked at the screen for less than a nanosecond, to see who it was and to also check and make sure the phone was on silent. From the left corner of my eye, I saw Emeka wince. I pressed the little red button and rejected the call. It was my sister, Vicky. I made a mental note to call her back. I looked at Emeka for a sign of disapproval. He winced again. Emeka did everything in excess.

He adjusted his sitting position and started burping.

"Come on, put that air conditioner on maximum immediately," he yelled at Obiageli and pulled up his jellabiya while undoing the waist ropes of his jogging bottoms.

Then Emeka winced again and again and again. The air conditioner circulated very cold air. Emeka started coughing, and the cough went on for quite a long while. When it finally subsided, he started burping again. What Emeka did next shocked me.

I saw him wipe his soupy fingers on the pure white table napkin by his side. My first instinct was to tell him that was gross but decided against it when I saw him open his eyes wider than usual.

Just when I thought it was all over, I heard a big loud sound as Emeka gulped in a huge amount of air and knocked his champagne flute and the water in the little silver wash hand bowl on to the floor. He started coughing again.

"Drink water!" a panicked and alarmed Mama instructed with a mouth full of chewed mixed meat and fufu. I was not sure if she forgot to close her mouth because after the drink-water instruction she left it hanging open for us all to see the slimy *agbono* soup, chewed meat and fufu food stuck to her teeth.

"Sorry, Emeka," Obiageli said as she carried on scraping a big piece of white cow-foot with her oversized front teeth.

Then the loud hiccups started. Bwaaarp! Burrrp! Bwaaap!

Unfortunately, when the hiccups subsided, the cough began again. Mama rushed to his side to massage his back and as if on cue, Obiageli dropped her piece of cow-foot on the pure white tablecloth, jumped up immediately and very quickly joined in the back-massaging business. I stood up. I was not too sure whether to join them or not, so I remained on my feet. I didn't think it made sense all three of us crowding around him to pat and rub one back. And so, I remained on my feet.

As the cough grew louder, I could tell he was gasping for air as well. All my first aid practical and oral knowledge suddenly evaporated into thin air, and when I eventually thought of giving him the five sharp blows between his shoulder blades with the heel of my hand, I couldn't because Mama and Obiageli were in the way.

The uncontrollable coughing fits violently shook the whole silver- and glassware on the table and the huge Swarovski crystal chandelier above the dining table. When Emeka finally stopped coughing, there was incessant wheezing and tears rolled down his fat chubby cheeks.

"It is enough," Mama screamed as Emeka reached for his champagne flute.

Emeka stood up, took off his jellabiya and flung it on the floor in anger. His bare, large breasts and drum of a tummy hung over his entire body.

He was on his feet and about to say something – but could not stand for too long. He slumped on the chair and did a big display of the hanging tummy of Kirikiri for all to see. His face contorted as he retched and this time around, he forcefully and uncontrollably ejected all the food from his stomach. The spewed meal was all over the white jellabiya on the floor, on the dining table and right inside the already slimy dish of *agbono* soup. I watched in disgust as fat lumps of fufu from his mouth settled on top of his potbelly while others slid from his hairy chest onto the floor. Finally, a light greenish mixture of champagne and soups dribbled out of his mouth as big fat tears rolled down his cheeks.

"My throat," Emeka croaked.

Throat? Which throat? I could not see any throat or neck.

"My throat. I can't breathe," he croaked again. This time he held his chin with his left hand as there was no throat to hold.

I could see he was struggling to breathe.

Akpan, the cook, and Ekwena, the driver, rushed in just in time. I was not sure if it was a bone that was stuck in his throat and he was trying to cough it out, or if it was the champagne that went the wrong way.

Ekwena panicked when he saw his master on the floor.

"Master should be taken to Manning Hospital," he advised.

"Let's go, Master," a panicked Akpan screamed as they tried to lift a short and fat Emeka that tipped the scales at about eighteen stones. Ekwena rushed out to bring the car to the front of the house and both men practically carried our very heavy and stout Emeka into the car.

Emeka was rushed to the hospital.

26

I called Emeka's phone several times all through the night, but he did not answer, neither did he call me back. I did not have the driver's mobile phone number, neither did I have one for Akpan, the cook.

I decided to have a shower and get pretty for his return. Emmy! I spent over an hour soaked in the bath and spent another half an hour deciding on which nightdress to wear.

Feeling all nice and warm inside me, I settled for a short pretty baby-pink, see-through nightie that had "Tonight is the Night" written in big, nicely joined, silver cursive letters. Strangely, with each new day, I loved Emeka more and more.

I sat by the window, gazed at the full moon and watched the bloated and overfed dogs roam around the compound. The estate was eerily quiet. The ticktock-ticktock of the gold-plated clock on the wall was the only sound that I could hear, and it showed that the time was five minutes past eleven at night.

Emeka was still not back.

I returned to the dressing table and carried on making

myself pretty. I put on a bit of my colourless lipstick, applied a teeny-weeny bit of my Si perfume behind my ears and returned to my position by the window. I promised myself that if they were not back by twelve midnight, I would ask Udo, the PA, to drive me to the hospital.

I knew Emeka was back when I heard the first and then the second gates clang, followed by the sound of tyres crunching on the gravel.

I looked at the clock on the bedside table – it showed the time was two minutes to eleven-thirty. I looked at the full-length mirror, smiled at my sizzling self in my sexy, plunging-neck, see-through nightie and gave myself thumbs-up.

I heard the car pull to a halt. I heard the loud opening and slamming of car doors.

"Too much money corrupts absolutely," I hissed. They always had to slam and bang the car doors shut. I left my position by the window and rushed to the bathroom to tidy my hair. I was relieved Emeka was back.

Must have a heart-to-heart talk with him about his bad eating habit. Must place him on the Atkins diet. I mean, who eats a whole chicken as a snack?

I stepped out of the bathroom and made my way back to the bedroom window. Then, I heard a high-pitched, piercing and anguished cry that shattered the quiet of the darkest night of my life. That blood-curdling cry stuck to my brain, and will remain there forever. I knew immediately that something terribly bad had happened.

"Ibusa people, come and help me, oh!! Ibusa people help me, oh. Ada has killed me, oh!! Ibusa o-ko-ko-kooo!! Ibusa people, help me, oh. Ada has killed me, oh!! Ada, oh. Ada, oh."

That spine-chilling scream that shattered the calm night at the Kirikiri estate will live in my conscious, subconscious and unconscious mind for the rest of my life on earth.

After that, everything was a blur. I heard so many doors open and slam shut at the same time. I heard footsteps. Running feet. Hurrying footsteps. Rushing footsteps. People crying. People talking. Dogs yapping crazily.

Horrified and alarmed I began the long, quick walk without shoes or slippers on the carpeted floor of the long grand hallway and made my way downstairs. When I was not moving fast enough, I started running.

It sounded like Mama's voice, but I was not too sure.

God, please let Mama be okay, I prayed repeatedly as I ran down the red carpeted steps, two steps at a time.

When I drew nearer, I heard the cry again. Louder and clearer.

"Igbo-uzo o-ko-ko-kooo. Ada oh!! Ada has killed me, oh." It was Mama. Emeka's mother.

I quickened my pace. The cry persisted even after Mama stopped. It boomed, vibrated and reverberated as if electronic effects were added to it.

Which Ada? Me? Or the other Ada? I was nowhere near that woman. I ran down the stairs. I rushed pass the two full-length portraits of Emeka on the stairwell. I raced through the front room. I rushed across the hand-knotted Persian rug and when my pace was still not fast enough, I started running and ran faster than Usain Bolt, or so I thought. I headed for the front yard. Obiageli and Udo and most of the house-helps ran out at same time as I did.

There was absolute pandemonium in the front yard. There were people everywhere. It was like bedlam. Something or

177

somebody was on the ground surrounded by the security guards, the mobile policemen, house-helps and Ekwena, the driver. They were all weeping and wailing. I moved closer and was shocked to see a screaming, inconsolable and shoeless Mama sat on the gravel driveway with her two legs stretched right out in front of her and arms flailed in the air. The little thin hair in the middle on her head was unruly, scattered and all over the place like a dried-up overused bathroom mop.

"The wicked have done their worst, oh." She cried. "Ada, you have done your worst. You have killed him. You have killed him, oh," she screamed loud and clear as soon as she saw me.

Everyone was weeping and wailing and shouting at the top of their voices. I found the cacophony of noise deafening while I tried to figure out what was happening.

"Now that you have killed him you can have the world to yourself. You have killed my son. Now you can carry all his wealth to London," Mama screamed louder from the ground.

I was too shocked to cry.

I was later told that Emeka's heart had stopped beating on the way to the hospital; that there was a traffic jam on their way to the hospital; that the hospital tried to revive him but all their efforts were in vain; that they tried CPR and defibrillation of ten electrical shocks to his heart to reset the heart rhythm back to its normal regular pattern but that nothing worked and he was pronounced dead.

There and then, the fabric of my life changed forever.

I blamed myself for not accompanying him to the hospital, but in the same breath told myself that as Mama and Obiageli were there and did not ask to go with him, I couldn't. Besides, nobody knew Emeka would die; after all, he had so much more mileage left in him.

"Wicked witch. You brought your bad luck from London," Mama screamed.

I stood rooted to the ground in total shock as I tried to take in and process what was happening.

The next second, within the squeezing of a lemon and the twinkling of an eye, eighty-year-old Mama became a cheetah. She most unexpectedly leapt off the ground and rushed at me.

I heard the loud deafening roar of a huge thunder right inside my tympanic membrane as my right ear went on fire – or so it felt. I suffered an immediate, temporary ear-blockage. I saw sparks of fire before my eyes and witnessed the sun, moon and stars collide forcefully in the dead of the night. Next, I saw a very bright red light and then I saw my grandmother that had died over twenty years ago at the far end of a pure white tunnel. I did not register what happened or feel the full impact of Mama's big, hot, front-hand slap on my right cheek, ear and eye until after about ten seconds – and those ten seconds seemed longer than ten hours. My head spun, or so it felt, like it had rotated round my neck and my chin was aligned parallel to my left shoulder. For a split second I forgot where I was.

I did not cry. When I regained my posture, I blinked my eyes thrice. After that, I spent ages massaging and rubbing my abused cheek in total shock.

I could not till the next day fathom how and where Mama got the amount of energy that she used to dispense such a big slap at that time of the night. Weeks later, when I told my mum about the slap, she said she felt the impact in her sleep; that she woke up at that instant and told my dad somebody just struck one of her girls in Lagos.

As I stood there in a daze, rubbing my cheek, wondering why I could taste blood in my mouth, Mama came for me again.

Fortunately, this time I threw my head and chest backward and all she got was the right sleeve of my nightgown which she ripped off. Mama had gone feral and lethal. She made one more attempt, spraying us all with spittle and the smell of *agbono* soup in her breath, but Ekwena, the driver, and the security guards restrained her.

In protest against the restraint, Mama slid back onto the gravels and sat there weeping and wailing like a baby. I remained rooted to the same spot where I felt my face was far away and safe from her.

Mama suddenly sat up on the gravels, and while still on the ground crawled up and rushed at me again. This third time she aimed for my bum. The most disgusting eighty-year-old grandmother and mother-in-law in the world put her hands under my nighty and grabbed my pants.

"Mama!! Stop!!" everyone screamed but Mama had gone coocoo. She had lost the plot. She pulled and tugged at my panty.

"Murderer!! Murderer!!" she screamed and continued to pull at my panties. "London witch. London prostitute." Mama had gone bunkers.

It took three hefty mobile policemen to pull her away from me. Mama remained seated on the ground panting and puffing with a piece of my white cotton pants in her right hand. She held the piece of fabric like a trophy for all to see.

"You killed him. You brought your bad luck from your London." Mama shook and ranted on the ground. "I knew that your cock and bull insurance story was all a cunning ploy for you to sneak back into my son's life and kill him. You have done your worst."

The gates swung open. A car drove in. Emeka's sister, Aunty

Adanne and their older brother, Brother Polycarp arrived. Aunty Adanne was in tears.

"Right!! Carry all the property. Take everything to London. London witch," Mama continued screaming and crying.

Adanne rushed at Mama and closed her mouth with a cupped palm while Brother Polycarp helped her up. He seemed stronger than all of them. Like me, he did not shed a single tear. I put that down to the fact that he was a man and that he already lost two brothers and a wife not too long ago. I heard Udo talk to some doctor on the phone. I heard her say Emeka was dead and that they needed to come and give Mama an injection. It was all surreal.

Dead?

I wanted to die with Emeka. I moved away from everyone towards the main house and stood alone by the door to the grand living room in total shock. I hoped and prayed someone would come in and say there was a mistake. Like a mix-up.

It was impossible. Emeka was invulnerable. He was indestructible. He was secure and safe. In fact, he was invincible. He was immortal. I did not see death in Emeka's eyes at all. He was not the type to die. How could he leave all of this? His fleet of exotic cars, his houses, his money, his Bitcoins, his aircrafts, all his petrol tankers, his petrol stations and his good life? His bubbly, his assorted dishes and chickens?

I remained by the door massaging my cheeks. Nobody even looked at me or cared about me. I could not understand how they could be so evil. Most of them were crying and grieving the loss of their ATM and that was it. What about me?

I was very angry with myself because my lacrimal glands refused to produce tears. Not a single drop of tear.

"Where is Emeka?" I finally asked Ekwena, the driver, as he walked up to me.

"Sorry, Ma."

"Where is Master?" I asked again.

"He is in the mortuary, Ma," he responded without looking at me.

Emeka in a mortuary? I wished I had died instead of Emeka. I blamed myself. I blamed the fire that engulfed his Ikoyi house and I cursed the raging inferno for ripping through the house that rapidly. If only it had been a small fire, maybe Emeka might have still been with us.

Everyone stayed in the grand living room downstairs and watched and listened to Adanne and Brother Polycarp as they made call after call. Nobody really slept. Unfortunately, I still could not cry or shed a single tear.

Emeka's PA, Udo, brought a doctor to give Mama, Obiageli and I injections and everything became hazy from then on. I remembered being in a daze and drifted off. It was a dreamless and restless sleep which must have lasted less than two hours.

"Ada, come and go put some decent clothes on," Udo advised as she pulled me out of the living room and up the stairs.

We made our way up the stairs. When I heard running footsteps behind me I jumped, thinking it was Mama.

"Madam, it is me, Ekwena…" The driver said as he caught up with us.

Udo and I stopped halfway up the stairs.

"Madam, this is Master's stuff."

Ekwe handed to me Emeka's Rolex and his eighteen-carat-gold signet ring.

Udo, the PA, and I returned to the bedroom where the smell of my Si perfume still lingered. As soon as we walked into the room and I saw my image in the log bedside mirror I immediately realised why Mama went for my underpants. I had run downstairs without my housecoat when I heard her scream. The contour of my entire body was visible through my see-through nightie. No wonder she went for my body. When her daughter, Adanne, later asked why she pulled at my panties she said she had wanted to take out Emeka's good luck that he passed to me through that channel.

27

Ibusa again.

There was no cavalcade of big black bulletproof supercars or mobile policemen, no bodyguards in shiny suits and no fancy earpieces or walkie-talkies. There was just the Black Maria that conveyed Emeka's body to Ibusa and our car.

We drove straight to Emeka's father's traditional, basic, no-frills Umute village house. The roof made of zinc seemed lower than it was twelve years ago. The only belonging I had on me was my Chanel handbag. No suitcases. From the corner of my still slightly swollen eye I espied five black Range Rovers parked on the other side of the road – the engines of all five of them were running. They were Emeka's black SUVs. I could not see inside the cars because of their blacked-out windows, but I soon understood why they were in Ibusa.

Obiageli, the PA and I were in the same car. We were asked to remain seated in the car until Emeka's body was taken out of the Black Maria.

Emeka's oldest sister, Aunty Adanne, and her husband were

already in Ibusa. I noticed she could barely open her eyes when she came out of the house. Her eyelids were almost the size of tennis balls – they were terribly swollen from crying. Unfortunately, I still could not cry. I tried to produce tears but they never came that day.

"Ah, this is not fair. We have been in this car for over an hour," Obiageli moaned in protest.

"Don't worry, we will soon go inside the house," the PA said slowly.

It was like Aunty Adanne heard Obiageli because shortly after she came to address us.

"You will be allowed in shortly. Let me usher the children in first," Aunty Adanne advised. I watched as she crossed the road, walked up to the Range Rovers and from each car a little child and a lady hopped out.

Five children in total. Could those be the five children on the insurance claim?

I watched in awe as Aunty Adanne led them into the house.

"Don't tell me our husband fathered all those children?" Obiageli asked sarcastically.

"Yes, he did," Udo, the PA, replied. "Five girls and they are all aged five... Sorry, the last one is four years old."

"What?" Obiageli and I asked at the same time.

"Are those their mothers?" Obiageli asked.

"Yes," Udo replied.

I saw people everywhere. Large groups of aunties in white blouses and hollandaise white and purple wrappers stood around the front yard where Emeka lay. They were all talking in low voices. In my entire life I never saw so much sadness, or so much shaking of heads.

Emeka's body was laid in state in front of his father's house.

I reached out to touch his arm, but before I could, I heard an Aunty scream from the crowd. "No. No. No. No. Don't touch him. You can't touch him."

Did they not know that Emeka had just shattered what was left of my heart into invisible tiny pieces? Plus, the five children! I knew they could not be his children because Emeka was unable to make babies. Obiageli and I were living proof. Those women must have tricked Emeka.

Emeka looked so handsome, cool, calm, peaceful and serene as he lay there with his eyes shut. If it was not for the cotton wool stuffed into his nose and ears, I would have thought Emeka was just sleeping. I wanted to remove the cotton wool that they used to block his ears so that I could call him his pet name – Emmy – and wake him up. I wanted to remove the cotton wool from his blocked his nose so he could smell my Si perfume from last night. I wanted to open the closed eyes so that he could see me and wake up. Most of all, I wanted to shout at him to get up and not lie there like a zombie. I prayed internally that he could just wake up and ask that we returned to Kirikiri.

"The elders said that we had to first and foremost pay the penalty for a goat that our grandfather stole over fifty years ago, before any burial can take place," Adanne cried.

Just then, Big Aunty, Emeka's big Aunty, emerged from the hut and broke into a beautiful dirge.

"My strength, my tower, my backbone, my pride and joy gone." She sang with tears in her eyes. "He is gone, the brother whose name I use to brag, show off and pose is gone." She cried and sang in the Ibo language.

Everybody started wailing.

Big Aunty continued until her voice became croaky with emotion and tears filled everyone's eyes.

"My brother, who knew how to write very well with a pencil and remove the written words with an eraser, is gone," she continued in a croakier and flatter voice. She walked up to me crying.

"Follow me, Ada," she said in a sing-song voice.

I followed Big Aunty out of the room. As I walked behind her, I heard dreadful sighs, hisses and kissing of teeth. I did not see the faces of the aunties behind me, but I felt the daggers and evil looks at my back, and imagined all their heads shaking sorrowfully, especially as I was not crying. I trailed behind her all alone.

"You will have to marry our older brother, Polycarp. Remember his wife died less than one year ago," Big Aunty said without turning around to look at me.

"What?" I screamed. "That is moral outrage."

"Moral outrage? That is English grammar you are speaking," she hissed. "Emeka's name will not be blotted out of history. Our brother Polycarp has a marriage duty to take you on as his wife."

Big Aunty was well known for torturing young widows. She was once married to a foreigner, that is, somebody from outside Ibusa, until the marriage had failed. I was later told that after the collapse of her marriage, she returned to Ibusa and brought back with her all the wicked ways of life in her ex-husband's town. Every time there was a death, she was the first on the scene, where she put into practice the foreign wicked culture.

Big Aunty opened the door to a tiny, windowless and airless room at the back of the house. The only source of light in the dimly lit room was a little kerosene lantern that was beside a raffia mat. There was also a metal pail by the mat. That pail was my make-shift latrine and there was an A4 sheet of paper folded into two on the mat. No chair, no bed, no table. The raffia mat on the floor was covered in ashes. It was like someone deliberately sprinkled them all over the room and on the mat. There were no pillows.

"We have prepared this room for you with the sprinkled ashes. All you need to do is take your position on the mat."

"Maaa?" I asked, not sure I heard right.

"You heard."

"What?"

"Yes. And you will remain in this room in isolation until the night before the burial… Except for an accompanied trip to the market first thing tomorrow for you to buy six white hens for the ladies in the family. Our daughter will use the hens to cleanse you."

"That is not possible, Ma. I have to be in London by tomorrow night, Ma."

"Oh!! Wait a minute. Were you planning to abandon your husband's corpse?"

"No, Ma," I stammered. "I will go for my meeting and return in time for the burial," I explained.

"Hahaha," she laughed aloud sarcastically. "My dear child, forget about London and work for the next fifty-two weeks. You will have to prepare for the burial. After the burial ceremony you will remain in the village and sit in mourning for one solid year."

"Aunty, please. Please." I fell on my knees on the concrete floor and pleaded. "Please Ma. I can't. Please Ma, if I don't, my name will go on the international fraud database."

"Story-story," she hissed and exhaled. "Read the paper on your mat," she said sternly.

Big Aunty slammed the door shut, locked it from the outside and left. I knelt in the centre of the room and clung onto my

Chanel bag very tightly. The room was eerily quiet.

There were 10 instructions on the list:

1. Day one – Hair to be shaved off.
2. Sit and sleep on ashes until day of funeral.
3. Day two – Purchase six white hens from the market.
4. Practise and prepare how to weep and wail on the day of funeral.
5. Lie with corpse the day before the funeral to ward off flies.
6. Must not leave room without ashes on hair.
7. Day nine – Corpse bathed and wife to drink the water from the corpse-wash.
8. Prepare for burial.
9. Burial ceremony.
10. After the burial, widow to wear black clothing, remain in the village and mourn late husband for one year.

I sighed aloud.

Unbelievable.

Incredible.

Impossible.

My whole thinking was that we would accompany the corpse to Ibusa, after which I would go back to Kirikiri, pack my stuff and go to London. If the dead could wake up and speak, Emeka would have said a big fat robust no to all of this. I lay down in the middle of the raffia mat and used my stuffed Chanel bag as a pillow.

28

I was on the fourth decade of my rosary beads when I heard someone unlock the door from outside. My Rotary watch showed it was twelve midnight on the dot. Big Aunty returned in the company of Ekwena, the driver. She had in her hands a tray of razor blades and Ekwena had in his hand a little stool.

"Good evening, Ma," Ekwena greeted as he sat on the stool, brandishing his blades. I was on the mat.

"Ekwena is going to shave your hair off right away."

"Aunty, it is not my hair – it is a weave."

"I don't care. Go on, Ekwena."

I thought Ekwena would dust off the ashes first, detach the sewn-on hair and then undo my weaves – but I had no such luck. Ekwena did not even bother to remove the attached Brazilian hair. He proceeded to shave me from the scalp; he scraped my cornrows and Brazilian hair off from the roots. I felt the scraping but could not see the result as Ekwena started from the back of my head. Reality smacked me in the face when he scraped the front and I watched the rows of matted hair and sewn-on Brazilian hair fall on the mat and mix with the ashes. The Brazilian weaves had cost me almost one hundred pounds and I paid almost thirty pounds to fix it.

"Ma, all these things are not our Ibusa culture," Ekwena protested.

"Shut up, Ekwena. This is what I want," Big Aunty snapped at him. "Everything I wrote on that A4 is what I want."

"Okay, Madam."

As soon as Ekwena finished shaving my head, both of them walked out of the room without saying a word to me. I was staring at the destroyed weaves and hair on the ashy floor, when Big Aunty popped back and said, "You will remain in isolation in this room until the burial."

"When is the burial?" I asked.

"We don't know yet."

"Aunty, my second interview at work is in four days' time. If I don't go, they will think I am guilty."

"We are keeping you in here for your own good. Whatever you do, do not go out in the sun any time soon, so you don't meet your dead husband. If you do go out in the sun and you meet Emeka, your whole body will just melt like chocolate."

"Aunty, please." I cried. "I want to die."

"Die, Ada. Die. That will be better for you. Die so that we can bury you with Emeka. After all, he really should not be buried alone. Die, oh, Ada. Die."

"Aunty, shouldn't we send a message to her family to let them know their daughter is here?" Ekwena asked.

She ignored Ekwena.

The door slammed shut and the key turned in the lock again. I touched my bald head and wept like a baby.

I was on the brink of suicide and prayed that death should come for me.

I hadn't even been married to the man for the last eleven years. I could feel the shaved-off hairs on my sweaty body but I was not allowed to have a bath. All I had to lay my head on was a raffia mat and my bulging Chanel bag which doubled up as a pillow. It was such an uncomfortable pillow because of the various contents, especially my phone and power bank and the wads of fifty-pound notes. I stretched out on the raffia mat and slept with my eyes open like a shark.

After a while, I sat up and told myself that I had to find a way out of the tiny little room. I knew that if I did not attend that final interview at work, PJ&PJ would conclude I absconded because of my guilt.

My phone showed the time was ten minutes past one in the morning. I called Malika, but she didn't pick her phone up. I was tempted to call Mama and Papa, but decided against it as I did not want Papa to have another stroke. And then I remembered Show-Boy-Ten-Ten's mobile number in my bag. I retrieved the piece of paper from the side pocket of my bag and called Show-Boy's number. Surprisingly, he answered and sounded wide awake. In fact, the phone barely rang when he picked it up. When I asked if he could drive me from a village on the outskirts of Ibusa to my parents', he laughed and said it would cost me money if he came at that time of the night.

"Not tonight. Tomorrow morning."

"No problem, Madam."

We agreed I would charter him for the day. Pay him an hourly rate, and he was to wait for me in the catholic church on the high road from 8am for further instructions.

Just when I gave up and said I would allow God's will to be done Malika called me back.

"Emeka is dead," I whispered into the phone.

"Dead?" And then there was silence. Malika was not speaking. Then she spoke and apologised and said the phone dropped from her hands. I did not listen or hear what Malika said or was saying after that. I just continued talking.

"He performed magic," I continued. "I did not see death in his eyes. He died on the dinner table while eating like a king. When he started coughing at the dinner table, I thought..."

"OMG!!" Malika exclaimed.

I went on to tell her about my whereabout, my shaven head, and the proposal for me to drink the bathe water. Malika waited for me to finish.

"You have to find a way to get out of that place immediately. Otherwise, you are finished," she screamed.

The line cut and the phone went dead.

The bottom had fallen out of my world yet again.

I heard people did irrational things when they were in a state of shock, but the irrational thing that I did next was classic. While everyone slept, I lay awake planning my escape. Plan A was to ask to use the bathroom and from there I would abscond on to the streets and run away. Plan B was to ask to use the bathroom, I would lock myself in there and wait until Show-Boy arrived to drive me to my parents.

I relieved myself in the bucket beside my mat and at 8am on the dot, Big Aunty arrived with a bowl of corn porridge, cornflour cereal and a plate of bean balls.

"I am not hungry, Ma."

"Alright then. Ekwe will use the *okada* bike to take you to the Eke market right away. You will go and buy six white hens for the female children in the family."

I sat up on the mat, grabbed my bag, slung the double silver

193

chain and leather straps over my right shoulder, rose and followed Ekwena out of the room.

There were people everywhere, talking excitedly like it was Christmas day. There were smoky fires and big cooking and frying pots at the back of the house. Five cows were tied to five different trees waiting to be slaughtered. Colourful canopies had been erected in the front of the main house and on the street. There would have been at least ten of those canopies. There were stacks of rented chairs and tables. Even Ekwena was in good spirits. I could not believe their sombre mood disappeared so quickly. He was excited about the wake that night and as I mounted the back of his motorbike, he reeled out names of dignitaries that would attend the funeral.

"Madam, I hope you have money for the hens?"

"No, I don't. I have only got pound sterling."

"Madam, we have to go to the bank to change the money. How do we do it? The bank is one way and the market is the other way."

"No problem. Let's go. I will give you two hundred pounds to change in the bank. You go and change the money, I will drop off, stay and pray in the church for Emeka's soul until you come back."

Ekwena's eyes lit up when I gave him four fifty-pound notes to change in the bank.

"Okay, Ma," he replied excitedly.

I mounted the back of the motorcycle. When I imagined myself seated with six live white hens in my hands on the motorcycle, I shuddered and almost fell off the bike.

As soon as I stepped into the old town church and smelled the familiar burning incense, I felt safe. The daily morning mass was on and the little congregation was singing the hymn "Do Not

Be Afraid For I Have Redeemed You".

How appropriate, I thought. That was the same church where I did my Sunday school, bible studies, my First Holy Communion and my Confirmation. The church where I raised my voice like a nightingale and sang as a young chorister. I found an almost empty pew and sat there. I tried saying the Lord's Prayer but could not pray. I sat on the pew and waited impatiently. I waited and pictured myself back in Kilburn. No work. Up in the morning… Walking up to Kilburn station… Armed with my five-pence, orange Sainsbury's carrier bag… Picking up the *Metro* from the station and carrying on to Greggs for two sausage rolls and a drink. All of a sudden, I heard running footsteps behind me. I refused to turn around, just in case it was Adanne or Big Aunty. The footsteps rushed pass me and headed for the altar. I recognised the face: it was good old Vero, one of the catechists. Then I saw the backward baseball cap. I wanted to leap for joy, but controlled myself. I watched Show-Boy come in from the side door to the right – he walked up the middle aisle and stood in the middle of the church. I watched him take his dark sunglasses off and look around the church. Show-Boy was looking for me. He looked at me but did not look a second time. He was expecting an Ada with a Brazilian weave. I got up, walked up to him and tapped him on the shoulder.

"Show-Boy," I whispered.

He turned around and looked at me.

"Jesus is Lord!! What happened to Madam's hair?" he exclaimed aloud. "OMG! What happened?" he asked alarmed and pointed to my bald head with his left and right index fingers.

"Shhh… Where is your taxi?" I whispered, desperate. I practically ran out of the church, followed him to his cab and jumped into the car where I sunk into the back seat.

"Lagos – straight," I commanded.

"Maaa? Lagos?" A surprised Show-Boy asked.

"Yes, Lagos. Lagos. Lagos. Let's head for Benin and on to Lagos. Move. Fast. Quickly."

"Yes, Ma." Somehow, Show-Boy caught on without asking any questions. He sped off, raising so much dust like a getaway car in a movie.

Ibusa was bathing in the most beautiful, glorious morning sun which blazed down merrily on an almost dried-out Oboshi stream when we left my hometown.

Show-Boy started humming "Amazing Grace," chewing his gum and kola-nut. He headed for Lagos in full speed.

I cried from Ibusa to Lagos nonstop.

We hit traffic inside Lagos. It was at a standstill. The air conditioner in Show-Boy's battered taxi was circulating hot air despite the fact that it was at its highest blast. The beads of sweat clung on to my face. I could no longer mop my perspiration because my handkerchief was soaking wet. My boubou was soaked and so was Show-Boy's shirt, but we had to wind up because of the thieves and the hawkers that shoved their wares in one's face. Bananas, oranges, mangoes, guavas, tamarind seeds, potatoes, cheese… All the fruits and vegetables I could think of were on sale on the roads. The one that tripped me most was the raw beef that was hawked on the road.

Show-Boy headed straight for the Murtala Muhammed Airport. When I gave him two hundred pounds on arrival at the airport, he leapt out of the car and prostrated on the ground in gratitude and refused to get up.

"God bless you a million times over, Ma."

"Thank you, Show-Boy. God bless you too."

I left him still prostrated on the ground and hurried into the airport. Of course, my flight had left as scheduled. After spending ages in the departure lounge at the airport, I eventually bought a one-way, first-class ticket back to London. I was the first to board the plane. All the things I went to collect for Mr Murphy – my childhood and graduation photos, my diaries, my scrapbook and all – were left behind in Kirikiri.

I must have been the oddest international passenger they ever saw at the Murtala Muhammed International Airport in Lagos because I boarded an international flight with no luggage whatsoever. The fact that I paid cash for my ticket also caused me a lot of problem, but Emeka's ten grand did the walking and talking at the airport as I bribed and tipped my way up until I boarded the aircraft. Most of the time, I didn't even know what I was doing. I was in a daze and just dished out the cash to anyone who asked for money. I bought a new one-way, first-class ticket, because the economy and premium economy seats were all gone. I also bought a head cap, a pink one because that was the only colour available at the duty-free shop. I did not relax until the plane took off.

PART 4

PART 4

29

Hopelessness.

When our plane finally landed at Heathrow Airport, my initial instinct was to get out of my first-class seat and do a twirl up and down the aisle; but I resisted the impulse. My heart was still heavy and I was not too sure returning to London was a wise decision. I knew I could actually end up in prison. I also knew my case was a hopeless one since, statistically, only five to ten per cent of identity fraud cases are ever solved. I did not find the cheque and what angered me most was that someone, somewhere, would eventually pocket hundreds of thousands of pounds.

It finally dawned on me that I was all alone and on my own when Vicky, my sister, who was supposed to meet me at the airport with a wig for my bald head, a change of clothes and some food, did not turn up. I had imagined us crying together, hugging and talking for hours, but that did not happen.

I was nauseous and queasy all the way to London.

*

Kilburn was still the same. The people on Kilburn High Road carried on as usual, oblivious to my predicament and as usual, they were all in a hurry. Life continued for them all. The flowers bloomed and the blackbirds chirped from the leafy trees on my road as I arrived at my Kilburn flat, still dressed in my capacious, black, ankle-length boubou.

My shiny black door was covered in dust. When I let myself into the flat, it looked so much smaller compared to my parents' house and the Kirikiri mega-mansion.

I stepped on a big pile of letters that had been posted through my letterbox. There were envelopes in assorted sizes and colours. I shoved them out of my way with my right foot.

I had a lot of me time to think while on the plane and in my head, I had drawn up and compartmentalised a list of all the people I was going to confront – starting with my next- door neighbour. She had a lot of dodgy teenagers and their posts for faceless names were sometimes mistakenly delivered to my address. I would also confront my two cousins who had used my address a few months ago without my permission. I certainly would challenge another cousin who had asked me for my date of birth, out of the blue, saying she needed it for the embassy. I planned to do a backtrack to all my old addresses as advised by Malika. Last of all, I reminded myself to confront Maureen from church who had asked if she could insure a car in my name.

My arms, face and legs were covered in big mosquito bites and prickly heat rashes spread themselves on my neck, upper chest, under my breasts and armpits. I lay in my bath and scrubbed my body until the bites started bleeding.

While replaying the incidents of the past few weeks, incredulity hit me. I could not believe that after so many harrowing days in Kirikiri and Ibusa, I returned with nothing to show for all the days and the money spent abroad. Unbelievable. There I was: jobless, husbandless, childless, about to be homeless and most likely imprisoned for an offence I never committed. Emeka, my only hope for a new life, was dead and gone and I still could not get Emeka's mother's cries out of my head. Those screams just refused to go.

My heart constantly ached for Emeka and his name resounded in my head every other minute. It was like a piece of firewood burned in me. The worst bit was that I never said my last farewell to him. I missed him and truly wished I could turn back the hands of the clock. I regretted the twelve years of separation. I kept hoping he would call, even though I knew that was impossible.

I got out of the bathtub and was shocked at my reflection in the mirror. My round, bald head looked like a clenched fist of Fullmer, the boxer. I was as bald as a badger. I stood and watched the tears from my sunken eyes run down my hollow cheeks. I looked in a sorry state. I stepped on the bathroom scale and was shocked at the number of pounds I had lost. I had shrunken four sizes; from a size fourteen down to ten, and my little voluptuous curves had all disappeared.

"Emeka is dead and gone," I told myself, trying to make a mental switch and give my stolen ID its place of priority on my mind, but the memory of his death refused to go to the back burner.

30

"Abomination!!" Papa screamed down the phone. "Your in-laws just left our house. You have poured sand into my eyes. You put us to shame."

I did not expect an angry reaction when I called.

"I am sorry, Sir…" I was shocked at the amount of energy in Papa's voice.

"Don't sir me, I am not a knight. How could you run and run all the way to London yet again? Ehn?? What is it with you and this London, eh?"

"Papa, I had to come back because of my interview."

"Which rubbish interview? When we remember death, we tread softly. Death is for us all."

"Sorry, Sir… Papa…"

"You passed our house in Ibusa, passed Benin, passed Lagos and went all the way to London again."

Mama came on the phone. "You have to come back immediately. Right away," Mama said slowly. "If you don't, you will be ostracised by Ibusa people. Ibusa people will avoid you like a plague."

"I will disown you if you do not come back and bury your husband," Papa threatened in the background.

"Okay. I have heard. Once I finish the interview at work, I will come back immediately. I also have a name to clear here, Papa."

"Come back now. Now. Now."

"Yes, Sir."

"Now!!" Papa boomed authoritatively and hung up.

Although I was disappointed in my parents, I was slightly relieved to hear Papa's voice sound very strong. I got off the phone feeling better than I did before I had called them.

Papa's health must have improved tremendously... And they must think it is all about them.

I, myself, was also upset because I abandoned Emeka in death and jumped ship, but that is because I had no choice. I had an interview to attend and they didn't seem to understand I could go to prison. Nobody seemed to care about me. I knew that Emeka would understand why I left, especially with the hideous and demonic instructions that were on the A4 sheet of paper.

Please forgive me, Emeka. I was not prepared to drink the water from a corpse-bathe.

I dug out an old wig from one of the bedroom drawers and settled down on the cold leather sofa in the living room to open my mail, leaving the killer brown envelopes till the last. They could wait.

The first white envelope was a letter from Ben, my solicitor, advising of the restraining order on all accounts in my name. He stated that, in an attempt to freeze the other Ada's accounts, PJ&PJ inadvertently froze all my bank accounts as well. It didn't matter to me at all because I still had a lot left from Emeka's money. I pictured myself back at Aunty Rhoda's once I exhausted what was left of the ten thousand pounds.

The second letter was from my internet provider, stating that my direct debit was returned unpaid. My mobile company sent the third one. They were unable to take the monthly payment. The fourth letter came from my bank stating that my account had been frozen as requested. Then there was a brown envelope that was addressed to Ada B. George, concerning the renewal of Children's Allowance. Children's Allowance? I had never applied for or claimed any form of allowance in my entire life. Then there was a new medical card – thank God for that. Another brown envelope addressed to me was about home insurance. There was also a letter from Bigwigs asking me to call them during working hours Monday to Friday 8am to 6pm. One letter was a refusal from a bank – they were refusing my recent application for a credit card, which I had never applied for. There were also five cards that were dropped by various bailiffs that had called, and there was a letter about my second interview at PJ&PJ.

I rang Malika. She was still at her friend's house.

"You were right not to disobey or argue with your dad because of his health," she whispered and agreed I did the best thing by coming back to London. "Forget those ancient mariners," she shouted when I told her about my dad's latest outburst.

I called Ramila, but her phone rang out. She sent a WhatsApp message shortly after, and the message read:

"There are five children, a husband and a pay-out of three-quarters of a million. Obtained birth certificates for children have you down as their mother. Housing records and documents were obtained for a property that you own in Abbey Wood and you sold one other property just before you died. The money for the property was paid into a bank account in your name. Speak later."

I put the mobile phone down and went to bed. I pulled the

duvet over me and never wanted to get up ever again.

Anything could happen, and I didn't care. I was ready to go to prison.

31

The next day looked promising. It was bright and fair. First, I dug out and tidied my old CV and then spent most of the morning trawling the internet, looking for another job. Thoughts of Emeka and the Samsung phone with the WhatsApp message that was burnt to tinder and ashes in the Ikoyi mansion drifted in and out of my head and I started charting Emeka's life in my mind.

He had come to Lagos after his secondary school education in Ibusa. His parents sent him to live with his eldest brother, Ignatius, on Montgomery Road in Yaba. After two years of sleeping on a raffia mat in the living room, washing cars every morning and being an errand boy, Ignatius got him a job on a demolition project. After that, he put Emeka in one of the ministries and from there Emeka bought a ticket and sponsored himself at TVU where he studied Economics and obtained an upper second-class degree.

I must have fallen asleep mid-afternoon, because I woke up from a terrible nightmare.

I was waiting for Emeka's call even though he had just

arrived at my flat in London with a wicker basket. In the basket was an array of goodies: a bottle of red wine, a jollof rice dish with lots of assorted meat, fish and snails; there were tangerines, guavas, mangoes and oranges, and a carton of orange juice. When he eventually called, Emeka asked to speak to Aunty Rhoda. He wanted to ask her about the vanity case because his university transcript and certificate were in it. He needed them to find work in heaven. He told me that the vanity case was black and that it contained my expired passport, our National Insurance number cards, our old payslips, university certificates, our marriage certificate, his love letters to me, receipts for the cars that we took to Nigeria from Germany, and an old tenancy agreement for our off-campus accommodation.

I hated siestas since my boarding school days because they always inspired bad dreams. I sat up, not too sure if I was dreaming or not – until I ran my left palm over my bald head. The bald pate said it all. I lay down again, but could no longer sleep, so I got up and started messing about with my iPad. I sat hunched over the it for a long time. First, I checked the internet and browsed guides to happiness, then I checked my inbox, which was full. I had two hundred and ninety-one messages. The last message was asking me to let Reon and Malika know I was thinking of them on their birthdays. Another message from Facebook asked me to help Reon celebrate his birthday on Facebook. I went on to Facebook and wrote "Happy birthday Reon" on his wall. I wrinkled my nose and muttered "Yuck" when I saw Reon's profile photo. The child had not changed. His hair and clothing wreaked of poor career, as did those of his friends. Out of boredom and curiosity, I scrolled through his friends' pictures.

I combusted. Apart from me, Ada Nneka George, there was also an Ada B. George among his friends.

Ada B. George? Ada B. George? Ada B. George? Unfortunately, Ada B. George did not have a profile picture and there was no indication of what the letter B stood for. I tried to access her Facebook account, but it was restricted. I decided to self-google my name and when I ego-surfed, there was unsurprisingly a google ganger with my name, associated to a second address in the south-east area of London! Also listed at that address were a man born between 1960 and 1965, named Ade Smith; an Adetokunbo Smith; an Emeka George and five children.

I carried on searching: my current address aside, I was also placed at Aunty Rhoda's address in Putney and six other addresses in South East London. Two of the addresses were in Abbey Wood and five in Peckham! Unfortunately, there were only the first two letters and first numbers of the postcodes shown, not the full addresses.

I had never lived-in South-East London. I tried accessing my supposed profile on Facebook through Google but the restrictions didn't allow me to access the thief's profile.

I made a mental note to contact Bernard Benson's office.

I had to go somewhere immediately and I knew it had to be Aunty Rhoda's house in Putney. But before then, I tried LinkedIn and I saw her face for the first time. There it was – the picture of a light-skinned, pretty lady with a lovely smiley face. She had the two, little, vertical marks on her face – one on each cheek. Her name was mine. Same date of birth. She was a nurse and was currently the CEO of a care agency with a staff strength of twenty-five carers. A telephone number was provided and so was a post office box. I rang the telephone number, but it went straight to an automated voicemail. A Mr A. Smith was down as one of the directors of the company.

I jumped off my bed.

All of a sudden, I developed a strong sense of bravado. I needed to visit the Peckham and Abbey Wood addresses, but I did not know the exact house numbers. Something told me to go to Aunty Rhoda's house. I called Ben, the solicitor, and he offered to go with me; if nothing else, to retrieve the vanity case.

32

I was fuming when we arrived at Aunty Rhoda's; but on Ben's advice, tried to remain calm. I pressed her doorbell repeatedly with all my strength.

After a while, a weak voice asked, "Who is it?"

"It is me. Ada."

"Bless!! My child! Welcome," Aunty Rhoda greeted warmly from inside as she fiddled with the lock.

My anger immediately vanished when I saw the diminutive, frail, old lady dressed like an Eskimo by the door. I could not understand how she could wear so many layers of clothing indoors and her oversized, red, winter hat covered almost a third of her little face.

It was a typical, old-school house. The walls of the short corridor leading to the front room were adorned with photos of the Queen and Prince Charles and Diana. There were no pictures of William and Kate, the Duke and Duchess of Cambridge. Aunty Rhoda still had the old television set with the two long silver antennae in her living room. On top of the TV was a centrepiece of plastic flowers and the same old picture of Reon in his bottle-green cardigan. The house was boiling hot.

"Good afternoon, Ma," I greeted and I introduced Ben as we walked in.

"Welcome, children of God," she replied, and just then Reon bounced down the stairs.

"Hey." He looked gaunt and his eyes were worryingly sunken and bloodshot. His beard was unkempt and he wore little square silver earrings on both ears. He was dressed in a black T-shirt that was full of holes and safety pins and his blue jeans were ripped at the knees. "You alright?" He asked warmly.

"Yes. And you?"

"I am good."

"How is work?" I asked.

"I am not working right now. Just came out."

"Again?"

"Yes, but I was in for something minor... Very minor... Handling stolen goods," he said nonchalantly.

"Oh no, Reon! Not again. And you don't call handling stolen goods minor. It is major!! I thought you had changed."

"He is very sober now. His eyes saw pepper in prison. They beat the living day out of him in there," Aunty Rhoda said aloud. "He says. I wasn't there," she added and turned both lips up.

"I am now a good boy. I am twenty-seven years old and I am now in the Lord's hands. I have given my life to Christ. I did so last week."

"Amen," Aunty Rhoda and I chorused.

I did not see any sobriety in the Reon that stood in front of me. First of all, he looked older than his twenty-seven years. Not only that, but he also oozed of poor career, irresponsibility and poverty. He had tattoos on both arms and the torn jeans that sagged down his bottom almost dropped off as he sauntered to the kitchen.

"How are you?" Aunty Rhoda asked.

"Not fine, but thank you for asking, Ma," I responded and went on to tell her everything about my parents and Nigeria. Everything, but Emeka's death.

When she asked about work, I told her we were still at it and that I could go to prison if found guilty because of the amount of money involved.

"Prison?" Aunty screamed aloud.

At the word "prison" Reon rushed out of the kitchen.

"Who is going to prison?"

"Your Aunty Ada. Someone committed big offences in her name."

"That's crazy. Too mad. Too bad," Reon said. "What happened?"

I ignored him.

"Do I have any letters?" I asked.

"Nope," he replied.

Ben and I looked at each other. His eyes begged me to remain calm.

"Emeka and I left a black vanity case here in the basement."

"It will be where you left it," Aunty Rhoda said confidently.

"Thank you, Ma."

"Reon, take your Aunty to the basement," Aunty Rhoda instructed.

The poorly lit basement was like a storage unit for every single person that had passed through the house. It was full of all sorts of suitcases, cartons, boxes, Ghana Must Go bags and various sizes of black bags. Books, crockery, more black bags, old bedside lamps, retro telephones, an old liquidiser, oversized pots and frying pans were stacked on rows of shelves. Initially, we did not find the vanity case, but Reon finally located my prized possession on the topmost shelf, hidden behind large cameo dishes, pots and pans.

I opened it.

It was empty.

There was not a single thing inside.

"Let me climb up and check on the shelf... The contents of the case might have fallen out," Reon said. I started crying and stormed up the stairs to Aunty Rhoda.

Reon swore he knew nothing about the contents and started crying as well.

"I would never steal Ada's stuff. I steal outside. I never rob family members," Reon whimpered and returned to his room.

Ben and I looked at each other and he shrugged.

A few seconds later, a visibly disturbed Reon returned to the living room. I went down on my knees and started crying.

"Reon, please! I beg you in God's name. I am on my knees. Please, help me. I don't want to go to prison. Please... Please, Reon. Please."

Reon's eyes welled with tears. "Sorry, Aunty Ada. Please, stop crying. Please. Aunty Ada. Please. I feel your pain."

I continued crying.

"Okay. I have a confession to make," he said without looking at me in the face.

"Yes, Reon?" Aunty Rhoda snapped.

"I always knew someone was using Aunty Ada's name to work. I didn't know they also did fraud with it."

"Pardon?" Aunty Rhoda asked impatiently.

"I passed all her post to Uncle Abbey Wood… He emptied the vanity case."

"Who is your Uncle Abbey Wood?" Ben asked.

"Brother Ade in Abbey Wood."

"What do you mean? You gave him my post?"

"Yes."

"Why?" Ben asked.

"Because I always did. Many years ago, when I found Aunty Ada's short birth certificate while I was cleaning her room, I gave it to Brother Ade and from then on, he collected all her post."

"Mr Lawyer, don't mind this boy, oh. He is a big liar. His lies can wake the dead up. I almost lost this property because of him, but for the grace of God."

"Grandma!! If you doubt me, let us go to his house now."

"Okay, let us go," I screamed.

Ben agreed to drive us to Ade's house.

33

It was a long drive to Abbey Wood. Reon co-directed us to the identity hijacker's house. It was in the middle of an extremely posh, tree-lined road on the outskirts of London.

Abbey Wood looked peaceful.

I had suddenly developed this reckless sense of bravado and I was desperate. I was ready to fight. To kill. To maim.

I started humming one of Eliza's war songs in the car.

I was trembling in my seat. "Once Reon knocked and gained access, we would storm the house very quickly," I said aloud and carried on scrutinizing each house as we drove past. Not one of them seemed fit for an ID thief. Stylish, luxurious cars were parked on every single driveway of the very upper-middle-class road. There were no shops, pubs, bus stops, tube stations or offices in the vicinity. I could tell that it was a highly affluent and quiet neighbourhood. In fact, it seemed too elegant a road for an identity thief.

"Arriving at destination on right," announced the beautiful voice of our lady navigator on the GPS.

Her house was one of the many big, identical, detached houses. I suddenly felt nauseous.

Men, I am going to seriously deal with the fraudster, I enthused. Headbutts and all.

"I can't wait to see these people," I announced aloud.

"No fighting. You are a gentle lady, not a fighter. All we will do is call the police if there really is anything, because I don't really trust this child," Aunty Rhoda advised.

"In fact, I plan to beat this girl to a pulp before handing her and her cohorts over to the police. First of all, I will deck her one hot, correct, back-hand slap." I paused and added, "Or maybe not."

"Good girl."

"I hope and pray to God that we are able to hand them over to the police peacefully and bring everything to an end," Reon muttered.

A Yoruba adage says a bad child also has its good and useful days. Reon was that proverbial bad child that entered its mother's womb from the evil forest, but he was very useful that day.

"Uncle Ade can be dangerous," he warned.

"We don't care," Aunty Rhoda and I chorused.

"Hm-hm-hm! This trip can lead to tragic consequences," he warned again.

"I don't care. In fact, nobody cares," I screamed. "This is my life that is at stake."

Ben parked the car at a vantage point on the left-hand side of the road, from where we got a very good view of the wide front door of the house. I felt my heartbeats quicken. It was pounding restlessly and all of a sudden, my tummy was in knots. It felt like it was colonised by loads of imaginary butterflies.

The house looked massive and so did the driveway. Surprisingly, the driveway, which could very easily fit at least six cars, had only one car in it – a metallic black Porsche Cayenne with blacked-out windows. The registration number was ADA001. I looked at Ben and pointed to the car as tears welled in my eyes.

Finally, I was going to confront the monster who had caused me so much grief.

We sat in Ben's car and watched in silence as Reon strolled across the wide tree-lined road lackadaisically. He pulled his hood over his head and scrutinised his phone as he made his way to the entrance of the big house. I prayed they opened the door of the house to him because Reon looked like a ragamuffin. He was so out of place in his hoodie and sagged, tattered jeans that were falling off his bum.

What if it was the wrong house? What if they were out?

Reon reached out and pressed the doorbell. It did not seem like there was anyone at home, but after a long while a stooped, bespectacled man dressed in a white, flowy, jellabiya kaftan opened the door. All his hair was white. Reon and the man stood by the front door talking for a while. It seemed like he was not going to allow Reon in, as if he wanted to make conversation at the doorstep and dismiss Reon. The man was talking, but I could not hear what he was saying.

"Oh my God. Oh my God. Oh my God," Reon screamed aloud. Repeatedly. Years later, I wondered if he had screamed that loud because he wanted us to hear him. He was loud and clear. I saw that Reon raised his two hands and put them on top of his head.

"No. No. No. Oh, no," Reon said again with both hands still on his head.

After about five seconds he took the hands down and hugged the man by the door. The man took his glasses off and wiped what I imagined were tears away from his eyes. Reon's shoulder movement indicated he was sobbing. Both of them walked into the house and slammed the door.

I punched my left palm with my clenched right hand and rocked my whole body impatiently. We sat in the car and waited for Reon to come back for us, but he did not return.

"Ah-ah!! What could be happening?" a puzzled Aunty Rhoda asked. "That was Tokunbo that answered the door," she said in a worried voice.

"I haven't got a clue," I replied, and added, "But whatever it is… It is not nice."

"Should we call Reon's mobile?" Aunty Rhoda asked.

"Aunty Rhoda, is this the same Toks that lived with us in Putney? Your tenant?"

"Yes. It is."

"Hm…" I exhaled aloud. "No. No time to start calling Reon's number. I am going in there," I said as I felt a sudden rush of adrenalin. I was raring to charge at my tormentor. I was going to beat her mercilessly. I jumped out of the car and ran across the wide road like a crazed woman. I turned around to see Ben running after me and Aunty Rhoda hobbled behind him.

I placed my index finger on the doorbell and rang it continuously until a teary-eyed Reon answered the door. He was sobbing like a baby. An obviously exhausted, white-haired man with a snowfall of dandruff on his collar stood behind him. Tears rolled down his cheeks and he stank of stale aftershave.

"Thank you. Thank you, oh. Thank you for coming. Please come in and sit down," he said bravely between sobs.

What was going on?

I walked straight into the front room, followed by Ben and Aunty Rhoda. There really was nowhere to sit. The living room was full of clutter – boxes of unsewn lace and guinea brocade fabric, boxes of shoes and packets of costume jewellery were all over the tomato-red leather sofas, dining and coffee tables and chairs. It was later Reon explained that the other Ada was also a trader.

I finally saw her; I mean, I saw her photograph and I could not stop looking at her picture.

It was a big, framed photo on top of a round coffee table. A photograph of a smiling, plump and very light-skinned lady. She was decked in jewellery. Her full and luscious lips were covered in Russian red lipstick and lip gloss, and her wide smile revealed a lovely set of big white teeth and a sparkling gold tooth that replaced one of the incisors – the right one in the front upper jaw. Her face in the palm of her hand was a lot fairer than mine. That hand and the fingers that held the face in the picture were in a sharp contrast to the face. The hand was darker than dark-brown chocolate and her knuckles were actually black. Her prominent, short, vertical facial marks stood out on either cheek; they were a lot similar to my faded ones. Her entire upper eyelids were intensely covered in terracotta eyeshadow and above them were tattooed eyebrows. The glued on false eyelashes were the thickest and longest ones I had ever seen.

The woman's flawless skin looked smoother than a new-born baby's bum. She had massive gold rings on her two middle fingers, and her gold earrings were thick and huge loops. It was like she wore a doughnut on each ear. Her voluptuous boobs looked as big as the papayas I bought for two pounds ninety-nine at our Kilburn market and the gold chain around her fat neck was huge and wider than a dog's collar. The stud on her nose was almost the size of a five-pence coin. I thought she had very long hair, but then, when I looked closer, I realised that what she had on her head were braids, the thinnest and tiniest ones – one million braids.

How could this showy person have stolen my life and passed for me? We had no resemblance whatsoever. The face of the lady in the photograph who had thrown an atomic bomb into my life and shattered it into tiny pieces looked vaguely familiar. I had seen the face somewhere; albeit without the marks and darker. I struggled in my head to put a name to the face but couldn't.

… And then it came back to me. Her name was Binta and both of us were once tenants in Aunty Rhoda's house.

The expensive leather sofas; the large, flat screen TV on the wall and the huge chandelier all smelled of pound sterling. There was a big stack of orange B&Q buckets with stickers that read "Happy 38th Birthday, Ada".

She was preparing for my birthday!

"Adetokunbo, what is happening?" Aunty Rhoda asked.

"She died, oh. Aunty Rhoda, Ada is dead," the man wailed.

"I reject death in the mighty name of Jesus. I am not dead. I will not die. It shall not happen. I will not die," I muttered under my breath. I was weakened by the news.

"She left me with five little children."

"What?!" Aunty Rhoda exclaimed aloud. "Who died?" she asked.

"Ada. Binta. My wife. She died."

"It is a lie. Don't say that again. No. No. Oh, no! When? How? Where? What happened?" Aunty Rhoda asked.

"Yesterday night."

I felt the shivers travel right down my spine as I looked at the faces of my companions with my eyes widened in shock. We were all shocked. That was most unexpected. Unbelievable.

Aunty Rhoda started crying.

When is all of this going to end? I asked God in my head.

"Thank you for coming," he greeted again. "Please, sit down."

Ben and Aunty Rhoda managed to push the stuff on one of the sofas to one side and perch on the edge near them. I remained on my feet and so did Reon.

"My fearless wife. My lioness. My crown. My jewel. The only fish in my ocean. My duvet cover, my blanket is dead."

"Dead?' a teary Aunty Rhoda asked again.

"Dead, oh," he repeated. "She died in Lagos yesterday."

I became nauseous again, although very briefly this time.

"Heart attack," Reon volunteered.

"Yes, oh. Heart failure. She was dealing with a lot of issues which were weighing her down," Ade explained.

I was dumbfounded. How could I be so unlucky? I remembered Adetokunbo from Putney. He had aged. He was all grey; even the stubbles on his chin and his eyebrows were grey. He did not recognise me. I took another look at the happy, smiley face in the photograph on the coffee table. How I wished she could rise from the dead. I wanted to knock the gold tooth out of her mouth for starters, and then use both of my hands to yank the big doughnut-earrings off her face.

Death, oh, death. Death, you have done it to me again. How could you be so unfair, so inconsiderate, so bad and so wicked? Where do I go from here? Eh?

I walked up to the TV and spoke to the photograph.

"Do you know what you have done to me? Eh? You ruined my life, my name, my career, my whole family," I told the picture.

"Sorry?" A confused Ade asked.

"Do you know who this is?" Aunty Rhoda asked.

"Toks?" I asked.

"Yes, Tokunbo. I am Adetokunbo. Toks for short."

He looked at me.

"Are you Tokunbo?" I asked.

"Yes, now. This face looks familiar." He took the misty glasses off and looked right into my eyes.

"My name is Ada. Ada George. I used to be Ada Chukwu."

"Jesus wept!" he exclaimed. "The original Ada?"

And before I could bat an eyelid he fell straight on to the floor, lay on his tummy, stretched his entire body, and in that prostrated position grabbed my left ankle.

I noticed Reon brought out his phone and started recording him immediately.

"Ada, please forgive us. Please forgive us. It is the devil and he will be put to shame. I am sorry. Please don't be angry. The devil used us."

"God will punish you," I hissed.

Still on the floor, he looked up and said, "We only borrowed your names."

"Indeed! Only borrowed! Plus, Emeka's name, too? You are both sick in the head – you and your dead Binta," I hissed.

He looked like a wretched lizard, or rather a scorpion on the floor. I wanted to stamp, trample and crush his reptile-like head with the sole of my feet and grind it until he became ashes, like the ones on my raffia mat in Ibusa.

Adetokunbo looked up at Reon. He fixed his gaze on Reon for about ten seconds and shook his head.

"I am sorry, Uncle. I didn't have a choice. Grandma asked me to bring them here."

"Leon, Reon or whatever his useless name is…is an animal. A very stupid boy he is. He is the architect of all this."

Aunty Rhoda sighed aloud.

"Shortly after Ada and Emeka left for Nigeria, Binta and

224

I were in our rented room minding our business and doing our thing our own way when Reon burst into the room. He showed us what he found in the basement. He showed us your expired British passport, your birth certificate and a marriage certificate… Oh, and you and Emeka's provisional driving licences."

"Where did you find them?" I asked Reon.

"The little box in the basement."

"Binta said to him, 'You better return them, you nonsensical thieving boy… Crazy boy. Why do you like ransacking people's stuff?' Reon returned the documents to the basement, but that night at about ten o'clock, the three of us, Binta, Reon and I, decided that Binta could use this Ada's details until she obtained her right of abode in her own name… And… Oh, that is not all. That day we dashed Reon twenty pounds for his generosity and thoughtfulness."

"Is that right?" Aunty Rhoda asked.

"Yes, Grandma," he replied with his eyes fixed on Binta's picture; as if his salvation lay with the photo.

Aunty Rhoda shook her head vigorously in disgust.

"And I must say that the Ada name brought Binta a lot of good luck," Ade mumbled.

I hissed aloud.

"But as soon as we got our papers we reverted to our names."

Again, I felt like crushing and dancing the twist on his little round reptile and mousy head as he lay stretched out on the floor.

"Emm," he stammered and continued talking. "Well… You seee, in fact… In short… She was only meant to use it for a few months but carried on for years."

His grip on my left ankle became stronger.

"Can you let go of Ada's ankle?" Ben asked authoritatively.

He let go of me and I started taking pictures of everybody

and everything, then I stopped. I stood and looked at the photo of Binta so many times and took photos of the photo so many times. I snapped away like a possessed woman. Suddenly, Ade got off the floor and decided to play macho.

"In fact, in short, ah-ah... What is the big deal, eh?" he asked arrogantly. "I beg, I have enough on my plate right now. It is not a big deal. People do it. It happens every blessed day in this London. Ah-ah. We are not the first and we will not be the last."

"Reon, call the police!!" I went ballistic and screamed. "Call 999!!" I screamed at the top of my voice.

"And please stop making noise. This is a no-noise area."

"I will scream. I will shout. I will scream. I am screaming. Arghh!" I yelled at the top of my lungs.

"Aunty, calm down. What is the reason for calling the police? There is no emergency here," Reon said calmly.

"There is an emergency. Call the police. They stole me," I screamed. "They hijacked my identity," I screamed louder. "He put me through a lot of palaver and turned my life upside down. They damaged my unblemished stellar career at work."

"Ada. You and I can go to the station to make a statement," Toks said in a very appealing voice. "Think of my neighbours. Think of me. Think of my children and think of my dead wife."

"He is right," Aunty Rhoda said very quietly...

"Neighbours? Your neighbours? Call the police!!" I screamed and carried on screaming until I could scream no more. "Call the police!!" I yelled repeatedly. "Call the police before he absconds!" I said.

"Abscond? To where? I have five motherless children in this house."

"Tokunbo? Does Tokunbo not mean that you were born abroad?" I asked.

Tokunbo ignored me.

"Yes, it does," Aunty Rhoda replied. "But he was born in Ghana."

"I was born in Ghana and taken back to Nigeria over the seas – hence the name Tokunbo," he said.

"Brother, how about the name Ade?" Reon asked.

"I am Ade. My full name is Adetokunbo. I was flown into Nigeria from Ghana."

"Reon. Are you deaf? Please dial 999. Now."

"I beg, Ma." Ade went on the floor again, rolled over and grabbed Ben's right ankle. "We are all one. Please. We are one Nigeria."

"Of all the people in London, why me?" I asked.

"Ada, I beg pity me. I beg you in God's name. I lost my wife less than twenty-four hours ago. Don't do this to my family."

"It will not be better for you and your entire family. Bad luck will follow you all for the rest of your lives."

"I have not touched the money. You can have it. Please. The cheque is upstairs. Take the Porsche Cayenne. It is brand new and is already in your name. Ada… Sorry, Binta only drove it about ten times."

"Look at me! I have been through hell. I am a nervous wreck. See me thinner than a rake, and look at your robust wife, fat and very healthy."

"But she is dead!" Toks protested. He added, "You can take the Porsche Cayenne and all the money in Binta's account."

I hissed.

"In fact, it is from when she reverted to her real name that sickness and problems set in." He was talking and singing like a canary. "The problems started when all her bank accounts that were still in your name were frozen, then the police executed

227

a warrant on one of her properties that she was trying to sell. As if that was not enough, she lost a lot of her foreign carers at her care agency because of Brexit."

I saw Aunty Rhoda looking at Binta's picture on the wall. It looked like an old picture compared to the condolence one. Binta looked very portly and her nails, like claws, were painted yellow.

"What a pity. May her soul rest in peace," Aunty Rhoda muttered and shook her head. "What happened?" she asked.

Tokunbo explained that they had locked the doors and gone to bed when the doorbell rang and how he and the children all rushed down to see who was at the door. He looked through the spyhole and espied Pastor Jonathan, the deaconess and the assistant pastor of their church.

"All three of them?" A puzzled Aunty Rhoda asked.

"Yes, Ma. Deaconess asked the children to go upstairs and Pastor told me I had to leave for Nigeria as soon as possible because my wife was very ill in the hospital. I even thought there was a mix-up and that it was this Ada that was ill, but then I heard one of the children scream upstairs and they all rushed downstairs crying."

"Oh no! What a way to find out," Aunty Rhoda said sadly.

"Heart failure, Ma. Heart attack. A lot had happened. For some unknown reason she could not get money out of her bank. All her bank accounts, her reward account, her bond, ISA and savings accounts were frozen. She had over three-hundred-thousand pounds in one of the frozen accounts. She worried so much, Aunty."

"I understand. Sorry. Accept my sympathy."

"Thank you, Ma. She was doing extremely well. But you know this country – they give you your pay in one hand and take it back with the other."

I totally agreed with him on that – we all had bills, income tax, road tax, council tax, prescription charges, standard charges, penalties, contributions, eye tests, car tests, TV licence, driving licence, and all sorts of insurance.

"It is a vicious cycle," muttered Reon.

I kissed my teeth and hissed loudly. I was sure if my mother was awake, she would have heard the hiss in Nigeria.

It turned out that Binta went to Nigeria to sell the house her family was building for her in order to generate income. When she got there, there was no house. Her family said they sold her land because they needed money to eat. They said that the pictures they sent to her over the years were photos of someone else's house. They never built any house. The shock gave her a heart attack and she died on the spot.

I wanted to tell Ade that I had no business with all the rubbish that he was vomiting. I wanted to tell him that it served her right.

"You destroyed my life – not just mine, but also my parents' and my entire family's. Everybody's," I screamed.

"I am sorry."

"Pocket your sorrow, please. Reon, dial 999," I shouted.

"Yes, Aunty."

"Leon. Wait. Eh. After all, we are in it together."

"*Tufia*," Aunty Rhoda hissed and spat at Reon. "So, the ant that was eating the spinach was inside the spinach?" she added.

"Madam, please do not spit on this child again," Ben advised. "I will not condone violence. Otherwise, I will call the police right away. In the interim period, I will take a statement from you, Sir."

If only we had come earlier, if only they had not kept me in Nigeria, if only I had googled my name earlier.

"Wait a minute," I said. "I remember Binta was about to get a British passport before I had left and she did not have those marks on her face."

"She scratched the marks on with a razor blade because you had marks on your face in your old, cancelled passport."

"Did she not apply for a British passport just before Emeka and I left for Nigeria?"

"She did."

"En-hen? So why my name? Why my name out of the millions of names in London? I remember she got a letter asking that she should pick up the passport in person…"

"Yes."

"And so?"

"She never went. She developed cold feet. She was scared."

"I see. Why then did I start getting her post all of a sudden?"

"She changed her correspondence address to yours. Reon gave her your new address."

"My Reon?" A shocked and tired Aunty Rhoda asked.

"Yes, Ma."

"Reon?" we all chorused, except Toks.

"Aunty Ada, you gave me your address when I saw you in Brent Cross."

After a long silence, I asked, "Where is the cheque?"

"Upstairs."

Toks ran up the stairs and returned within seconds with the cheque. I snatched it off him. It was an unusually hefty cheque. Light green in colour. It was issued to Mr Emeka George. The payable amount was seven hundred and fifty thousand pounds. I brought out my phone and took so many pictures of it. I continued snapping pictures of the cheque until Ben tapped me very gently on the shoulder.

"It is enough," he whispered.

I gave the cheque to Ben.

"Sit down, Mr Ade. I would like to take a statement from you. I will ask you questions and write your answers on an A4 sheet of paper. After that we shall call the police." Ade sat down as instructed by Ben and provided concise answers to all the questions that were put to him.

The picture of the three-page statement remained stored in my photo gallery for a very long time. I will never forget the contents of the document for the rest of my life. I read it over and over until a copy of it was imprinted in my memory word for word. If I would be woken from a deep slumber at 3am in the morning fifty years from now, I will be able to recite the statement off the top of my head. It read:

"My name is Adetokunbo Smith. I am also known as Ade or Toks or Tokunbo. I am over eighteen. I am currently unemployed.

Binta Ogu, also known as Ada George, and I did not set off to commit insurance fraud. I met Binta Ogu who was to later become my wife and who became Ada George at a bus stop in Peckham Rye. I never in my wildest dreams thought she would ever become my wife and go on to bear five children for me. At the time I met her, she had just left the home of a very rich family in the Golders Green area of London where she was working as a servant. I met her when she came to Peckham to learn hairdressing in a salon. She used to visit me at Aunty Rhoda's house when Ada and Emeka lived there. She moved into the address when a room became vacant.

I knew the original Ada from when I lived at Aunty Rhoda's house as a student. After Ada left Aunty Rhoda's address to go to university, a credit card arrived for her. I intercepted the card and approached Binta to run it for me. After Ada and Emeka went back to Nigeria, her last payslip and P60 arrived. I advised

Leon to put them in her vanity case in Aunty Rhoda's basement. It was then that Leon found Ada's old passport, birth certificate and marriage certificate in the vanity case. He gave Binta these documents for work purposes only.

Binta did not do any fraud to become rich. She became very rich from her hard work. When she became Ada George, she worked very hard. She started off with early 'momo', that is early morning cleaning of offices and then went on to work as a catering assistant. She later became a care assistant and eventually became a nurse. She opened her care agency a few years ago. The agency was in distress because of Brexit. Virtually everyone in London knew her as Ada George. She got the marks tattooed on her face in Camden Lock so that she could pass for Ada. Binta applied to the Home Office for a stay in her name. She lived and worked as Ada until she got her right of abode. She bought properties in Ada's name and had our five children in Ada's name. Binta reverted to her real name immediately when she obtained her papers. Binta invested and contributed a lot in Ada's name, including the National Insurance contributions she made in Ada's name. She believed she was entitled to benefit from all the taxes she paid in Ada's name, and also a benefit from the life insurance she took out in Ada's name.

Binta was the one that took out an insurance policy in Ada's name. She did not provide any ID at the time. She tried to change it to her real name when she got her papers. She killed Ada off when she couldn't do anything to claw back her payments from the insurance company. Binta bought the death certificate in Ada's name from a place called Oluwole in Lagos, Nigeria. I have never been to Oluwole. Binta sold the properties she bought in Ada's name to herself. Binta maxed out all the credit cards in Ada's name because she thought Ada was in Nigeria.

We never knew Ada was in London. We thought she was in Nigeria and was never going to come and live in London because Emeka was rich. If we knew she was in London, we would never have used her name. It was when my wife and I ran into Leon, aka Reon, at Dalston market not too long ago, that he told us Ada was back and had lived in London for over ten years. Prior to us meeting Leon, we did not know that she was back in London. Leon gave my wife Ada's current address and phone number. My wife panicked and she must have changed her address with all her debtors to Ada's address. I do not know why she stopped paying on the maxed-out cards. I did not cash the insurance cheque because I no longer have an account in Emeka's name. The cheque was in my briefcase in my bedroom. I have handed the cheque to Ada's solicitor. Neither my wife nor myself cashed the cheque. We did not cash it because it was issued in Emeka George's name.

My wife died of a heart attack late last night. Yes, she committed all the insurance fraud in Ada's name. I am a widower. I have five children to feed.

I am sorry and apologise for the inconvenience we caused Ada. I wrote the letter to the insurance company in Emeka George's name. We are not bad people. We are very religious and important people in our church. I am willing to make whatever necessary amends required. My wife was in the process of changing all the documents to her real name when she died. In fact, she had sold some of the properties in Ada's name to herself and also started taking driving lessons in her real name. We do not have any monies stashed anywhere. We live from hand to mouth and on overdraft.

I agree for a copy of my statement to be handed to the police. Please take the Porsche Cayenne on the driveway for free.

Signed, Adetokunbo Smith.

34

Ben drove into the PJ&PJ's car park and eased his Ford Focus next to Debbie's black Vauxhall Mokka. The tastes in my dry mouth were of fear and anxiety. A big black Rolls Royce that reminded me of Emeka's supercars was in the disabled bay. As Ben pulled the hand brakes, I reached for the large empty cardboard box that I got from Iceland on Kilburn High Road.

"Leave the box. I will come for it after the interview," Ben said quietly.

I wondered why he was almost whispering when it was just the two of us in the car. My plan was to fill the box with my personal belongings in the office. I left it on the back seat. Out of the car, I pictured Mr Murphy in Mary's swivel chair with his PJ&PJ dongle around his neck, the bright-red silk tie and the matching bright-red pocket kerchief. I was going to face him one more time and I seriously did not care anymore about whatever happened.

A copy of Adetokunbo's statement was in Ben's briefcase and I kept a laminated copy in my second-hand Chanel handbag of life.

The night before, I dreamt I was found guilty and sent down…
And, quite frankly, at that stage, I didn't even mind going to prison
for a break from all my calamities.

We were met at the initial reception area by a uniformed
security guard – he must have been newly recruited because I did
not recognise him.

"Come with me. The meeting is on the first floor." He led
us to the visitors' lift.

I quickly looked away when I saw myself in the full-length
mirror in the lift. The person in the reflection was a total
stranger. I looked again. My extreme weight loss was shocking.
I could not believe the image in the mirror was mine. I saw very
visible streaks of uneasiness, worry, fear, nervousness, restlessness
and tension stamped all over my face. My cheeks were hollower
and my eyes were redder, duller and sunken deeper than when I
first got back from Nigeria. The sadness written all over my face
was totally unalloyed.

My black blazer hung limply from my skeletal body. It
dropped off my shoulder to reveal scaly heat rashes over my chest
and neck.

Mr Murphy was waiting at the other end of the lift to meet
us. There was something different about him; he seemed to have
put on a bit of weight or maybe it was the lapels of his navy-blue
suit that made him look different. Those lapels were wider than
the Watford Way and I noticed a funny twinkle in his eyes. His
face was like one of those smiley potatoes Reon ate when he was
a child.

"Bernard Benson. Ada George's solicitor," Ben said as he
reached out his right hand and shook Darren's hand.

"Darren Murphy. Hello Miss George."

"Good morning," I greeted.

Darren led us to the second consulting room on the first floor, where all three of us sat down. There was no red folder on the table and there was no PEAL tape machine. The desk was empty.

"How are you today, Ada?" he asked with a pleasant smile on his face.

"I am okay. Thank you." Don't smile back, I cautioned myself. These people are deadly.

"Did you go abroad?"

"Emm?" I stammered and looked at Ben.

"Yes. She did," Ben cut in sharply.

"We thought so. We tried calling you several times."

"She went to see her aged parents."

"Very good." Mr Murphy shuffled on his chair. He cleared his throat and placed his two palms on the desk. "Now let's get down to business," he said as he took his hands off the desk and rubbed them together.

"Hmm." I sighed out aloud and waited.

"First of all, congratulations on your promotion. You are now a substantive senior manager. PJ&PJ is very proud of you."

I looked at Ben. He placed his right index finger on his lips, indicating that I should not say anything.

"I must let you know that you are a big asset to the company."

Neither Ben nor myself said anything.

"Second of all," Mr Murphy continued, "after a robust, in-depth and thorough investigation, we found out that your identity – that is, your name – was stolen. I, or rather we, have passed the identity thief's details to the police."

I heaved a very loud sigh of relief, and grabbed Ben's left hand.

"We have here a copy of the statement that was provided by the culprit's husband."

"Yes. Mr Ben, my solicitor got the statement from him."

"I know. But that doesn't mean we did not do anything to help your case."

I nodded in agreement.

"You are well loved in PJ&PJ."

"Am I?"

"Yes, you are. Some unknown colleagues of yours decided to write an anonymous letter to the head office in Watford accusing us of a poor investigation, of unfair suspension, and wastage of salary because you were still on our payroll."

Really?! I was tongue tied.

"They did? Bless!!" an impressed Ben said.

I was flabbergasted. Did that mean my horror was over?

"We carried out an in-depth investigation. The mortgage application forms for the properties in your name were obtained and so were the life insurance papers and the children's birth certificates… The entries on the birth certificates show three of the children were born on days that you were at work. Here."

Darren Murphy and Ben Benson laughed. It is not funny at all, I felt like saying.

"We contacted past employers for the ID hijacker. The last employer for the supposed dead lady stated that they paid a gentleman named Mr A. Smith her death benefit. Pictures of the lady and her husband at office parties were also obtained."

I could not say a single word.

"Our case on you is now closed and the suspension has been lifted." So, saying, Mr Murphy tapped on the desk again and shifted positions on his chair. His body language pronounced the issues were closed.

"Is that it?" I asked overwhelmed.

"Yes. It is. You can now return to your desk…" He chuckled

and added, "Just joking. I believe you would be given some form of leave and you can resume in your new band whenever you want to."

"Can I ask what full names your findings revealed?" Ben asked in the best professional tone I had ever heard.

"Well. Yes, you may. But at this stage I am not in a position to provide names."

"That's okay."

"I have quite a lot of important documents on my file. But because of the Data Protection Act…"

"I understand," Ben cut in.

Mr Murphy reached into his briefcase and brought out a red file; he opened it, and as he flicked through the papers, he reeled out some of the evidence.

"We have photos of the identity thief and we got statements from her previous employer. We got her job application, her pay details and we got statements from her past and present neighbours. We also carried out covert surveillance of her at her Abbey Wood address."

I wanted to jump up and give Mr Murphy a big hug for a job well done, but restrained myself. After all, I had been through hell all because they decided to find me guilty until they had evidence that proved I was innocent.

"Thank you very much," Ben said and stood up for us to leave. "Come on, Ada, let's get out of here."

"Before you leave, Ramila said to ask you to pop in and see her in the staff canteen upstairs."

"No. I just want to get out of here."

Mr Murphy ignored me and winked mischievously at Ben.

"Ah. Let's go and see her," Ben advised.

We got up and as we were about to leave, Ben spoke.

"Darren, Ada has something for you." Ben reached into his briefcase and brought out a brown envelope; he whispered, "The cheque," in my ears and handed the envelope to me. I gave it to Darren and watched his face very closely.

As he tore open the brown envelope, my mobile phone started vibrating, I got it out and looked at the screen. The displayed calling name was Home Wrecker. I stored Emeka's mum's number as Home Wrecker. I allowed it to ring out.

"Wao!! You got it back?"

"Yes," Ben and I chorused.

I could tell he was well chuffed. He put the cheque in his briefcase.

We made our way up the stairs to the third floor.

35

I heard lots of voices and laughter as we approached the canteen. Then I saw it. A big banner on the canteen door. It read "Welcome back Ada." A second big banner on the wall scripted "We missed you dearly." And a third banner read "We love our Pretty Ada."

We walked into the canteen. Shocks! I was taken aback by the amount of phone-camera-wielding colleagues in there. Cheers resounded everywhere and we were greeted by a loud applause that carried on for such a long time. Virtually every single member of staff in the building was there, including the mail opening staff from the post room, the messengers, the cleaners, the drivers, the security guards, front of office staff and the entire admin team. The canteen was packed. In my eleven-and-a-half years at PJ&PJ, I had never seen a gathering of everybody in the building in one room; neither had I seen so many happy faces in a long time. I was overwhelmed. They were all beaming. There was food everywhere. Gone were the gruesome pictures of Mary McGee's bandaged head and broken arm that had defaced the pretty white noticeboard; they were replaced by photos of my staff award in 2016.

And then Daisy got up as if on a cue. She was in another of her skimpy mini dresses. Daisy cupped her right fist and pretended she had a microphone in her hand. She looked at me with pure love and admiration in her eyes. Everyone went quiet as she cleared her throat thrice and belted out.

"Welcome Ada, welcome. Welcome Ada, welcome. We have been praying-praying-praying for your return. We have been praying-praying-praying for your return. Welcome Ada, welcome. Welcome Ada, welcome."

She looked so angelic in her yellow cotton pinafore dress and she sang like a nightingale. I used to think Aunty Eliza's voice was the best, but Daisy's voice beat Eliza's hands down. The applause that followed was louder than the first round. Ben and I joined in and clapped for Daisy.

I looked around the canteen. I could not believe the amount of decoration. The walls and tables were beautifully embellished with lots of lovely red, blue, yellow, pink and gold hearts. There were colourful balloons hanging from the ceiling and the walls. I was in cloud nine.

"Congrats on your promotion" was written in royal-blue cursive on the biggest fuchsia-pink balloon I had ever seen.

"Hola!!" my Spanish colleague, Maria, screamed aloud from the back of the crowd.

I smiled and nodded. I looked around and my mouth watered. I had never seen so much food in PJ&PJ. The array of edibles: big silver trays of spring rolls, samosas, pakora, Bombay mix, chapati, chicken biryani, fried chicken, roast chicken, jollof rice, fried rice and paella on the decorated table tennis table made me hungry. I was later told it was a potluck and everybody brought something.

Debbie and Ramila walked into the canteen. In the crook

of Debbie's hand was a big and colourful bouquet of flowers. Ramila held a card that seemed bigger than the twenty-six-inch TV screen in the staff room.

A chorus of "Speech… Speech… Speech!" filled the room. Colleagues beat rhythmically on the tables, clapped their hands and tapped tumblers and mugs with their cutlery.

Debbie spoke, "Please, sit down everybody."

We all sat down and everyone kept quiet.

"Welcome back Ada. Words cannot express how happy we all are to have you back. We felt the vacuum."

"Yes," everyone chorused and clapped.

"Headington House has not been the same without you."

"Yes," they chorused and clapped again.

"Those welcoming words of Daisy's song were from all of us. That God that you serve at your Quex Road church is a living God. Do not stop serving him. After a thorough investigation you were found not guilty… And I always knew that."

She went on to say that they had since found out and confirmed someone hijacked my identity and that the person died while using my identity.

"It is one of those freaky unfortunate things that happen in life," Debbie continued. "And I believe God wanted to make you a stronger person. Ramila will give you a letter from the office and we look forward to your resumption as a senior manager next week."

More clapping.

"Our pretty Ada Nneka George is innocent," a happy Ramila said aloud as she came up to me and gave me a big hug and presented me with the flowers and a welcome card that was signed by everyone.

"I will not keep you for too long as I know Mr Benson and

Mr Murphy have work to go back to. Here is a welcome card from everyone. I believe there is a voucher for your favourite store, which we all know is Debenhams."

"Thank you, Ramila," I muttered. "Thank you."

Everyone clapped.

"Incidentally it is my favourite store as well." Ramila chuckled and continued, "Congratulations on your promotion to senior manager. PJ&PJ has decided to give you two weeks paid annual leave."

I pinched my left wrist to make sure that I was not dreaming.

"Thank you," I said quietly. "Thank you all," I said again loud and clear. I took the envelopes off Ramila and handed them to my solicitor.

"We were all rooting for you," she whispered into my ears and gave me another big hug with tears of joy in her eyes.

One by one, everyone came up to me and gave me a hug. I felt genuine love and care all around the room. In fact, I had never experienced so much love in my whole life. I thought my heart was going to burst with elation. I gripped and held on to Ben's hand tightly. I didn't want to fall off the moderately decorated chair, or on the big Costco cake which was on top of a nicely embellished table with lots of balloons and flowers.

More impromptu speeches and words of praise and recognition followed. "Ada is one of the most honest persons… Ada is very kind and sympathetic… Hardworking… Encouraging, caring and nicest… Ada's character is impeccable. We love you Ada," and many more.

After the last speech I began to feel slightly uncomfortable because all of a sudden, I noticed that my manager, Ramila, Mr Darren Murphy and Debbie kept looking at the clock on the wall and also at the door. Everybody suddenly went quiet and if a pin had dropped in that canteen, we would all have heard it. Time stopped moving.

I was just wondering if it was all another set up when the door burst open and Mary McGee came in and held the door open. I heard Daisy gasp aloud. A kind of nervy Debbie stepped forward and a handsome tall grey-haired gentleman probably in his early sixties walked in. He was dressed in a well-fitted, tailored, navy-blue blazer with gold buttons, immaculate white shirt and pleated chino trousers.

"Hello everyone," Mary said with a wide smile on her face. "May I introduce Sir Peter Johnson to all of you."

"Good morning, Sir," Debbie said aloud.

We all chorused "Good morning, Sir."

In all my eleven years plus at Headington PJ&PJ none of the Johnson twins had ever been in the building.

Oh my God... The smile on his face was like it was imported straight from heaven. It was just warm, serene, immaculate and divine.

"Good morning, everyone. Good to see you all," he said in a soothing, deep, calm and very eloquent baritone voice that reverberated throughout the room. Sir Peter Johnson could have easily passed for a middle-aged Irish priest. His winning, angelic smile and his aura exhumed peace, holiness, contentment and genuine happiness. No wonder he was so rich. I could tell he did not have one single bad bone in his body. Most of all, he was arrestingly handsome.

"Welcome back Ada..." he said slowly in a very rich voice. A strong wave of warmth and bubbles ran through my entire inside as he focused on me with his smiling eyes. Everybody was clapping and I joined in the loud applause.

"You don't know me." He paused, smiled and looked around.

He had dazzlingly piercing eyes. "But I know you. On a few occasions, I heard you take the first and second readings at my church on Quex Road." He hesitated and continued. "I am also a north-west Londoner like you and Mary, albeit I live on the other side of Kilburn High Road. I live in West Hampstead…"

It was all like a dream. More waves of warmth and bubbles ran through me and little butterflies fluttered and floated in my stomach. Sir Peter Johnson carried on talking with that fixed angelic smile in his eyes and on his face.

"Now, Pretty Ada…"

Pretty Ada? Ooh la la!

"… Because your accounts are still frozen, and I can actually feel your pain…"

He could? I felt an instant emotional connection when Sir Johnson said he could feel my pain. He paused and continued slowly. "I mean, I know that no amount of money can obliterate all that you went through, but there is a cheque in one of those envelopes from Sir Paul and me. It is a little compensation cheque for the sum of five thousand pounds from us."

There was a loud applause that went on forever. Sir Peter Johnson had us all in the palm of his hands.

"… And a ticket for a sponsored city break for two."

More clapping.

Tears welled in my eyes, but I held them back and felt an instant connection with Sir Peter Johnson.

I cleared my throat and stood up. "Thank you so much, Sir Johnson. I am overwhelmed. I feel greatly honoured and I am extremely grateful, Sir. I can't believe you came all the way to Headington because of little me. And so much money? Thank you again, Sir." I bowed my head in appreciation, placed my right hand on my heart, turned to my colleagues and spoke out loud and confidently. "Thank you, everybody, and please join me in thanking Sir Peter Johnson again."

Everybody got up and screamed, "Thank you, Sir Peter!!"

"You are all welcome." Sir Peter said with another peaceful, angelic smile. "Thank you all for the hard work... And for all this food. Please keep it up. Emm, I promise you all that we will have a big Christmas party this year." He paused humbly and then added. "Enjoy the rest of the day and I should see you all soon." He walked up to the decorated table tennis board, took a samosa, did a royal wave by raising his right hand in the air, twisting it slightly from the wrist, and he left.

Ben walked up to me. Oh Ben! "Congratulations Ada. I have to go now." I attempted to get out of my seat to escort him. "No, don't worry," he said very quickly. "I will send you my bill," he added with a smile.

"Okay. Party over. We will leave the food in the canteen. You can pop in and grab whatever you want as and when you need to," Debbie announced loudly.

Hot tears stung my eyes and all I could do was blow plenty kisses, place my right hand on my heart and bow my head in gratitude.

Back to the grind, I thought as I sat at the old desk. It felt very weird being back in Room 348. There was a new computer decorated with pink ribbons and there were large helium balloons by my desk. I sat there while they got the office manager's room ready for me.

Everything around me was annoyingly new – from the black gel keyboard wrist rest, to the incoming and outgoing post trays. Even the pens and the pen holder were all new and alien to me. All my old stationery was gone. My good old single hole punch, my 2017 Columban missionaries' calendar, my blank envelopes and stapler were also gone.

I switched the computer on and the log in screen flashed up. For a long time, I sat hunched at my desk trying to remember my password, but Emeka's face evaded my screen as I drew a blank on all three passwords. I knew that was no zone for Emeka but all I could do was stare sadly at the brand-new computer and wish they never removed my good old faithful PC. I was in no mood to ring the IT department because the mere thought of dealing with them made me nervous.

My colleagues had not changed. In fact, the banter was worse than it used to be, but just hearing them jabbering away as if everything was normal was a breath of fresh air.

I decided to call it a day.

I exited the office through the back door and walking through the office car park I looked at the alleyway. There was a big gate at the entrance. It was locked.

Whatever happened there?

36

"Which stupid *yeye, yanmayanma, jakujaku, jagajaga, nkpokolo,* rubbish resolution?" Malika raged when I got home. "You must take them to an employment tribunal for treating you so unfairly and unlawfully."

I did not say anything.

"Five thousand pounds? Five thousand miserable pounds," she repeated again. "How very daring of them? That is chicken-change. Pittance in comparison to what they put you through."

"Seriously, Malika, I don't really care about compensation or no compensation. I am just happy I cleared my name and also very happy I had the privilege to meet Sir Peter Johnson. I will look for another job or contract like most Londoners do. In fact, my gut instinct tells me to resign and that is what I will do. They can always find another jackass in PJ&PJ."

"Jenny ass you mean?"

"Well, a female donkey."

I went to the bathroom to sit and look at the pictures that Mr Ben forwarded to me – in the quiet of the four walls of the toilet. My bum had barely landed on the toilet seat when my phone started vibrating. To my utmost shock, it was a WhatsApp call from Emeka. When I saw his picture and name, I flung the phone into the wash-hand basin and ran out of the bathroom.

"Malika," I screamed at the top of my voice as the phone carried on vibrating in the basin. "Malika. Emeka is calling me."

By the time a panicked Malika arrived the phone had stopped ringing. I pointed at the phone.

"I bet it is his mum or Obiageli," Malika hissed as she looked at the phone. "Just ignore them."

I retrieved the phone from the wash-hand basin and looked at the screen – there were forty-two previously missed calls. Four of them were from my mum, five from Home Wrecker – that is, Mama-in-law – one from my dad and the remaining other calls were from Emeka's phone.

I decided to call my mum back.

"Good afternoon, Ma."

"Ada."

"Maaa?"

"How are you?"

"Fine, thank you, Ma. Is everything okay?"

"I hope the weather is not too cold out there…"

"Why is everyone calling me? Eh?"

"My daughter, everything is not okay."

"What?"

"There is a big-big problem out here… Nothing to do with any of the Chukwus. All the Chukwus are fine. Your father is doing very well and your sisters are fine… But your husband's people need your help."

"What now? What do they want Mama?"

"Your mother-in-law and your junior wife just left our house.

There is a big problem on the ground and only you can solve it…"

"What is it Mama? And please speak up and get to the point."

"They cannot access Emeka's accounts."

"En-hen? What's that got to do with me?"

"You are down as his next of kin in all the banks."

"Incredible!! He never changed those details?"

"No, he didn't. All the bank accounts, properties and assets are in his name and yours."

"Oh my God!!"

Mama asked me to come back to Nigeria. When I refused, she told me the downside of me not coming back and the effect it would have on my dear Papa's health. She promised she would be there for me on the day I returned.

"I will face your mother-in-law. Afterall, her bum is not bigger than mine."

Nausea overcame me. I was sicker than a parrot when I put the phone down. I rushed back to the toilet and threw up.

One by one the days went by. Lent and Palm Sunday came and went. The clocks sprang forward and Easter Sunday followed suit. The only thing that remained permanent was the Easter egg from Malika. And that was still on the granite kitchen worktop. Uneaten.

I knew that I had to go back to Kirikiri to go and take inventories and give Emeka's family access to his monies. I felt sorry for Mama-in-law and Obiageli for their untimely displacement. The tenants in Emeka's properties blatantly refused to pay the rent to his family members; they carried on paying their rent into Emeka's bank accounts like they used to do. And I was the only one who could take money out of the accounts.

Spring sprang and came laughing over Kilburn. And while

the residents of Kilburn packed their woollies and winter warmers away, I got busy in readiness for my return to Kirikiri.

A few days before I flew out to Kirikiri, I armed myself with that same empty box from Iceland, went back to PJ&PJ and cleared all my stuff. I sent my letter of resignation to HR by recorded delivery and enclosed a cheque for one month's salary in lieu of notice. I knew in my head that I would go to Kirikiri and open an office where the wrongly accused are defended. I would also set up a shelter for the widows and abandoned wives in Nigeria.

The next afternoon, a heart-warming letter arrived from a company called Data-Log. My heart leapt with enormous joy when I opened the letter.

"Dear Ms George,

We write to formally advise you that after a thorough, robust and in-depth investigation, we can confirm that your name and/or address have been used fraudulently by parties unknown, to obtain products from our company.

I have therefore closed the account(s) and have also informed the credit reference agencies to remove any related information to ensure that your credit rating is not affected in future.

We shall keep an electronic record of the account for our own purposes in our efforts to prevent, detect and combat fraud.

We very sincerely apologise for any inconvenience we might have caused and trust this matter has been resolved to your satisfaction.

Signed, S N Phillips."

Soon after that, other letters started arriving from various companies to fix things. My heart soared higher and higher with each new day, and each new letter buoyed me to a dizzying height of happiness and incredible joy.

It felt like a joyride in Thorpe Park when five similar letters arrived in one day.

PART 5

PART 5

37

Good old faithful Show-Boy-Ten-Ten met me at the Murtala
Muhammed Airport in the punishing heat. He drove me straight
to my new home in Kirikiri.

The first disturbing sign I saw on arrival that afternoon was
on the top metal bar of the unattended gates. It was a bold sign
that read "This house is not for sale." The high gates to the drive
were surprisingly wide open. I did not see any mobile policemen,
neither did I notice any security guards as we drove up the
long, deserted drive. In place of the two, ferocious and well-fed
Alsatians, a duo of docile, skinny and mangy dogs lay curled-up,
looking half-dead. They were badly emaciated and surrounded
by flies. In their canine foetal position, the animals seemed
unperturbed by the arrival of a strange car in the compound.
They did not even flinch or acknowledge our arrival. The darker
Alsatian, whom I later named Sky, reluctantly raised its head,
looked around and lay back down; while the brown one, whom
I named Apollo, raised its hind legs, scratched its head and ear
vigorously, looked at the car, shut its eyes and went back to sleep.

I could tell they knew that Emeka was gone.

Show-Boy followed my directions and drove his battered taxi up the drive to the mega-mansion.

A long row of big petrol tankers parked along the way up, against the furthest wall in the compound, covered in thick layers of dust. They were not there before I left. I counted and there were nineteen tankers in total.

It was all so uncanny. What a wicked ruin of wealth.

I could not believe so much change had happened in such a short time.

From afar, the back of Emeka's gleaming, flashy, attention-seeking cars in the carports looked like they too were masked in dust. I saw the helicopter. It was parked on the lawn and also covered in dust. I was very pained when I saw the once lovely rose garden had turned into an unkempt lot, and overgrown shrubs and wild plants displaced the landscaped lawns.

The eerie stillness, the smell of desertion and the havoc wreaked by Emeka's death were everywhere. How could everything change within such a short period?

There was not a single person in sight; not even a lone servant or house-help. I became very scared and full of nerves. After a few seconds I turned around because my nostrils were hit by an unpleasant, distinctively foul stench. It was from the two nonchalant, malnourished dogs. They walked behind our car sluggishly. The emaciated Alsatians reeked of poverty. They reeked of filth and neglect. I sensed their fear from the way their ears were pulled right back and glued to their heads.

More shocks! I noticed the red Ferrari was gone.

I mopped my face with my wet hanky and fought back a deluge of tears. When I got out of the car, the two dogs shuffled all the way to the front door and suddenly, their sad eyes lit up and they started wagging their tails. I knew then that they remembered me and were happy to see me. If dogs could talk, they would have told me that they had not been fed for weeks.

"This house is not for sale" was also etched on the front door of the mega-mansion in bold, capital letters.

I walked up to the main house, almost slower than the dogs. I was very apprehensive; unsure of what was behind the closed door. It was slightly ajar. I pushed it open very slowly and stepped in with Show-Boy right behind me.

I almost jumped out of my skin when a plump, furry rat scurried out of the opened door. I walked into darkness and total silence. I turned the light on, and the portrait on the wall was immediately illuminated by the chandelier. A live wall gecko resting beside the portrait of eighteen-stone, champagne-loving Emeka scuttled away.

Emeka! He looked so alive with his overgenerous jowls and his come-hither eyes that seemed to smile at me.

I stood and looked around. The big, flat screen television that was mounted on the wall above the mantelpiece was also gone.

"Who is that?" Mama, the not-so-weak-and-feeble octogenarian, screamed from where she stood on top of the stairs.

"It is me, Ma. Me. Ada," I called out as I smothered imaginary creases from my black linen dress and prepared to meet her. I was not sure if she was going to greet me with another front-hand slap, or walk me out of the house. "Good evening, Ma." I greeted and went down on one knee, ready to bolt if Mama tried any violent moves.

"Aw. Ada. My dear Ada. Ada darling. Ada sweetie. Ada puff-puff. Welcome my lovely child," she greeted in a warm voice that was sickeningly unusual and scary. I was oh-so-nauseated by the change in her sentiment, I almost asked for a sick bag.

"Please forgive me for leaving, Ma." I pleaded as I bent and knelt on the other knee. Mama looked different. Her radiance and glow had diminished and she looked a lot thinner and paler than I anticipated. No push-up bra. No make-up. No jewellery. No Hayes or Jubilee head tie. She had aged in such a short time.

"Forgive what? There is nothing to forgive, my daughter. It is the way God wants it all. Whatever he has written can never be erased. Destiny will always be fulfilled. Please, get up."

Mama was dressed in a white lace blouse and she tied two white and purple *nkpulu-oka* wrappers around her waist.

"Good afternoon, Ma," Show-Boy greeted.

I started to get up. Udo, the PA, came in from the back door. Her voluptuous curves had thinned out, and she was about three shades darker. She pulled me up and gave me a big hug.

"Welcome Ada," she greeted.

"What is happening here? Where is everybody?" I asked in exaggerated surprise and alarm.

"Hm!!" Udo sighed.

I sighed as well, and so did Mama.

"Welcome my daughter. We have been waiting and praying for your coming," Mama said and added, "Hunger has almost killed us."

"Where is everybody?" I asked again, sitting back on one of the dining chairs. "Oh, this is my driver, Show-Boy."

"Good afternoon, Ma."

"Afternoon Boy," Mama said with another sigh. "The bean ball has scattered inside the frying oil. The party is over because Emeka is no more."

"How now?" I asked Udo.

"My sister, I am fine, oh. I will fill you in later."

"Is my Mum here yet?" I asked her.

"No, oh. Was she supposed to be here?"

"Yes, oh."

"No. We have not seen her."

I wrinkled my nose. There was a foul smell in the living room. Udo looked at me and her eyes wandered towards the other corner of the room. I saw a mouse trap with a dried-out rat in it.

"That is where the smell is from," Show-Boy, who stood behind me like my personal bodyguard, said. He walked up to the trap and removed the rat with his bare hands.

"Where is everybody?" I asked again.

"They are all gone. No money for salaries. No food," Udo replied.

"Where is Obiageli?"

"Gone. Forever gone. She killed my son," Mama cut in.

"Pardon?" I asked, not sure I heard Mama properly.

"I drove her away. She killed Emeka," Mama snapped.

Did she?

Udo, the PA, excused herself and left the room.

"Obiageli killed Emeka, but no problem, he has gone to rest in a better place."

Typical! I thought. Nobody ever died of natural causes in Nigeria. They always blamed some poor person or relative for every single death in Nigeria. First, I was the murderer and then Obiageli. Next it would be Udo.

Mama said a soothsayer told them that Obiageli killed Emeka. She also said that when Obiageli realised Emeka died intestate and everything was in my name, she turned very nasty.

"I didn't see the Ferrari outside. Where is the Ferrari?" I asked.

"Obiageli sold it. She said she needed money to eat."

"And the ninety-inch flat screen TV?" I pointed at the bare wall.

"Obiageli sold it," Udo replied as she walked back to the front room.

"Hmm, my child. Forget about that animal. Let us talk about more important things. We could not bury Emeka, oh."

"I heard so."

"My son's office is closed down."

"I heard so."

"We are yet to bury my son."

"I heard so."

I wanted to tell her that God wanted me to get a chance to say goodbye properly; instead, I asked for everybody else.

I noticed Mama kept staring at my expensive wig of one million braids. Her roving eyes focused on my hair and then darted to my tummy.

"How did you do Bob Marley on your hairless head?" she finally asked.

"It is a wig, Ma."

"A wig?" she asked surprised.

"Yes, Ma."

"Sorry. I am so sorry about your hair. Please don't be angry."

"That is all passed, Ma."

"Good girl. Did you see 'The house is not for sale' sign?"

"Yes, Ma. What is all that about? I was surprised when I saw it."

"Obiageli and her sisters tried to sell the house with us in it!"

"Wao!! Where is Ekwena, the driver?"

"We fired everybody. Him as well. We could not pay their wages," Udo said sadly.

"You are a very lucky girl. God just wants you to bury your

260

husband," Mama-in-law explained.

These people will never ever go hungry again for as long as I live.

I also vowed not to allow the work of Emeka's hand fall apart. He must have left all the bank accounts and the main company, the custard factory, in our joint names for a reason. All the houses and cars, even the helicopter – which were not in my name – were in the name of the company – our custard business which was in my name.

I didn't care about those though; I was just glad I was given the opportunity to say goodbye to Emeka's physical being before he was finally laid to rest.

"If Emeka was buried in your absence, that would have been a big abomination," Mama said as she gnawed hard on a chicken leg that she retrieved from some dirty tissue paper in her handbag.

"And you would have been ostracised by all Ibusa people," Udo added.

"We thank God." I chuckled.

"The villagers also said the family had to pay a certain fine that was outstanding since the death of Emeka's grandfather. The fine was imposed because he stole a goat from a neighbouring village when he was young, and it was never paid," Mama said sadly.

"Don't worry, we will pay all the fines," I said consolingly.

"And that aside, he could not be buried in his father's house because it is too small, ancient and in a state of disrepair. We need a mansion where dignitaries and Emeka's timbre and calibre friends can attend. The only way out of the dilemma is to quickly replace the old house with a new one for the funeral, but this cannot be done because no one can gain access to Emeka's money," Mama added.

"Don't worry, it will all be sorted."

I remembered the goat story. My dad had told me many years ago; about how Emeka's grandfather, the village outlaw, actually stole a goat and ran away with the stolen goat tied to his back. Pa Eluemuno pretended he was carrying a child on his back. The more bizarre part of the story was that because the crafty man did not want traces of the goat seen, Pa Eluemuno ate the goat meat with the goat hairs on. He was very rebellious, I was told.

38

Udo and I went up the stairs to Emeka's room. She handed the keys to the room to me at the door and stood behind me as I very slowly opened it. We walked into a cold, lifeless room. The silence was deafening and the room was exactly how he had left it. Not even the curtains were drawn. I was not too sure if my nose was playing tricks on me, but I seriously thought the fragrance of Emeka's cologne, mixed with vomit, was still in the room.

Emeka's nicely folded set of striped pyjamas was still on the left arm of the leather chair. His bottle of aftershave, two walkie-talkies and a bunch of keys were on the dressing table. His mobile phone chargers and iPod dock were as he had left them. An unopened bottle of Moët and two champagne flutes were on top of the bedside fridge. I knew for sure that if Emeka had not died that night, he would have popped open the champagne at about twelve midnight and said "One for the night," as he guzzled all the contents of the bottle.

The white jellabiya that he wore that fateful night was on the bed; no one had bothered to wash off the vomit and food stains.

No wonder the room smelled of rot and cologne. My packed suitcase, my old photos, my scrapbook with glued on pictures and the food stuff from Mama to Aunty Rhoda were still in the Ghana Must Go bag on top of the chaise longue.

I spotted my Si perfume on the far-left corner of the dressing table – I grabbed it and very quickly sprayed some. I carried on spraying it as I walked around the room and finally stopped sprinkling when I sat on the high chair in front of the tallboy. That was the same high chair that I had sat on that fateful night. I had never opened the drawers of the tallboy, and out of curiosity I opened the first one. Neatly arranged and still in their wrappers were stashes of layered monies in different currencies. There was a layered row of hundred-dollar bills, a layered row of fifty-pound notes, one row of euros and a fourth row of naira. I had never seen that much money in my whole life.

"OMG!!" I exhaled aloud.

"Shh," Udo instructed. "Keep quiet. You know, these people have a narcistic sense of entitlement."

"I understand."

There were documents for all of Emeka's luxury cars nicely arranged in the second drawer of the tallboy. The third was full of wristwatches including three Rolexes. I could not understand why Emeka had three Rolexes plus the one Ekwena handed to me. He could only wear one at a time, for crying out loud. And then my head started spinning at the sight of so many wristwatches. I became dizzy. I threw my head on the back rest of the high chair. I could not believe I was the custodian of such a vast empire. So much money. So much wealth.

No fainting spells, I cautioned myself.

"There will be drastic changes after the funeral," I said almost to myself as I shut the drawers and stood up. I did not want to sleep in the master bedroom that night. I was too scared to sleep there because there were memories of Emeka everywhere.

Udo said I could stay in her very spacious room for the night. She called it her bolthole. It turned out Udo had a thing for sleeping with the lights on – that explained why I espied Emeka very easily on the night of their rendezvous. She offered me her bed and made a makeshift one for herself on the floor. I felt very guilty and said she could share her bed with me, but she refused.

When the rain began to fall in the middle of the night and Udo started with a rattling cough, I once again asked her to come up to her bed. She refused again, but after about an hour on the bare floor, she eventually climbed onto the bed.

I moved to the wall and gummed my body to it; I did not want any part of me to touch Udo's body.

I tried to sleep, but sleep refused to come so I lay awake and listened to the rhythm of the pouring rain and Udo's gentle and soft breathing. I could not believe I was on the same bed that Udo had shared with Emeka not too long ago all because I was too scared to sleep in the master bedroom.

Loud thunder and lightning struck in the middle of the night and I thanked God I was in Udo's room. I very gradually and eventually made myself comfortable on the inner side of the bed, although, I lay tossing and turning for hours. When Udo got up and went to turn the light down, I started sobbing. I cried for the position and situation I was in. After a while, Udo stretched out her hand. She patted and consoled me like a baby until I dozed off, but I did not sleep for long. I woke up in the middle of the night and started crying again.

"It is enough. Stop crying," she whispered into my ears. Every time she begged me to stop crying, I cried more. I cried and cried and cried until I could cry no more.

"Things should not have turned out the way they did," I said.

Udo patted my right shoulder. She rocked her body as she patted me.

"I am just too scared to close my eyes," I whispered.

"I understand," she said with a soft voice. "It is okay." She very gently nibbled at my ear affectionately and kissed me lightly on my forehead. It felt so safe and warm on Udo's bed. Our warm breaths steamed up the room until the electricity ceased and we both opened our mouths to chorus "NEPA!"

When the generator came on and Udo knew no one in the house could hear us, she opened her mouth and told me so much that night.

"Apart from his entire estate being yours because he never did a new will or change any of the documents since you had left, you are also very lucky because you are the sole beneficiary of an insurance policy that Emeka took out while you were still married."

If only she knew I would willingly give up all the white houses, the cars, the helicopter, the business and everything, to have Emeka back to life.

That night, the heavy pouring rain lashed against Udo's windows and made so much noise on the roof. It rained continuously all night, and the next day and the day after.

After that first night, I slept in Udo's bed every night. I clung on to Udo as if she was another saviour.

She told me so many things I didn't know about Emeka – there were the good, the bad, the ugly and the horrendous horror. I refused to believe the not-too-good ones.

"So how did Emeka become so rich?" I asked.

"He made his money from his brothels, his property empire and the Bitcoin currency."

"Bitcoin?"

"Yes," she said. "Okay. I will tell you the whole story."

"I am all ears."

"His late brother bought land and built properties in Emeka's name."

"Yes?"

"His brother could not but build the houses in his name because he was a civil servant."

"Yes?"

"Then he died intestate and Mr Emeka played a very dangerous game. He sold all the properties and invested the proceeds in Bitcoin currency."

"He did?"

"Yes. Initially, he bought and sold the cryptocurrency, and then after a while, he took a chill pill. He kept all the proceeds in a digital wallet and then sat back and waited patiently for a rise. Once there was a huge rise in 2013 – just before the bubble burst – and before that ghastly crash he sold up and closed shop."

"Whoa!!"

"Yes. It turned out to be a huge success and he made a very massive profit. Large fortune."

"Hm! Smart man. Emeka had always been very smart."

"Correct. And now you are the only one who can access Emeka's wealth."

"Oh my God! This is scary. I feel like a fraudster, especially as I was away in London when he amassed all that wealth and became so rich."

"Don't say that. You laid the foundation with him. Afterall, both of you started the custard factory and you never stayed to enjoy the fruit of your labour."

"It is well," I said after a very long silence.

"You are the only living signatory to his accounts because he never removed your name. He did not put Obiageli down because she is not really from Ibusa and he wanted his wealth to remain in Ibusa and be spent wisely."

She told me so many more things that I never knew about Emeka, including the fact that he, Emeka, was a habitué of dens for prostitutes and that we were both lucky we did not catch any sexually transmitted diseases from him.

I slept in Udo's bed every night until day four.

39

On the fourth day of my stay in Kirikiri the rain came tumbling down again with a bigger vengeance and I spent most of the day gazing out of the window.

Later that afternoon, from the front window, I saw a drenched, lone, stooped figure walking towards the house, clutching what looked like a little black nylon bag in one hand and a stick in the other.

I flung off my flipflops, opened the door and ran barefooted into the pouring rain. The rain blew in my face but I kept running until I got to her. My Mummy. My London Mummy. My Tea Mummy. She looked frailer and thinner and limped as if in serious agony. I was pained to see my mum in pain.

"Mama," I cried.

We stood and hugged in the pouring rain. My first instinct was to lift her up, put her on my shoulder and carry her right into the house – but feeling tired myself, I slowly led her towards the house.

"Our taxi broke down by your first gate," she explained. "My load is in the taxi."

"Mama welcome," I greeted. "Don't worry, Show-Boy will go and get your load."

I relieved her of the little black bag that contained a big loaf of Benin bread. I helped her to the porch and sang "Mother Is A Priceless Jewel" in my head.

"There is God," Mama said repeatedly as we very slowly made our way to the mansion. "Show-Boy?" Mama suddenly stopped and asked. It was as if her brain just received and processed the name.

"Yes, Mama. Show-Boy. That is that driver I told you about. He is now a permanent fixture in this household."

"Hmm!! Just like that? You children of nowadays!"

"Yes, Mama. Us children of nowadays. He is cool, you know."

"Okay, oh. If you say so."

Seeing my mum was as if I won a million pounds on the lottery. She arrived in her very humble way and her presence transformed my life in the Kirikiri mansion. She brought with her a breath of fresh air, new hope and a new lease of life.

From when my mum arrived, Emeka's mum automatically became Mama-in-law in my head and my mum became the matriarch of the mansion. "My darling wife," Smart Mama-in-law hailed me. She grinned like a Cheshire cat every time we ran into each other on the grand corridor and in response, I always wore a polite smile.

Mama-in-law knew I was their bread and butter and she was most annoyingly all over me like a rash. On my part, I pretended all was well between us, but my guards were permanently up.

270

In fact, in my head, I blamed her for everything. She was the one who set off the chain reaction that culminated in Emeka's death. If she hadn't brought Obiageli to our house twelve years ago, my late husband and I would have carried on coasting like we did prior to her interference.

I listened as Mama and Mama-in-law chatted away like old buddies most of the evening.

They called each other My-In-Law.

"You must return to the master bedroom to establish your position," my mother insisted that night. "Don't worry, you don't really have to perform most of the funeral rites, money walks and talks in Nigeria," she added.

Mama and I moved into the master bedroom that night.

And some very strange things happened that same night.

Firstly, as I sorted out Emeka's unwashed shirts, trousers and socks and sniffed each item of clothing to decide whether they were dirty or not, I felt a lot calmer and seemed to draw some inner strength and succour from the scent of his worn clothing. I very surprisingly found the smell of his clothing extremely therapeutic.

"For as long as I live, this kind of thing will never happen to you again, or any of my other girls. Never again," Mama vowed with tears in her eyes.

"It is okay, Mama."

"It is not okay. I took my eyes off the ball for a split second and they treated you like a poor child without a family. They behaved as if you fell from the skies."

"It is in the past now."

"No." Mama sobbed. "It is not in the past. All my children were born in Great Britain. They did not treat you like a child that was born in Great Britain."

271

Mama was on fire that night – she gave me that old time religion and prayed fervently like the old prayer warrior that I knew back in the days.

Secondly, after prayers we hugged one another and shared the peace of the Lord by shaking hands. I grabbed hold of Mama's knobbly right hand, but she instantly drew back like she got an electric shock from my hand and quickly pushed my hand away.

"What?!" she asked alarmed.

"What now? What is wrong, Mama?"

Mama stood still and looked at me for a while, and then she came closer and placed the back of her right palm on my neck. Next, she felt my forehead, and looked into my eyes.

"Why are you so warm?" she finally asked.

"How...?" I felt my forehead.

"Your body is piping hot."

I checked again with my right palm. "No, I am not. Stop it, Mama. You are scaring me, Mama."

"Show me your hands."

I stretched both hands out to Mama.

"Why are they so pale?"

I was so relieved it was nothing sinister.

"Stress." I chuckled... "I even felt very dizzy again this morning."

"Stress?" I saw Mama's wrinkly face split into the biggest grin I had ever seen in over thirty years. She looked as pleased as a punch and prouder than a peacock. "No wonder you look robust." She proudly raised her bony shoulders. "I could almost see your kidneys when you came to Ibusa."

"What are you on about, Mama? I haven't put on weight."

"You have. And that is because you have swallowed a cockroach, and a very big fat cockroach at that," she said proudly.

"Yeeuk," I said disgusted.

"You have. When was your last time? When you last had a time?"

"Time?"

"Your menses."

And then it clicked. I realised she meant when I last had a period.

"I don't know." I could not remember when the last time was.

"Emm?" And then I remembered that my last menstrual period was months ago, when I was preparing for the result of the paperboard promotion at PJ&PJ.

"Quite a while. Before the suspension," I replied.

Mama went down on her bony knees and touched the floor with her forehead. She looked up to the ceiling and muttered words I did not hear. When she stood up, I saw tears trickle down her face.

"To God be the glory. His time is the best."

"What is wrong, Mama?"

"Shh," she said and placed her index finger on her lips. "You have swallowed a cockroach."

"In English please, Mama."

"Yess. In English. You have a bun in da oven... Coo-chi-coo-chi-coo."

"Meaning?"

"You are pregnant," she whispered.

"I am?" I asked astounded.

"Shh."

No wonder. That explained the nausea, the excess sleep, the weight gain and my big boobs, the lower abdominal pain and the throwing up on the plane.

Mama said victoriously, "Sometimes in life we lose to win."

My thoughts wandered off to Kilburn and Headington and the buses. I was brought back to the present when I heard Mama sneeze aloud. I looked at my mum and said, "Bless you, Ma."

"Ah-choo," Mama sneezed again.

"Is the air conditioner too much for you?" I asked.

"No, Dear."

"Mama, I will do a reasonable funeral service for Emeka – after all, he was devoted to me at the end," I said in an attempt to change the topic.

"I agree. Even if you have to mourn for one year and shave your hair off again, it does not matter," my mum advised. "And the mourning period will also be cut down to one month anyway," she added.

Mama and I talked till the early hours of the next morning.

40

I got builders to demolish Emeka's father's house in Ibusa and erected a mansion – a replica of the Kirikiri mansion – within three weeks. I added a state-of-the-art gym, a ten-car garage and seven bedrooms with private terraces. All seven bathrooms had mirrored walls and standalone bathtubs. I knew I was a winner when all my sisters and their husbands arrived in Ibusa for the burial. I became gutsy just before the funeral and asked to see Emeka's body; I was happy with what I saw because it was well preserved. I made a mental note to call and thank the proprietor of the best morgue in Africa and for a long time, I sat beside the body all alone and talked to him.

On the actual day of the burial, my sisters and I pulled out all the stops and honoured Emeka with the most befitting and elaborate funeral that the people of Delta State ever witnessed. We had five live bands on the street. All the invited and uninvited guests at the burial were fed on assorted Nigerian, Chinese, Japanese and Caribbean dishes till they could eat no more. There were takeaway containers for people to take home as much cooked food as they wanted and live cows were given out to prominent families to take home and slaughter. We gave out irons, fans, buckets and assorted plastic containers to the guests and the dancing and merriment went on till 7am the next morning.

After the burial, I never for once saw Emeka in my dream and I never remembered the pains he caused me; it was like his death erased them all and I only remembered the good times. I did not just bury Emeka, I also buried the love I had for him that had refused to die. The funeral brought a final closure to my entire saga and I was able to say my final goodbye properly.

Everything else moved so quickly after that.

I became a millionaire by default and I promised God that Emeka's pot of money would be shared to every single member of the George Izuchukwu family; no matter how small. I got rid of all the gas guzzlers that polluted the air. I also sold the SUVs with the thick bulletproof windows and even the ones with the sealed cabins full of oxygen supplies.

Obiageli returned like a prodigal wife. I got on with things and planned to convert the south-wing servants' quarters to a granny cottage for Mama-in-law, all because I felt sorry for their horrible experience and displacement from Ikoyi.

The spring gradually returned to my footsteps and my hair soon grew long enough for me to fix Brazilian hair on again. I forgave Mama-in-law for her personal vendetta, and grabbed a second chance to coexist with her. As for Obiageli, I swore to ensure she was well looked after.

My tummy grew bigger and bigger by the day, and so did my nose, my lips, my cheeks and most especially my fingers. My scans showed that I was expecting a baby boy. Being pregnant at quarter-to-forty was not a walk in the park. My strength and energy levels were pretty low, despite the fact that I ate like a horse.

EPILOGUE

November 2019

I knew I would never walk alone when I strolled unhurriedly from one end of the estate to the other with two-year-old EJ – Emeka Junior – in tow.

On the day that millions across the world revelled in the good news that Harry was going to marry Meghan, my plump Prince Emeka George the Second was born on a cold November afternoon at St. Mary's Hospital in Paddington. And as Britain downgraded her national terrorism threat level from severe to substantial, I welcomed a period of relative calm and the change in my fortune. I also launched my charity for widows and abandoned-cum-battered wives.

One lovely Thursday morning when the volatile Bitcoin was at a ninety per cent high, I cashed in Emeka's remaining cryptocurrency and my fortune exceeded thousands of millions of naira. I joined the centimillionaires' club. People said I secured a huge Emeka bonus, but that was not true as it was sad to be in such a beautiful mansion without Emeka.

I still received congratulatory messages two years after

the hijack of my identity and I will forever count myself lucky because, statistically, only five to ten per cent of identity theft cases were solved. Luckier still, I was able to retrieve and hand-deliver the yet-to-be-cashed cheque to Darren Murphy.

Adetokunbo was found guilty of aiding and abetting Binta Ogu in the commission of a criminal offence and for false representation.

I know that one day Prince Emeka George the Second will ask me what everyone asked over the last fourteen years: why I did not divorce his father and remarry. I will tell him that I took the vows I made in a catholic church before God and in front of over one hundred people very serious.

Strangely, my only regret in relocating to Kirikiri was that I did not stay in Kilburn to enjoy a ride on the Elizabeth line. There were times I missed my little flat in Kilburn and my simple no-frills, stress-free life. I sometimes wished I could turn the hands of the clock back and EJ and I be transported back to my freshly laundered beddings on my little double bed. I missed so many things about my old life. I missed even the simplest things I enjoyed on a Saturday afternoon, like rubbing my legs against the smooth, silky feel of my fresh white bedsheets from the discount shop on Kilburn High Road. I missed reading *The Daily Mirror* in bed on a Saturday afternoon. I missed going through my box of broken jewellery searching for missing studs for broken earrings. I missed listening to Radio 4 on my Pure radio in my little kitchen. I missed the smell of fried chicken and chips on Kilburn High Road. I missed my colleagues at PJ&PJ, the baking competitions, the chats by the tea point, water cooler and coffee machines. I missed the Diwali parties, the whirr of the printers, the sound of keyboards, the office banter and most of all, I missed Daisy and the office gossip.

Papa and Mama visited so many times and eventually moved into one of the cottages behind the tiered rose gardens. They missed Emeka so much. I could never tell if they were pleased with how things panned out for me, but one thing I knew for sure was that they were very happy I finally got a child – a male child for that matter and a carbon copy of Emeka.

Some of my windfall was spent on Aunty Eliza. She got an artificial eye and did dental work to replace the two upper front teeth that her ex-husband knocked out.

I bought new pews for all the churches in Kirikiri and its environs. I also gave a lot of cash donations to the nearby catholic churches. I stopped hiding my facial marks. I enhance them with black-coloured pencils and they stand out like number eleven.

I am still waiting to see Emeka in my Kirikiri dreams, but the last time I saw my mesmerizingly beautiful image in the mirror, I said:

"You are stupendously and obscenely richly blessed, Pretty Ada Nneka Chukwu-George."

ACKNOWLEDGEMENTS

To my most amazing children Vanessa, Peter and Paul Onyemem. Thank you for your support and unconditional love.

Thank you my dear family and friends for your immense and unwavering support over the years.

Thank you Dr Olabisi Gwamna for taking time out of your busy schedule to read through and edit this novel.

A special thank you to Claire Ellis and the SilverWood Books team for their hard work.

Also to my creative writing course mates and tutors at City Lit Holborn, I would like to say a big thank you for the invaluable feedback, contributions and helpful criticism.